OTHER HALF

OTHER HALF

PSYCOP 12

Jordan Castillo Price

JCPBOOKS.com

First published in the United States in 2021 by JCP Books
www.JCPBooks.com

ISBN 978-1-944779-20-7
First Edition
Also available in audiobook

You don't marry the person
you can live with.

———◆•◆—◆■◆—◆•◆———

You marry the person you
can't live without.

CHAPTER ONE

Weddings are joyous occasions. At least, they're supposed to be. But ever since we discovered Jacob's initials in the notebook of the late and unlamented Dr. Kamal, Jacob had been anything but happy. I don't suppose I'd ever thought planning a wedding would be a walk in the park...but this one felt more like a sprint through a minefield.

Jacob needed answers—specifically, how his family tree ended up in that book and what it actually meant. Yes, it made sense to do some digging and find out more about his family's involvement with Kamal. And yes, our wedding would be a perfect excuse to visit...and, incidentally, poke around. But I'd be lying if I said the thought of what we might find didn't make me want to drop the whole thing and elope.

In fact, it was tempting to suggest we forget the fanfare and do the deed at City Hall post haste. Unfortunately, once Jacob's sister Barbara texted us about some extracurricular Clayton activity in hopes that we could attend, there was no way to weasel out of heading up to Wisconsin to announce our "good" news.

If you're ever hoping for someone to mother you, just show up in a clunky plaster cast. Not your other half, of course. They soon forget all about the big, heroic sacrifice you made slamming your hand in a car door, and get inured to the sight of you hauling around an awkward and painful burden. Plus, they tend to get sick of it smacking them in the ribs every time you roll over.

But if Jacob's mom pampered me before, she positively spoiled me now.

While Jacob was doing our dirty work, I kept his mom out of his hair. Shirley hovered beside the couch and watched me as I sipped the mug of coffee she'd just put in front of me. "Is it strong enough for you, Vic? Do you need more cream?"

"I'm good. It's great. Listen, why don't you come sit down? Jacob and I wanted to talk to you guys before we go to Clayton's... thing."

School play? Soccer match? Science fair? I'd been told at some point, no doubt, but had forgotten the details on our way up to Wisconsin. Who could keep up with whatever it was we were supposed to endure on behalf of Jacob's nephew? The kid was so entrenched in various character-building activities, it was a wonder he was even allowed to sleep.

Shirley paused, and a look of alarm flashed across her face. "What is it? What's wrong?"

"Nothing's wrong," I said hastily. I'm not quite sure she believed me, so I tried for a reassuring smile as I patted the cushion beside me clumsily with my crushed hand. It was mostly healed—these days, it itched a hell of a lot more than it hurt. "No bad news. Really, I'm sure you'll all be pleasantly surprised."

I've never been good at doing comfort. I'm told my

reassurance-face looks like I've eaten something dubious from the back of the fridge and am currently regretting that decision.

Off in another part of the house, the sound of conversation rose and fell. Uncle Leon and Jerry were engaged in a rambling debate about walleye fishing spots as the three of them made their way to the living room with a few boxes of mementos (and Jacob) in tow. The basement was crammed floor-to-ceiling with all the stuff from three dead grandparents, plus a heap of things that didn't fit in his grandmother's assisted living apartment—dozens upon dozens of boxes no one had figured out how to deal with, so they were thrilled that Jacob wanted to take some of it off their hands. An old wrestling trophy protruded from the uppermost box. Jacob set everything down, flapped the trophy halfheartedly in my direction and said, "It's a lot smaller than I remembered."

Jerry took the thing from Jacob and buffed some cobwebs off the little figure in a wrestling singlet. "Yeah, but you really creamed that other kid—and he was an obnoxious, rich-kid, private-school brat. So that's what's important."

Money is relative. Jacob had always struck me as having come from a higher social strata. College educated. Expensive taste in furniture. Better table manners. But getting to know his family had shown me that while we'd grown up in radically different cities, he and I were both raised in unassuming, working-class households. His parents had both held unremarkable jobs, Jerry in a paper mill and Shirley in an office. And while I frittered away my high school summers dicking around by the railroad tracks and replaying the same four punk rock albums, Jacob had been bussing tables and mowing lawns to save up for his first car. And if it weren't for a scholarship, the college of his choice would have been well out of reach.

Jacob took the trophy from his father and they both scrutinized it. They didn't just look like each other, they moved like
each other. And while Jerry was paunchy and graying and not
so limber anymore, they still had their moments where genetics
couldn't have been more obvious. Sometimes, during these
moments, I felt like I should wonder what my own parents
might have looked like. But I was so well-resigned to the fact
that I'd never get any answers in that regard that I didn't think
of my birth parents as actual people. Even theoretically.

Leon pointed to my mug...with his etheric arm. Given that
non-physical entities are easily as scary as ghosts, you might
think I'd find the term "etheric arm" just as creepy as "ghost
arm." But since I'd decided it was really just a human arm, a
normal part of his subtle bodies I was seeing (and not a demonic
parasite), it didn't much faze me anymore. "Say, that coffee
looks pretty good. A half-cup would really hit the spot. How
much time till we need to leave?"

Jerry checked his watch as Leon's etheric arm mimicked the
gesture. Jerry said, "Ten minutes, then we'd better head over.
Otherwise we'll be stuck parking halfway out to the cornfield.
Unless you take it to go."

Everyone seemed so focused on Clayton's big event that I
was sorely tempted to forget about the whole announcement
and tell them about the wedding some other time. But I'd
already let the cat out of the bag with Shirley, at least partway.
Mothers' intuition has never been clinically proven one way
or another—but Shirley always seemed to know when I was
holding something back. And she knew when I was uncomfortable, too.

The wedding is good news, I reminded myself. Anyone would
think so. Good. Freaking. News.

I gave Shirley a smile.

It felt pained.

"Jacob—before we go, you wanna fill everyone in?"

"Good idea," he said. "So, Vic and I...." Indecision fleeted across his expression. I saw it on him so seldom, I couldn't be sure it wasn't a put-on. "We decided to make things official."

His father and uncle both blinked as if they hadn't quite figured out what this had to do with a wrestling trophy or a cup of coffee. But his mother lit up with equal parts joy and relief. I can only imagine the potential announcement scenarios that must've been playing through her head—and the worst part was, she didn't know the half of what we dealt with.

"We were thinking we'd have the ceremony up here," Jacob added. His father and uncle went wide-eyed as what he was saying sank in. "Next month." Eyes went wider still. "At church."

At the mention of church, the mood in the room ratcheted up from mild confusion to bafflement. Neither of us was churchy...but a church wedding would give us way more opportunity to snoop around in Wisconsin.

Of course they were all happy for him—for us. But gobsmacked didn't even begin to cover it. And then, as if to verify that they'd heard what they *thought* they heard, all three dumfounded relatives turned to me.

I stared back stupidly for a heartbeat...then I nodded. Smooth. "That's the plan. Tie the knot. At the altar. Once the cast comes off, anyhow, and I can jam a ring on."

I'd figured Shirley might cry, but no, it was Leon. And those tears nearly set off a chain reaction. But he hurried off to the bathroom to save face—old-school Midwesterners like to think they're a stoic bunch—leaving Shirley to grill us while pretending not to pry.

"Why so soon? Don't you need more time to plan?"

No doubt, but Jacob didn't handle frustration well. The notebook situation had become so unbearable, and tempers so short, that pretty soon one of us was gonna start sleeping in the car. I said, "We're going for small and simple. There's really no need to make a big fuss."

"I suppose you've talked to Pastor Jill? No? She'll be real glad to see you again." Though, apparently, planning a June wedding from the middle of May was no mean feat. As Shirley rattled off a list of things a church wedding would involve—with the caveat that she was sure we had everything under control—I wondered how obvious I'd look if I took a few deep breaths from a paper bag.

Ideally, so we could have a chance to talk in private and re-strategize on the way to Clayton's thing, Jacob and I would meet everyone else over by the middle school. But his mother insisted on riding with us. And we couldn't just leave her at the curb.

Shirley was brimming with excitement, and as I listened from the back seat, she filled the car with breezy chatter about guest lists and banquet halls and honeymoons. There was an edge to her tone I couldn't help but notice. A thread of anxiety running through the monologue. I could think of at least a dozen valid reasons she might be anxious, so I was relieved that when we pulled up to the parking lot—within spitting distance of an actual cornfield—she said to Jacob, "This is *your* good news, but...maybe I should be the one to tell your sister about your big plans."

Jacob was about to climb out of the car, but his mother's suggestion gave him pause.

Shirley hastened to add, "I'm sure she'll be very happy for

you—especially that you're having it at church. You know how devout she's always been. But even though it's nearly a dozen years since her divorce, her knee-jerk reaction to these sorts of things can be a little...harsh."

Jacob didn't seem particularly convinced. "She's better off without Derrick."

"Even so, being left alone with a baby like that when you were planning on being a family—that's not something you just bounce back from."

Not surprising. Barbara is plenty of things—*resilient* is not one of them. I'm not one to jump to her defense, either. But even I would admit that the life she'd been stuck with wasn't exactly a walk in the park.

We caught up with Jerry and Uncle Leon and headed in. Clayton's middle school was small by Chicago standards, and there wasn't even a metal detector inside the front doors. A hand-lettered poster in a rack beside the gymnasium doors clued me in on which specific tortures awaited me. Band concert. But if we were supposed to be listening, at least we'd be spared the discomfort of talking...once the music started, anyhow.

The gym was half-full of people milling around, either catching up with old friends or finding somewhere to sit. I spotted Barbara right away, standing over a cluster of seats she'd saved for us with her hands on her hips and a "don't even think about moving my purse" look on her face. I personally wouldn't have cared where I sat. But since we'd driven all morning to be there, the family was hell bent on all six of us sticking together like glue.

Between the fact that we'd left at the last minute and the walk from the edge of the cornfield, we'd shown up with no time to spare. This was good. We couldn't exactly have a lengthy conversation during the concert.

Jacob's sister was forty, like me, though she acted like she'd never been anything but middle-aged. Maybe it was her divorce, or maybe raising a kid on her own. Or maybe the stars had aligned to give her a naturally bitchy disposition. Whatever the reason, for as much as Barbara grumbled about never seeing us, she sure went out of her way to make us regret showing up.

As we filed in and took our seats, Barbara said, "Took you long enough," and then glared at Jacob and me as if we must be the cause.

Normally, at this point, Leon would attempt to lighten the mood with a silly remark, or Jerry would minimize the situation, or Shirley, if well enough provoked, would flat-out tell Barbara to stop being such a sourpuss. The fact that all three of them just stood there and smiled at her set off her internal alarms.

"What?" Barbara demanded of them. "What is it?" She looked at Jacob and me again. It was the same look Jacob got when a bunch of evidence that would let him bring down a bad guy was sliding into place. Genetics. Crazy. Barbara hadn't just inherited the same dark eyes, though. Mentally, she was just as quick as her brother. "Well?"

"We'll talk after the concert," Jacob said.

Barbara leveled him a look. "And how am I supposed to concentrate on the music if I'm sitting here wondering why everybody's being so weird?"

Her voice wasn't exactly raised. But it was starting to take on an edge, and the people from the row in front of us were glancing over their shoulders in hopes of getting a more interesting show than they'd bargained for. I wasn't gonna volunteer any information. If push came to shove, I'd take a bullet for Jacob—or at least crush my own hand to provide a distraction. But Barbara was *his* sister, not mine.

Not yet, anyhow.

Jacob's practiced cop-veneer slid into place. "It's fine, Barb. It's good news."

Barbara took in the whole group of us—the over-60 crowd had zero practice in schooling their facial expressions—and again, just like Jacob, she managed to fit a bunch of random looks and a vague reassurance into a cohesive conclusion. "Oh my God. You're getting married." And before I could wonder if she was an undocumented telepath, she glared at her brother and said, "Isn't that just *great?*"

I never thought I'd be glad for a middle-school band concert. I'm no maestro, but even I could tell that whatever the kids were struggling through was off-tempo, and sour notes pummeled us with surprising regularity. It saved me from having to avoid saying anything, though, and by the time the band squeaked and squawked its way to a "grand" finale, Barbara had calmed down enough to offer Jacob a sincere congratulations, and he'd chilled out enough to accept it. And if I'd been expecting a big reaction from Clayton, I was sorely disappointed. He'd received the latest iPhone for his thirteenth birthday, and he only looked up from the thing long enough to avoid walking into traffic.

Dinner was hardly awkward at all. And on our way back to Chicago, I couldn't help but point out to Jacob, "We both expected your sister to say that fifty percent of marriages end in divorce, but she managed to resist."

"Low-hanging fruit."

True. But it deprived me of the opportunity to thank Barbara for handling that fifty percent herself. In the interest of keeping family relations civil, that was probably for the best. "Any luck in the basement?"

"We'll see. It's like a landfill down there. I have no idea what I even grabbed." Jacob shook his head in frustration and glared at the road. "I was hoping something would go smoothly for a change."

Like anything ever went smoothly—but, admittedly, I'd been hoping the same.

Normally, I would've given his knee a reassuring squeeze. Not only was my clunky plaster cast in the way—but the fingers of my left hand probably wouldn't squeeze so great anymore. Not without a bunch of grueling physical therapy we all knew I'd try my hardest to avoid. "Don't be preemptively disappointed before we've even had a chance to go through your haul. And even if you've only managed to grab some old magazines and a bundle of receipts, you'll have plenty of excuses to go back for more, what with the wedding on the horizon."

Jacob sighed heavily.

Everything was a lot harder with family than it was with mere acquaintances. I hated not giving them the whole truth, but Jacob was beyond invested in vindicating his parents. Unfortunately, it would be a lot harder to do that if they got the chance to reinvent the past. Jacob is a shark. So, I had no doubt he would get to the bottom of things and find out exactly how their initials came to be in Dr. Kamal's notebook.

What I dreaded—and what I sincerely hoped never came to pass—was discovering they'd been privy to the experiment all along.

CHAPTER TWO

Since that damn notebook came into our lives, Jacob had been running himself ragged trying to prove his parents were as unaware of how they'd ended up in its pages as he was. While I was definitely eager for him to get to the bottom of things, I was also afraid of what he'd find once he got there. If that discovery came through my filter, though, at least I'd have a chance to put a spin on it that would leave the majority of his childhood intact.

In other words, I had to do *something*.

Kamal was out there, and he owed us some answers. Unfortunately, Kamal was no longer on the same physical plane. And since we drove him to the other side, I had no way of extracting an explanation from him—not in my current state of mediumship, anyhow. But my old crony Dead Darla could talk to ghosts long-distance, so I knew it was possible. I just had to get myself super-pumped on white light, then figure out how to do it.

The problem was powering up, since there was only so far imagining white light could get me. Luckily for me, I could give umpteen reasons why I wanted my employers to help power-charge my mojo...the existence of parasitic "etheric entities" being one that I didn't even have to lie about.

My office at the Chicago regional FPMP headquarters was a lot nicer than I probably deserved. Big, too. That must've been my assistant Carl's doing. Back when he worked with Richie, he'd needed a space large enough to keep from strangling the guy. I used to think all that elbow room was a little excessive. But now, in the weeks since the big blowout at The Clinic, we'd rearranged things to accommodate our latest attempt to get a handle on mediumship, and I was thankful for the square footage.

The building was an old industrial cube of brick just west of the Loop, overlooking the rail yard. The interior was exposed ductwork and high ceilings. My office had white walls, gray berber carpet, and a radiator that gave off the occasional startling clang. There were three desks—Carl's, Darla's and mine—though we could have made do with only two. Not because Darla popped in from Indianapolis only every couple of weeks or so, but because I hardly ever used my computer. I found it a lot less mind-numbing to scroll through all the tedious reports my job entailed on my phone.

The desks were all pushed against the walls, and the center of the room, all the way over to the windows, was empty.

Because that's where the yoga happened.

Everyone knows natural solutions leave something to be desired. But what choice did I have? It was Russian roulette to swallow pharmaceutical psyactives, and F-Pimp National made off with my TV set.

And I did yoga myself into a pretty badass state of mediumship one time. Only that once, mind you. But it did happen.

Not only had the FPMP brought a dedicated yoga teacher onboard, but they hired the specific one whose poses sent me into a superconscious state, which is what the F-Pimp scientists call it when my ghost-vision spikes. Bethany Roberts had jumped at the chance to quit Jacob's gym for a gig at the FPMP. Not because she was particularly eager to advance the field of Psych, and not because she wanted to explore her own abilities... but because the FPMP offered pretty solid health insurance.

Bethany Roberts was also a "Light Worker." And on her, the new-fangled terminology didn't feel quite so lame. As far as we could tell, she had no more sensitivity to repeaters than your typical non-psychic NP. But she could occasionally achieve and remember some pretty detailed astral projections.

I'd had a glimpse of her by the glow of the GhosTV back when she'd made the unfortunate decision to try Kick, right before the feds at The Clinic hauled the damn thing away. She'd sure as hell *looked* like a medium to me. And my own limited experience with the astral plane confirmed that projection was something in a medium's arsenal of tricks. Our practice wasn't geared toward trying to make me project—though I wouldn't complain if that happened, since it might give me some kind of edge. But I hadn't gone astral lately, not even once. And we'd been doing yoga three, four times a week since The Clinic imploded. So far, all I had to show for it was relief from my persistent, nagging sciatica.

Bethany showed up for yoga at eleven o'clock on the dot— she's the poster child for precision—with her scientist sidekick in tow. I'd found these tag-alongs from the lab intimidating, at first. Just goes to show how a person can become inured to just about anything, given enough exposure.

Bethany was a tall woman around my age, with long, dark

hair, a Mediterranean complexion, piercing dark eyes, and intimidating posture. She takes her yoga very seriously. In fact, she doesn't even gloat that she gets to come to work in stretch pants while the rest of us are in suits.

Since so many different types of certified Psychs worked at the FPMP, there was a big pool of subjects to use in their study of the effects of yoga. The NPs weren't left out, either, since it wouldn't be an experiment without a control subject to use for a baseline.

I draped my jacket over the back of my chair, took off my tie, ditched my shoes and socks, and unbuttoned my shirt's top two buttons. The lab tech handed me a bundle of electrodes and I proceeded to stick them where they needed to be stuck. Not only was I less likely to trigger a panic attack and sweat them off if I put them on myself, but we'd done this routine so many times now, I had a good feel for exactly where each one was supposed to go.

Carl and Bethany got wired up, too, and we unrolled our yoga mats and assumed the position.

Bethany stood quietly for a few moments, eyes closed, centering—then said, "Today, we'll focus on Manipura, the third chakra. Let's begin."

I spread my feet, extended my arms, and settled into warrior one. The lab was having Bethany alter one variable at a time to try and determine what exactly had triggered my power-up back at the gym. Postures. Breathing. Chakra focus. So far, we hadn't figured much out, even when we reconstructed the specific routine that was so helpful before—or portions of it, anyhow. Thanks to my dumb injury, the postures I could do were limited to things that didn't require the support of my forearm or hand. But part of me was starting to worry that we weren't seeing any progress because yoga simply wasn't the natural psyactive I'd hoped it would be, and that whatever brought on my superconscious state back at the gym was a result of some other combination of triggers...or just dumb luck.

Bethany scrutinized my position, then nudged me into a more accurate semblance of the pose. She seldom did this with Carl. Not because he was NP—after all, we could very well hit the yoga jackpot and discover he was secretly a telekinetic all this time, and the reason he hated people pawing through his belongings was that he could feel the residue of their touch. But I strongly doubted it. I've only been on a first-name basis with one TK in the course of my life. And between Camp Hell, the PsyCop program and F-Pimp, I've met a *lot* of Psychs.

No, Carl was just way better at yoga.

Bethany went back to her mat, stretched into a perfect warrior one, then flowed into warrior two. As Carl and I mirrored her, she said, "Focus on your spine, above the navel, below the ribcage. Imagine a field of energy there, tucked behind the solar plexus against the front of the spine. Vic? It's just potential energy. Nothing is spinning. Not in any direction."

This was the thing about personalized yoga lessons. A hyper-observant teacher like Bethany gets to know your which-way-is-clockwise face.

"Imagine the energy as a beautiful sphere. A warm, rich yellow. And visualize the image of a lotus within."

Did most guys know what a lotus looked like, or was it one of those things women were great at and men just nodded along and hoped to change the subject before they revealed that they had absolutely zero clue? The cannery had decorative brick along the roofline that was supposed to be a lotus pattern—Egyptian Revival, and a weird attempt at it, to boot—but they were incredibly stylized. Still, I'm visual to a fault. When Bethany said the words *lotus* and *sphere*, the image of a big, round marble—the size of my fist, with a fake lotus in the center—popped into my head. Belatedly, I mentally painted the thing yellow.

"Vic? Did you have a question?"

It always felt funny to speak up during F-pimp yoga. But Bethany was big on "dialog." And our boss was really keen on her helping me figure my shit out. "Isn't this the *digestive* chakra?"

"That's right—Manipura is associated with metabolism and digestion."

"Great. But we didn't really touch on it that one time—"

"You're leaning forward," she said calmly. I straightened myself. "As you well know, chakras are merely a way to understand an abstract concept. Yes, digestion is one of the third-chakra functions, but Manipura is also the seat of dynamism. It represents your personal power. Isn't that exactly what you're hoping to activate?"

Well...when she put it that way.

"Can you picture the yellow sphere?"

"I guess."

"Breathe in."

Bethany was big into breathing, and she acted as if the majority of people were doing it wrong. But if I could forego the dangerous horse-pills and shove my psychic ability into another bracket by breathing in a certain way? I was all for it. I dutifully forced air in and out of my lungs according to her direction as we flowed through a few more poses. And when Bethany murmured, "Good," I felt a ridiculous sense of accomplishment. Because she wasn't effusive with her praise...and I really dug the thought of being *good* at something other than seeing ghosts.

Once our session drew to a close and the woman in the lab coat peeled the electrodes from my temples, Bethany said, "Have you spoken to Jack lately?"

I always had to do some mental gymnastics to figure out who we were talking about whenever someone called Jack Bly by his first name, even though he'd been my fake husband for a month. "Monday's staff meeting. Why?"

"Our focus on the Manipura reminded me of his digestive issues. I think he'd benefit from a session like this."

"Yeah...that thing I told you about him having irritable bowel syndrome was just a part of our undercover identities."

"It was?"

"His bowels are fine."

"Oh. Well. Good. That's good to hear. Very...good. Anyway. Remember to check in with your breath periodically, and I'll see you Friday."

"Will do."

Bethany and her scientist left Carl and me to roll up our mats and stow them in the cabinet with our exorcism gear. I shrugged into my jacket and was adjusting my necktie when I realized Carl was giving me a look—and quiet guys like him can say a heck of a lot without uttering a word.

"What?" I said.

The look intensified.

"Spit it out, Carl. What did I do now?"

"She's looking for a reason to talk to Agent Bly. Would it kill you to make that happen?"

"Wait, what? How did you get that from...?" Scratch that. I knew where he got it. Carl was excellent at reading people. Mostly, he'd trained to figure out who was carrying a hidden firearm or a suicide bomb. But he was also ten steps ahead of me in any given social situation.

I grabbed my phone, scowled it open, and said, "Tell Bly, *The yoga lady's hot for you.*"

"Sending."

Carl shook his head.

"What? We shared a freaking bed. I don't need to waste mental energy trying to be diplomatic."

"Sending," the phone repeated as it helpfully appended that last statement to the message.

The reply, *WTF?* appeared beneath the inadvertent second half of my message. I sent him a thumbs-up, then navigated away from the messaging app.

Mission accomplished.

CHAPTER THREE

While my back might have felt fantastic, my mood definitely did not. I'd come home from work prepared for a night of picking through old rolodexes and yearbooks, both hoping I'd find something, worrying I wouldn't...and dreading that if I did, I'd regret it. But when I walked in the door, Jacob called out from the kitchen, "Zoom meeting with Pastor Jill in fifteen." Oh, right. The wedding. "Soup's on the stove if you're hungry."

"Remind me again what your priest wants."

"Not a priest—that's Catholic. Pastor Jill is a Lutheran Minister."

"And that's different how?"

"She's a woman, for one. And she's happy to marry us in church, for another."

"You're just gonna overlook the obvious dig about groping altar boys?"

Jacob ignored my sorry attempt at humor.

I said, "Isn't Christianity all basically the same?"

"I have no idea—what I know about Catholicism doesn't amount to much. My father converted when my parents tied the knot, and according to him, he never looked back. When my sister and I had sleepovers at my grandparents' place, Grandma would drag us to mass...to my mother's great annoyance. Barbara and I were intrigued by all the statuary and stained glass. It felt mysterious. Taboo."

"So you're *sure* there was no altar boy type action?"

Jacob gave me an exasperated look.

Satisfied I'd finally landed my awful joke, I dropped an ice cube into my soup so I could pound it without cooking my own esophagus, then dragged a dining room chair upstairs so we could video chat with the pastor side by side. I hadn't exactly been thrilled to find out our church wedding involved actually meeting with the pastor—frankly, I would've preferred to write a check and call it good. But apparently, this was how things were done.

Jacob pulled up the app to make sure the audio was working while I futzed around with my chair and fantasized about pretending I didn't fit in the video frame. Unfortunately, it was a small office. And I could tell by the little picture-in-picture image up at the corner of the screen that no matter which way I leaned, the pastor would be able to see me just fine.

"I'm a little nervous," I admitted.

"We're not undercover. Just answer her questions as yourself."

I considered this advice. "Yeah. Not any easier."

Jacob had been gearing up for go-time—I could tell by the set of his shoulders and the laser focus of his dark eyes. But something in my small admission worked its way through his armor, and he turned to me and touched my cheek just as the computer started bleeping the pastor's imminent arrival. "You'll be great," he said softly. And then his game-face was back.

I'm not sure exactly what I expected the pastor of Jacob's

church to look like. Chicago is predominately Catholic, and what little experience I do have of church is steeped in ceremony, prayer candles, and elaborate stained glass. But the churches where Jacob grew up were mostly Lutheran. And to an outsider like me, the Lutherans seemed somewhat more approachable.

A generic person-silhouette popped up. Something circled a few times in the middle of the screen and then resolved into Pastor Jill, a sturdy woman in her mid-fifties with short, no-nonsense salt-and-pepper hair. Caucasian—though that was practically a given, since nine out of ten people in Jacob's hometown are white. The type of middle-aged Midwestern woman you'd encounter at a hardware store, or maybe a tractor pull.

"Good to see you again, Jacob." Her voice was really assertive. She would've made a good cop. "And to meet your future husband."

"Hi." I gave a stilted wave. Ugh.

"I was so glad to hear the two of you chose to have your marriage blessed in the church. Church weddings are falling out of favor these days. Young couples think the venue is old-fashioned and predictable. They want to get married in the park, or at the beach, or hurtling down the hill of a giant roller coaster. But as a same-sex couple, you guys having your ceremony at church sends a positive message to the whole community: that you're willing to stand up and declare your commitment. And that you have the same right to do so as any other couple."

Jacob agreed with her. "Absolutely. It's important to us to set a good example."

Talk about laying it on thick.

But Jacob is great at faking sincerity, and Pastor Jill didn't seem to notice. "I'm sending you a PDF of our pre-wedding guide that's got a series of exercises for you to complete, and we'll touch base to discuss any topics that come up. We can start with one of the exercises together to help you get a feel for them."

"No one said there was gonna be a quiz," I said. Jokingly. More or less.

"There are no right or wrong answers, guys. These exercises give you a chance to communicate about your important issues up front, with support and guidance."

Holy hell.

I checked our picture to see what the heck my face was doing. It looked encouragingly neutral.

"We'll start with the pecuniary questions." Pecuni-what? The pastor looked at us expectantly while I wondered if I should've spent my afternoon boning up on Christianity instead of doing yoga. The pause stretched awkwardly, and then she cracked a smile. "That's another word for *financial*. It was on my word-of-the-day calendar. I was excited to get a chance to use it."

I quelled a sigh, settled into my chair, and resigned myself to another forty-five minutes of sheer awkwardness.

Pastor Jill said, "Money can be a huge source of conflict in a relationship. It's important to understand where your spouse is coming from in *pecuniary* matters."

I went for a grin. It looked more like a wince.

The pastor said, "I'm sure it's no surprise that money can be such a loaded topic. Money isn't just about money. For instance, an issue that seems pecuniary on the surface might actually be about status. How much do you agree with the following statement: I compare myself to others financially."

"I don't find income to be particularly relevant," Jacob said.

"Right," I said.

Pastor Jill waited for me to add something, and when I shrugged, she said, "Can you elaborate on that?"

I racked my brain for an answer. "Income is something I only notice in a general sense. A person who's strapped for cash will react differently than a person who's flush, and my main point of comparison is myself. And a homicide with no financial motive could be a crime of passion, or a cover-up for something else—"

"Remind me what your job is?"

I shifted uncomfortably. "Federal agent. Before that, thirteen years on the force."

"Homicide," Jacob added.

The pastor looked flustered, but only momentarily. "As it relates to your *personal* life," she clarified. "How much comparing do you do?"

Could I answer, *A normal amount?* Probably not without raising a bunch of red flags. "Once in a while I might notice income, I guess. But I don't really dwell on it."

That seemed to satisfy her enough to move on to the next question. "Money issues can also be about security. How much do you agree with the statement: I feel more secure knowing we have enough money to pay our bills."

Hard to say who she was looking at through the video camera, Jacob or me, but Jacob answered first. "It's a legitimate concern, obviously. We're fortunate enough to have decent incomes."

Pastor Jill said, "What's your take on it, Vic?"

I couldn't very well say it was a non-issue for me. It would sound like I was covering up some deep-seated pecuniary anxiety I wasn't willing to admit, even to myself. But I wasn't. "We really have been pretty lucky. When big-ticket problems have come up, one of us has had the wherewithal to handle it."

"Does that mean you had reserves at one point, and now you don't?"

"Not like I did when we first met. But, you know. Houses cost money."

Jacob added, "We're pretty comfortable."

Pastor Jill said, "And what does that mean to you in terms of a safety net? A month's worth of expenses? Three months? A year?"

"We've had some car issues lately," Jacob hedged. "Ideally, at least a year."

"And you, Vic? How much savings would it take for you to feel financially secure?"

It seemed like a trick question. Because I'm insecure about everything from the fit of my pants to the sound of my own chewing. But money is just...money. "A month or two, I guess. If I had to take on a pay cut for some reason—or if our house fell in, or some other major expense smacked me upside the head—I'd deal with it. I'd cope. I'd adjust."

Pastor Jill jotted a few notes, then said, "Another thing money can represent in a relationship is control. You both work, you each have your own source of income. In the questionnaire you filled out, it says you have your own bank accounts, and a joint account for the household. How do you both feel about this?"

"It's fine," I said.

Jacob added, "We each came into the relationship with our own finances. It seemed easiest to add the joint account instead of completely dismantling systems that already worked for each of us."

The pastor said, "Vic, can you elaborate?"

Not only had I never given our pecuniary arrangement much thought, but I couldn't even tell you which one of us said, "Why don't we set up another bank account for the bills?" when we moved in together. If I can set something and forget it, I do—and our mundane finances were a prime example. Everything was on auto-pay. My personal debit card was never declined. And once in a while, I grabbed some cash at the ATM and noted that my receipt showed I still had money in the bank. Not a fortune. But I could buy another latte if the mood struck me, no problem.

"It really is fine. I don't give it much thought, and I'm not what you'd call a big spender."

"Spending is another important area to explore. How would you rate this statement: I check with my partner before I make a major purchase...?" As if Jacob ever asked anyone permission to do anything. Apparently, I was smirking. "You find something funny in that, Vic?"

Jacob answered her. "Like I said, we're fortunate that buying the wrong washing machine won't leave us choosing between prescriptions and food."

You were the one who insisted on a front-loader, I thought. But since he did all the laundry, I didn't indulge myself in the dig. "Look, I trust Jacob. And maybe it's adrenaline burnout, or maybe I'm just oblivious—but given what I deal with day to day, I just can't bring myself to get worked up about shopping."

Thankfully, that was the last awkward question we had time for. We got an assignment to do the first section of the marriage workbook before our next meeting, said our goodbyes and signed off. When the video call closed and the camera light winked out, the dark desktop photo of a starry galaxy let me see our reflections in the monitor glass. Not as clear as the tiny video picture-in-picture. But a lot larger. We both looked slightly spooked, as if we hadn't realized that while we were grilling the family, someone would be grilling us.

Once the computer powered down, I said, "I wasn't aware there'd be a PDF involved. No one said anything about a test when we signed up for this. Are we being graded? What if we fail, do we lose our big church wedding?"

Jacob shrugged wearily. He clicked over to his email and found the booklet waiting for us: *Wedded Bliss*.

CHAPTER FOUR

The reflection of our expressions in the monitor was priceless. Jacob hit the download button. "Our wedding's not in jeopardy. We'll just power through the booklet, say the right things, and everyone will be happy."

"Sounds good to me," I said...and then wanted to take it right back once I got a load of the table of contents. "Expressions of intimacy? As in sex? And we're supposed to talk about this with your priest?"

"Minister." The correction was halfhearted, as Jacob was too busy navigating over to that section to see exactly how mortified we needed to be.

Emotional and physical intimacy go hand in hand, but not everyone has the same expectations where intimacy is concerned. Discuss the following:
- What makes you feel appreciated?
- Who modeled affectionate behavior for you?
- How do you define affection?

Ugh. My first impulse was to leap up, run down to the kitchen, and scour the fridge for some leftovers. But before I fled the scene, it occurred to me that they wouldn't ask what affection meant if the definition was universal.

"How *do* you define affection?" I asked.

Jacob seemed puzzled—but also willing to talk it through. "Physically?"

"I don't know. You tell me."

"Closeness." He wheeled his chair up against mine and leaned into my side. "Touch." He ran his fingertips along my thigh. "A kiss...."

His lips brushed mine while his whiskers tickled my chin. Tongue. Just a hint. No, an invitation. It would have been so easy to lean into that kiss and avoid a potentially awkward conversation—but I was looking at a chance to find out how Jacob really ticked. It would be a real shame to throw that away.

I eased back and said, "So affection is sex." I glanced at the monitor and read, "*Affection can be verbal and nonverbal.* So, the nonverbal part—?"

"It's not just sex." He took my hand in his—the hand that wasn't hauling around a heavy plaster cast—and traced my life line with his thumb. His gaze went soft as he searched his memory. "Remember back at the old apartment?"

"How could I forget?"

"It was a Saturday morning. We both had the day off. I was heading out to the gym and you stopped me at the door. Not to kiss me goodbye...but to tuck in the tag that was sticking out on the back of my T-shirt."

"Gee. How romantic."

He smiled to himself. "Sometimes, back then, you hardly seemed real. More like a character out of a movie come to life.

I fell for you so hard, so fast, sometimes I worried I might wake up some day and find that the whole thing was an elaborate fantasy of mine, some crazy, vivid dream. And when you'd do something psychic—it was always obvious to me you weren't talking to yourself—this thing we had together felt just a little more fragile every time. Like eventually you'd wonder why you saddled yourself with some useless Stiff."

"Jacob—"

"But then you'd do something mundane like tucking in my tag, and I'd realize there was more to you than the high-powered medium who could literally see ghosts. Sure, that phenomenally rare psychic was you. But you were also just a guy." He looked up and met my gaze. It was hard, with so much tenderness there...but I managed to keep myself from looking away. He cupped my jaw and smoothed a thumb across my temple. "A guy with incredibly sexy blue eyes."

Okay. That earned him an eye-roll...but I was smiling while I did it. It's hard to kiss someone when you're smiling, but I guess the added challenge just makes it all the sweeter.

Once the kissing got hot and heavy—and once Jacob's office chair threatened to roll out from under him—he swung out of his seat and dragged me to the floor on top of him. I wasn't only straddling his hips, but also the pronounced bulge our kissing had encouraged. The office carpet was decent enough, though nowhere near as cushy as a bed, so when things started hurting, I rolled onto my side to take some pressure off my knees. A box of file folders prodded me in the kidney and an old rubber band was sticking to my neck, but I ignored them.

Our awkward tangle of limbs—and our sudden spike of need—was enough to distract me...at least until it was obvious that my non-broken hand being trapped beneath us was seriously cramping my style. There was only so far I could take things by grinding my thigh against him.

We adjourned to the bedroom and ditched our clothes. Unfortunately, the pause in the action was allowing words to slip in. Jacob asked, "Did you notice the next question on the list?"

"Whether we'd discussed family planning?"

Jacob treated me to a relatively tolerant smirk. "What sexual activities do you enjoy?"

"If anyone's figured that out about me, it's you."

He shook out the comforter—we don't generally make the bed these days, since no one sees it but us—and shoved an extra pillow out of the way. "I can go first. Even though I already spilled my heart out once tonight."

"No, it's fine. I'll take a stab at it." Maybe I was feeling cocky, what with our first premarital gauntlet successfully navigated. "I like it when you pound me."

There. I said it.

But before I could be too pleased with myself, Jacob threw me a curveball. "Why?"

What kind of question was that?

And yet, when I really thought about it, I had to concede the answer might not be so obvious. Jacob could physically over-power me if he wanted to, and we both knew it. Oh, I might get a few jabs in, but in the end, he was bigger, bulkier, and way more athletic. And the thought of him pinning me down and slamming into me? I dug it. Given my history, the mere thought of being overwhelmed should leave me tearing off in the opposite direction. But not with Jacob. "I like it because... sometimes it feels good to finally let go," I eventually said. "Because I trust you."

We left the lights on.

Not usually my preference. I don't mind seeing Jacob, but it can be distracting to know I'm being seen. Tonight, though—after talking more about our feelings than we had since...well, since ever...why bother hiding in the darkness?

He did me on my back, with my legs hitched loosely over his thighs. A slow, easy fuck, face to face, hands clasped together on the pillow. My plaster cast was still in the way, but he wove together what he could of our fingers. If I had a favorite position, this was the one. As sex goes...pretty basic. And eventually I'd need to reach down between us and help myself along to the grand finale. But maybe certain things become the standard for a reason.

Afterward, we lay there quietly for a moment, considering ourselves. I wasn't thinking much of anything other than *wow*, but Jacob was still ruminating on the meeting. He said, "When we were talking to Pastor Jill about our finances...did I come off too glib?"

"You're always glib—although the pastor's bullshit meter did seem pretty sensitive. But since when are you nervous about money?"

"I'm not." He dragged a finger through the jizz drying on my belly. "She's right, though. Money is about so much more than just money, and I want to make sure you really are good with our finances, and not just saying you are to avoid a confrontation."

I gave a silent laugh. "I'm a ball of anxiety about practically everything—so I'd advise you to sit back and enjoy the one area of my life where I'm not a complete basket case."

"You don't see it, do you?" Jacob drew a few more swirls. "You're really easygoing in so many ways."

Maybe. But wasn't that like saying the stern of the Titanic

stayed pretty dry as the ship went nose-down?

"I'm serious, Vic." Jacob nudged my jaw with a tacky forefinger to make me look him in the eye. "I realized just how lucky I am when you said you trusted me."

"In bed?"

"That, too. But the first time you said it, about our finances—especially the way you were so sure of it with Pastor Jill. It means a lot."

Funny. While the minister was raking us over the coals, I'd been blurting out whatever came to mind, while Jacob was busy curating his answers to make our relationship sound as healthy as possible. But the exercise got to him anyhow, and now he was feeling all sappy. I kissed him gently, deliberately, then told him, "We're solid, mister. We're good."

We lay together like that, basking in our big moment—and our big-O—at least until the pecuniary concerns started drifting in.

I said, "We need a safety net. In cash. In case we ever need to pull a Con Dreyfuss and disappear."

"Agreed." Jacob pushed himself up reluctantly from the dent he'd been putting in the mattress. "Let's go hit the ATM."

CHAPTER FIVE

Was it entirely rational to go grab fifty bucks right that second?
Obviously not. But it would make us feel a hell of a lot better.
So we threw on some clothes and headed out.

"I'll find out the best way to start skimming," Jacob said. That
was just one benefit about being Internal Affairs. Your co-work-
ers can teach you all kinds of cool tricks. "But a few dollars here,
a few dollars there would be really hard to track."

We headed over to a walk-up machine on Lawrence, the
one that was right outside the hardware store where we had
fake keys cut whenever a sensitive conversation needed to
occur. This particular ATM let you choose the denomination of
your withdrawal, and we'd decided it was best to go for bigger
bills, which would be less bulky to hide. We parked and made
our way up the block. As we did, I said, "I've been on enough
busts, back when I was on patrol, to know that anyplace you'd
think to hide something is the first place anyone's gonna look.
Particularly the toilet tank."

"And the freezer," Jacob said. "Those fake cans they sell
for hiding valuables aren't realistic, either. Plus, it's gotta be

something we can grab in a hurry. So prying loose a brick in the basement won't do us much good. We'll start by keeping our wallets topped off, and then scope out a few good spots near the front door."

Jacob ponied up to the machine and stuck his card in the slot. As he did, I wondered how obvious it would be if I took out some money too. What would I normally do? Not that anything about me is normal. But typically, if we stopped for cash and I was low, it would only make sense for me to grab some, myself.

Overthinking everything is exhausting, so I was pretty stoked about coming to a decision without too many mental gymnastics.

But I was so focused on patting myself on the back that I didn't notice anything was wrong until we had company.

The ATM was lit up bright to encourage a false sense of security in its customers. While a well-lit location in plain view is safer than a dark, out-of-the-way alley, a desperate enough crackhead might very well be willing to roll the dice and take their chances.

I saw Jacob's shadow. And my shadow.

And another shadow.

With no one casting it.

I was more startled than afraid—until the temperature plummeted, and my breath left my body in a frigid curl of air.

Most of the spirits I run into can be handled by convincing them to cross over, or urging them through the veil with Florida Water and salt. But then I stumble across a scary, messed-up ghost that reminds me it never pays to get too complacent. And judging by queasy feeling in the pit of my gut, this was one of those times.

Instinctively, I grabbed Jacob by the back of his sweatshirt and hauled him away from the shadow. Since I wasn't holding a reserve, white light didn't jump from me to him in a burst, but *flowed* instead—and that drain was just as disconcerting. Energy surged in through my third eye and out through my fist, like I was nothing but a big, hollow drinking straw.

I let go, fast, but Jacob felt the zap. And while he might not be able to see when something dead was crashing the party, he could sense it. He swung around one way, then the other—fast, like he was clearing a room.

Like he thought he damn well should be able to see. But, of course, he couldn't.

"Get behind me," he snapped. He was the True Stiff, the human shield. Not me. But of course I wasn't about to let him take charge. He couldn't *see* it.

Though, for that matter, neither could I. Not until panic-induced white light thundered down to refill my reservoir, and the shape of a man flickered into being. I caught a glimpse of a guy in a hoodie, with the hood cinched up tight and his face in shadow like the Grim Reaper. Just a flicker, then the visual was gone again. "Don't be stupid," the ghost barked out—holy shit, they read minds now? "Gimme the fuckin' money, asshole, or I'll blow your fuckin' head off."

My perceptions rearranged themselves as an array of ghostly flash cards sprang to mind. Repeater? Not with that temperature drop. Slippery? Definitely, a half-seen thing that was only partially tuned in, hard to get a bead on. Sentient? Maybe, but not particularly self-aware, not if it thought our money would do it any good. Something in between a repeater and a lucid spirit. A screwed-up ghost that hadn't figured out it was dead.

A ghost you wouldn't want to stumble across even back when it was alive.

"Talk to me," Jacob ground out between clenched teeth.

"Hostile—my visual is for shit—two o'clock."

Jacob inserted himself more deliberately between the dead thing and me. I let him.

"You think I'm playin'?" Its voice was garbled and wet. "Huh? You think I'm fuckin' playin'?"

It couldn't actually shoot me with a ghost gun...*could it?* Jesus. White light.

My neurochemicals scrambled into fight-mode, and as they did, my visual came back. Still flickery. But this time, I was looking right at the spot where the thing appeared.

And I could see a bullet hole where one of its eyes should be. As I glimpsed the bloody socket, the wall behind it lit up with spectral blood spatter. Just for a fraction of a second. But that was more than enough.

I centered myself as best I could as I grabbed for a baggie in my coat pocket and tore it open with my teeth. Salt scattered down my arm. White light found the conduit I'd opened moments ago with Jacob, and mojo poured into the salt so forcefully, the baggie lit up to my mind's eye like it was radio-active. I lobbed the open bag over Jacob's shoulder...but as I did, Jacob sidestepped. Not only did he jostle my arm, but another surge of white light arced between us. The baggie smacked the brick wall in a burst of activated salt.

Did I hit my target?

No clue.

And now I wasn't amped up enough to see the damn thing anymore.

Jacob scanned the area, and scanned again. "I think we got it."

"You think? I'd *know,* if you hadn't grabbed my freakin' light."

Jacob stiffened. Muscles jumped in his jaw. But he kept his

attention on the task at hand: making sure no one went home possessed. Namely, me. I opened up my crown chakra and pulled. It might all be symbolic, the thing I do when I power up, but I've done it enough that it feels like a physical strain—one with very little outward evidence. Like holding my breath, or engaging my "core."

We both attempted to see if we could tell whether or not the dead guy was still around. The temperature had normalized, and more importantly, I didn't see telltale hints of ghost peeking out from between the bricks. The more my tank filled back up, the more certain I was that we'd exorcised the crackhead mugger.

Unless we'd only scared him off.

A pedestrian crossed the street to avoid the two of us—me covered in salt, Jacob stiff with anger, clenching and unclenching his fists like he'd pummel the next thing that crossed his path.

"We've done all we can do right now," I said.

Jacob spun around to face me. "My name was in that book. I've got a talent. But what good is it if I don't know how it works?"

"We'll figure it out."

"Really? And how do we manage that? Especially with you shoving me off to the sidelines."

I cocked my head toward the store. "C'mon. Not out here." Not in front of the ATM surveillance where God-knows-who was watching.

Jacob's better at holding onto his anger than I am. As my adrenaline ebbed, I was already ruing the fact that I'd snapped at him. Normally, he could tolerate the random pissy remark. But his abilities were a notorious sore spot—and I'd just given that lingering bruise a good, solid kick.

We threaded up the aisles looking for something loud to camouflage our conversation. The old man who normally cut our keys was helping someone over by the nails and screws. But then I spotted some big metal rolls of chain you could purchase by the yard. I gave one a tug and it made a grinding metallic noise. And, bonus, we wouldn't have to shell out any of our hard-skimmed cash to buy it. We could just roll it back up when we were done talking.

Jacob and I angled ourselves so the cameras couldn't see our mouths. I gave the chain a few more yanks, then he rolled it back up. Over the clattering and clanking, I said, "Listen, we both want the same thing here. We're on the same side."

"I know."

"I get that you're frustrated. There are no practice ghosts, and spirits don't sit around waiting to be exorcised at our convenience. They take us by surprise and they need to be handled on the spot, and there's no room for trial and error."

"That's not it." Jacob hauled on the chain and several yards of it unspooled, dropping to a loud pile at our feet. He stared at the chain pile for a moment, then said, "What *am* I?"

I touched his hand tentatively. Nothing jumped between us, and I gave it a squeeze. "We'll figure it out," I said.

Though how we'd go about doing that, I had absolutely no idea.

CHAPTER SIX

Taking up with the FPMP had felt like a pretty strategic move, at the time. Not only would I have access to all the latest and greatest in Psych research, but I'd be able to keep an eye on all the spies who used to be spying on me. Too bad none of these resources were any use in me figuring out what the hell Dr. Kamal had been up to.

A few days after the big ATM blunder, I was called into the Director's office before I even made it to my desk. Right from the start, I got along with Laura Kim—probably because I was the type of hot mess The Fixer was just itching to put right. But once she found out she was a low-level psychic medium, our power dynamic shifted. Even though she was my boss, I was the only one who could tell her with any degree of accuracy whether or not she was blundering into a random ghost.

Laura Kim sees a lot of me. Not because I'm a particularly high-ranking agent, but because she feels better knowing her office is free from any stowaways of the dead variety.

Ghosts have their ways—they're unlikely to just crop up out of nowhere—but given Laura's position, I figure it's safest to give her office a periodic scan.

We exchanged bland morning pleasantries while I poked through the credenza and gave her miniblinds a quick shake. "All clear," I said, and then launched into a request while I was still on Laura's good side. "And so, I was thinking, now that all the weirdness at The Clinic has calmed down, maybe Archives can dig a little deeper on Dr. Kamal. Has anyone looked at the microfiche—?"

"Vic? We've been through this already." Laura took off her glasses and pinched the bridge of her nose. "Our talent is stretched thin as it is. I'm not going to allocate resources to investigating a closed case that's not presenting any current threat." She locked eyes with me. "Unless there's anything additional that's come to light."

I knew full well Laura didn't have the ability to read my mind—but sometimes she sure seemed like she could. "Kamal was at the forefront of psychic research," I hedged. "If you're keen on figuring out what makes us tick, maybe his original findings would give us some insight."

It seemed like a great argument to me, but Laura plowed on ahead without even pretending to consider it. "If you want more insight into your talent, then start looking somewhere that might actually do you some good. I've managed to secure a few hours of time from Agent Davis today. I suggest you use it wisely."

Special Agent Darla Davis rode shotgun with me in a standard black FPMP Lexus sedan. Darla looked more like some casting agent's idea of a fed than an actual government employee. Her black pantsuit was tailored within an inch of its life. Her hair was a shade of auburn never before seen in nature. And her pointy heels could double as a lethal weapon. In some ways, it wasn't a far cry from the Hot Topic goth chick she'd been back when we first met. Just more subtle, more expensive...and infinitely more authoritative.

The only time I saw Darla was when she was between top-secret assignments. I wouldn't go so far as to say we were friends—she'd specifically asked me not to invite her to the wedding—but thanks to our shared experiences, we understood each other pretty well. "How'd you end up on Richie duty today?" I asked. "I hope you're not being punished."

Darla rolled her eyes. "Director Kim likes to keep an especially sharp eye on him, just in case. I suppose I can't blame her. Personally, I can't imagine how your Jennifer Chance would manage to find him from the other side, but if there's anything we've figured out about mediumship...it's that we've hardly got half a clue how it all works."

"I guess. Still—not that I'm angling for your assignments, what with you running off to play ghost hunter every time some VIP decides their house is haunted—we've got a pretty good idea of our own capabilities."

"And?"

I shrugged.

Darla arched an eyebrow. "And you wonder why they'd pick me over you for the high profile cases." Maybe, back in the day, eclipsing me was something Darla would have gloated about. But although she spent her early career being overlooked and passed over, lately, she'd finally come into her own. "Politicians. I'm the ranking agent, so I'm the one they want. Lots of diplomacy involved, since half the time there's nothing there to find.

Trust me, you see the inside of one governor's mansion, you've seen 'em all. Though it is fun to poke through their cupboards and closets under the guise of checking for nonphysical energy."

"Energy that you could hear from anywhere in the room just by focusing on it."

"Exactly."

Maybe Jacob would do better to develop his mystery talent with someone like Darla—someone who wasn't as dependent on their visual perception as I was. I didn't always enjoy Darla's company, but I did trust her. And she'd seen what Jacob could do first-hand when the three of us tracked down The Assassin together at the FPMP. Be that as it may, it would be careless to discuss Jacob with her in an agency vehicle where the whole surveillance team would be privy to my innermost thoughts.

Unfortunately, in terms of keeping anything I wanted to say off the record, Richie's place was no better. Richie lived in a retirement home where all his needs were met...and where F-Pimp could keep an eye on him. The surveillance was in place mainly for his protection, but also to ensure there wasn't a replay of the time good ol' Einstein suddenly jumped three hundred IQ points. I could see the wisdom in not letting the guy just run amok. But all the surveillance definitely cramped my style.

We found Richie in the TV room watching a banal daytime variety show with a few well-to-do old ladies. Did they feel maternal toward him, I wondered? Or would they just keep their hearing aids set low so as not to throttle him for continually talking over the host?

Richie spotted us and groaned, "Oh no." Melodramatic, as always. "It's not time to fill out reports again already."

"You used to be happy to see me," I said.

"That was before you guys started writing your boring book. Now the only time you ever come to see me is when you need my help."

Darla met my eyes and smirked. Glad someone found him amusing.

"Come on." I cocked my head toward the conference room we'd reserved. "Let's leave your neighbors in peace."

Richie led the way like he owned the place. Heck, the FPMP had paid him so exorbitantly all these years, maybe he could have...if he hadn't blown his money trying to buy other people's affections with random gifts and endless rounds of overpriced drinks.

Like everything else at Richie's care home, the conference room was ritzy. An urn of coffee and an assortment of pastry was waiting—and not the cheap-o donuts you'd find at a convenience store, either.

"This sucks," Richie announced. "There's no whipped cream. It's bad enough that every time I turn around I'm answering your dumb questions, but no whipped cream? And would it kill them to have some chocolate sprinkles? I'm retired, you know. After fifteen years of outstanding service. That's what Director Dreyfuss said. Outstanding." Oh, I'll bet Richie's service stood out, all right. "It's usually twenty years before you can retire, y'know. But Director Dreyfuss had them make a 'section just for me."

Was this how I sounded when I asked Darla why she'd been chosen over me for a mission? If so, I wished I could go back in time and slap myself. "Listen," I told him, "I'm sure the coffee's fine."

"Even without sprinkles," Darla added. She was enjoying this.

Probably because she only had to deal with the guy a few scant times a year.

"The coffee shop on Irving Park got sprinkles. You have to ask for 'em special...but they got 'em."

Obviously, Richie had some sort of ulterior motive for trying to steer us toward a coffee shop. If he absolutely needed sprinkles in order to function, the facility's kitchen could probably dredge something up. I hate to admit to taking any cues from Constantine Dreyfuss—but in dealing with Richie, sometimes instead of trying to figure out how his mind worked, it was easier to just appease him.

And that was how I ended up in the world's dingiest coffee shop with not just one, but *two* of my old cronies from Camp Hell.

I may be no coffee connoisseur, since enough cream will make anything drinkable, but I could tell by the smell alone that the coffee back at the home would've been a heck of a lot better than whatever they served here. This made me even more leery about the fact that Richie had asked for this joint specifically. Was there possession involved? Or maybe some non-human etheric entity pulling his strings? I was pondering all the stuff we well and truly didn't know when I felt him perk up beside me...just as a cashier waved at him.

An extremely *busty* cashier.

Darla caught my eye and treated me to another smirk. I suspected it was only one of many I'd receive before the day was out.

Richie insisted on paying for our order—one regular black coffee for Darla, one regular coffee with cream for me, and one double-mocha extra whip monstrosity that made my teeth ache just looking at it. The FPMP would've been happy to pick up the tab, but Richie was eager to look like a big shot, so we let him pay. No doubt the tip he scrawled on the credit card receipt was outrageous. Hopefully, it would leave him in a less obstinate frame of mind.

Once we were all settled well out of earshot of the neighborhood book club, Darla and I consulted our notes. She was on a spiffy tablet. I still preferred good, old-fashioned paper—it made a more satisfying sound as I riffled through the pages. "On the subject of possession," I said, "we're trying to get an accurate idea if there are any preliminary warning signs involved that a medium could use to his or her advantage." If it was anything like a migraine, for instance, where a brief aura preceded the event, it would give the victim time to act. I, for one, would appreciate enough fair warning to zip-tie myself to the nearest heavy object and toss my sidearm across the room.

"Possession of what?" Richie asked.

"Spirit possession." I thought I sounded pretty patient.

"Why would you ask me about that?"

"Because you're a medium." That statement was met with a look that seemed too dense to be serious. "A medium who's experienced an instance of—"

"Nuh-uh. Nothing like that never happened to me."

Darla emitted a very lengthy and heartfelt sigh.

I pretended Richie Duff wasn't already dancing on my very last nerve. "It might feel like a time jump—like realizing you don't know how you got where you are."

"I dunno nothing about that."

"Or you might retain some awareness of what you're doing but feel like you're in a daze—"

"Nope. Sorry. Can't help you."

"Okay, how about this? Let's think back to your last place of residence. You disassembled a television set—"

"That's not a crime. It was *my* TV. I could do what I *want* with it."

"Look, this isn't an accusation. We're trying to establish a baseline of experience—"

"It was *my* TV," he insisted...and then he sent his big, syrupy mass of coffee toppling so it disgorged itself all over the table. Darla grabbed her tablet and I grabbed my notes—now christened in the upper left corner—while Richie feigned remorse. "Oops."

"I'm moving to that table by the window," Darla said with only a modicum of disgust, as if she hadn't really expected much from Einstein to begin with.

I grabbed a wad of napkins and joined her, leaving Richie to flit around the mess he'd made while the buxom cashier came over to help contain the spill. Gingerly, I blotted the edge of my notebook. "I don't think he's gonna give us anything."

Darla considered. "I don't think he has anything much to give. We want to find out what the precursor to possession might be... and maybe there's nothing to find."

Frustrating enough to make me understand, in some twisted way, how I'd come to be locked in a room with a dead body at the tender age of twenty-three. Seeing the people I'd known way back then always left me a touch maudlin, eager to devolve into victimhood and self-pity. Fortunately, I had more pressing issues than my pathetic origin story—and I suddenly realized that here, now, in this off-the-beaten-path location, I finally had a chance to talk to Darla without the entire FPMP listening in.

And hopefully, a chance to recruit her to help me get some answers.

"So...Darla...you read my report about the possession at Mid

North Medical pharmacy?"

She flicked through her tablet. "That sounded like a real barrel of laughs. Non-physical entities?"

"Forget about the habit demons. What do you remember about Dr. Kamal?"

"Why? What did you leave off the report?"

For all that we didn't spend much time together, Darla knew me pretty darn well.

I meant to make a negligent "oh, you know how it is" gesture— but only succeeded in thumping my plaster cast against the table, which very nearly left us with another coffee tidal wave on our hands. "What I saw when he was possessing the pharmacist wasn't a hundred percent Kamal, because he'd merged with the entities. But what was left of him...it recognized me." I glanced down at my notebook with its coffee-stained corner, which reminded me of another notebook—the one Sergeant Warwick diverted from evidence so I could investigate. The one with Jacob's initials inside. "It got me to wondering...can you help me find out what Kamal was after?"

"What are you saying—you want me to arrange for the two of you to have a chat?"

"You don't have to make it sound so ludicrous."

"Anwar Kamal was terrifying enough when he was alive. I can't imagine he was any less horrific as a ghost covered in etheric remoras."

"Terrifying how?"

"God complex. Devoid of empathy. Borderline sadist. Take your pick."

"But it's not like he can actually touch you from across the veil, can he? I thought your talent worked more like a telephone."

Darla gave me the sort of look she'd normally reserve for

Richie. "Channeling is less like a phone call and more like long-distance possession. And unless I've got a damn good reason to make contact, I'm not keen on sharing my body with the likes of Kamal. What is it you're hoping to get from him, anyway?"

The reason Jacob's initials were in that damn book. Not that I could say as much. Even if I did pull Darla into the loop, if she was this dead-set against channeling Kamal, my actual reasons might not be enough to get her to help me—so I did my best to make it seem like we both had something to gain.

"Aren't you interested in understanding what happened at Camp Hell?" I asked. "Especially now that we're all grown up?"

"What's there to understand?"

I thought back to the post-mortem glimpse I'd had of Director Sanchez, strangled in his office. "People died there. And for what?"

Darla blinked rapidly. Her eyeballs looked wet. "Even if we knew what the hell they were hoping to achieve at Heliotrope Station, it wouldn't bring anyone back, would it?"

Guess she was a lot fonder of Sanchez than I ever was. But before I could figure out how to massage that into a good reason for Darla to conference call with our late doctor, Richie bounded over with an even more excessive coffee-like drink and said, "When the cashier lady bent over to clean it up, I could see right down her top. Heh heh."

I tried to catch Darla's eye and exchange a look, but she was lost in thought now. I guess I really didn't take into account that she'd come through Camp Hell as scarred and embittered as me.

CHAPTER SEVEN

I managed to keep myself from throttling Richie...barely. In terms of the book Darla and I were valiantly attempting to write, he was pretty much useless—but that didn't mean he served no purpose at all. My hope was that I could bond with Darla over our mutual dislike of the guy. Unfortunately, sharing an exasperated eye-roll is one thing. Allowing someone to puppeteer your body is another.

Darla was at least willing to share her trade secrets with me. We were so different, though, that even armed with her detailed description of long-distance calling, I had no idea how to make it happen. From the sound of it, she put herself into a receptive state. Likely alpha, which I could do with the Mood Blaster app on my phone. And then? She searched...and listened.

That's where I lost my grasp on the instructions. Not because I'm visual while she's auditory—after all, I can hear ghosts too. But because there was a key step in the process that was so intangible she couldn't even articulate what it was.

That vague step was the part where training fell away and psychic talent took over—the switch that flipped when a clairsentient picked up a thought or a telekinetic successfully moved a paper clip. The part where you'd *try*...and something happened.

Except when it didn't.

After work, I was anxious and frustrated by the time I pulled up in front of the ATM. Not for pecuniary reasons, either. I had the vague sense that the ghost with the shot-through eye socket was only gone for now, not gone for good. Whether that fear was based in actual evidence, or if I was just spooked about the clumsy way Jacob and I had handled things, hard to say.

I gathered my white light, aided by fear-induced adrenaline, and approached the machine. There was a guy in front of me who seemed none too pleased with my presence. But there are lots of low-level empaths sprinkled throughout the population, and I can only imagine how freaky my energy must feel to them.

But what if he wasn't empathic? What if he was a low-level medium, and he was reacting not to me, but to the eye-shot mugger?

He shot me a look and scuttled away with his twenty bucks, and I belatedly fumbled out my bank card and keyed in my pin. Part of me was wondering how much I could withdraw without sounding any alarms. And part of me wondered if the shadow on the wall belonged to me, or to a scary dead mugger. But the thing about mediumship is that even someone as tweaked out as me can get things wrong.

Was I cold? Yes. But that could've been due to the weather. Once in a while, May seems like it can't decide whether it's finally willing to become summer. Did I have that creeping sensation on the back of my neck? Again, yes. But any hee-bie-jeebies I felt might be nothing more than my limbic system reacting to the memory of the gory ghost, and not its actual presence.

The touchscreen lit up, asking if I wanted a receipt, and I jabbed at it until it reset for the next customer. When I stuffed my money into my pocket, I felt the reassuring bulk of a baggie filled with salt. My mojo sparked and activated the salt crystals, but I didn't feel drained, not like I did when the spark leapt from me to Jacob. No, I felt augmented. Enhanced. Ready to rumble.

So, naturally, the stupid ghost didn't show his face.

Maybe the other night, he crossed over.

Yeah, maybe.

Too bad I couldn't call him long-distance and make sure.

This must be how Jacob felt, having a talent but not the first clue how to use it. They say misery loves company, but I wasn't so sure. Knowing that I was in the same boat as Jacob only made me more determined to contact Kamal. If only I could power up better, try harder, grasp the knowledge that was always just out of reach.

If only I hadn't lost that goddamn GhosTV.

While it was true that I'd never long-distanced anyone by its lambent glow, I'd performed several other impressive party tricks that weren't normally in my repertoire. I discovered habit demons. I saw people's psychic talents like Halloween masks. I even astral projected. So it stood to reason that somewhere on that dial, there was a setting to help me play telephone.

The TV snatched away by F-Pimp National was history. Even if Laura Kim agreed to lobby for its return, I doubted any of her superiors would listen. But there was one GhosTV still at large...and I had a sneaking suspicion her predecessor knew where it was.

Con Dreyfuss, however, was another ball of wax. One that hadn't been seen in months.

But there was more than one way to play telephone. Hopefully I could get him a message.

I swung by the cannery and picked up Jacob. My official reason was to invite Crash and Red to the wedding. Red was enthusiastic and supportive about the whole idea. Crash...not so much. While neither Jacob nor I looked forward to telling him we'd finally set the date, we'd both agreed it would be best to do it in person. And since I was already dreading the conversation, why not kill two birds with one stone?

Curious Curios is Crash's latest business venture. It's a funky second-hand shop in the back of an antique mall that seems to stretch on approximately forever. You've gotta hike through room upon room of displaced junk and horrible hand-me-downs to get there. And he doesn't even sell metaphysical goods anymore...not officially. But the items that gravitate to him and Red tend toward the artistically spiritual: carvings from Nepal, tapestries from India, and dangly wind chimes that might or might not be made from the bones of long-dead shamans. The place is a riot of color, style and taste, and nothing matches anything else. Yet, somehow, all of it's been curated and cared for in a way that makes it look like it was styled for a photo shoot in a magazine—a magazine too hip and young for the likes of me.

Come to think about it...did the kids nowadays even read magazines?

I've never seen a ghost in the vicinity, but I figured I should be on the lookout, since antiques would be the perfect vessel for a stowaway spirit. You can't take it with you, it's true. But someone with a deep enough obsession might very well try.

We found Crash alone, lounging in a papasan chair, tapping at a laptop in the cradle of his crossed legs. I've never been able to sit in those things without throwing out my back, so of course, he made it look effortless. Incense was smoldering, tunes were playing, and he was the picture of purpose and ease. He may never admit to it, but he's a workaholic of the highest order—even if that work involves posting artsy photos of papasan chairs on social media.

"Two federal agents at once?" he called over as we cleared the threshold. "What is this, a raid?"

It was so much easier back when he sold herbs, and I could pretend I was there to top off my mugwort.

Jacob was more accustomed to verbally sparring with Crash than I was. Plus he was immune to Crash's empathy. Major advantage. "Maybe we're shopping."

"The guy who buys everything brand spanking new—and the guy who then throws it away because he's afraid of owning anything? Try again."

Jacob allowed himself to look chagrined, but only somewhat. My anxiety was a low, constant churn. But maybe that was normal for me. "Where's Red?"

"Rainbow Dharma. Don't get me wrong, I'm down with everything the group stands for, and I'd gladly have a drink with most anyone there. But a ninety-minute meditation? I'd crawl out of my own skin."

I was fully aware of Rainbow Dharma's schedule. I'd been counting on it. Dealing with an empath was bad enough without also having a telepath in the room.

Crash closed his laptop, then pushed a ceramic zodiac platter aside and slid the computer onto a nearby shelf. "If you were hoping for a yoga lesson, we could swing by later tonight."

"No, it's not that." I looked hard at a framed poster for a sideshow "mind reader" from vaudeville days. It pictured a middle-aged white guy in a showy turban. "We've been doing some planning, is all...."

Crash squinted at me to see what I was hedging about, and realization dawned. "*Wedding* planning?"

"We've set a date," Jacob said. "It's in Wisconsin."

"Are you inviting me, or trying to make excuses as to why I'm not welcome?"

"Of course you're welcome," I snapped—and I didn't have to fake the spike of annoyance I felt. "You and Red. You know you're our closest friends."

"Then why didn't you just send us an email?" He lowered his voice to a dramatic whisper. "Or is this a super-secret affair you're keeping on the down-low to make sure Big Brother doesn't find out?"

Jacob said, "We just wanted to deliver the news in person. That's all."

I said, "You get that I can count the people I trust on one hand, right? And the ones that are cops have no desire to see me getting hitched to another guy." As I heard myself speak, I spotted my opening: the one where I could slam-dunk the seed I'd come to plant. "Bad enough I won't have Lisa there with me. So stop being a dick and say you'll come."

"All right, all right, don't get your panties in a twist. We'll be there—with bells on."

Once Crash plugged the date into his laptop, I said, "And no wedding gifts. We mean it."

"Did you not hear the part where I acknowledged your pathological aversion to material objects? No gifts. Understood. You'll just have to make do with the pleasure of my company."

We said our goodbyes and headed to the car before the telepathic half of the couple showed up. Jacob might be a True Stiff, but my mind was an open book. Red might only receive flashes of imagery, but between that and Crash's empathic advantage, I couldn't risk the two of them figuring out the main reason for my visit.

"Is there anything you need to tell me?" Jacob asked as we pulled away from the curb.

Crap. I thought I'd been smoother. "Was it obvious?"

"Only once I considered how much you *love* confrontation, once Crash pointed out that sending an email was way more your style."

Damn Crash and his perceptive judgement of character. "I miss Lisa, is all. It's hard to imagine doing this without her."

"And you think he's got a way to contact her."

I shrugged awkwardly. "If not her, then Dreyfuss. He was close to both of them."

I really did miss Lisa. And if her husband couldn't tell us what to make of Kamal's notebook, her sí-no would.

I strongly suspected that as soon as we left, Crash was launching a private chat that began: *Get a load of this*. So, while it might be underhanded, playing telephone—through Crash—was my best shot at calling in psychic reinforcements.

CHAPTER EIGHT

We were due to Skype with Pastor Jill, so we grabbed some take-out and ate it in the car on the way home. Not because we were in danger of being late, but because we had so much work to do. While Dr. Kamal's notebook was a pivotal piece of evidence...it was becoming clear that it wasn't going to decode itself.

Since Jacob and I have a combined experience of nearly thirty years investigating the kind of crap everyone tries to keep buried—and especially since we've each had high-level training at the hands of both the Chicago PD and the FPMP—you'd think the two of us could figure out what Kamal's notes actually meant.

Apparently not.

Obviously, I wasn't expecting anything along the lines of, *Dear Diary, here is my super-secret mad scientist plot in a hundred words or less*. But the pages were cryptic to say the least. Charts. Figures. Scientific notations. Jacob had a couple of science classes in college. I had less than that, just a few continuing education workshops in basic forensics.

And as family trees went, the records were spotty. Barbara

was missing. Uncle Leon, too.

Oh, and did I mention that some of the notes were in freaking *Arabic*?

And that Arabic has umpteen dialects?

We knew this because we actually watched a YouTube intro to the language...and immediately realized that neither of us stood a frozen cadaver's chance in hell at learning Arabic well enough to translate squat.

Even more daunting—some pages were missing. But Jacob's page was still there, and the initials, at least, were in standard English letters.

Every code has its key. If we could crack just one more set of initials near Jacob's, it would allow us to start tracking down commonalities that person might share with him. Like what? Teachers with unconventional methods involving flash cards that weren't technically part of the curriculum. Family friends who resurfaced every few years and took unusual interest in the kids. Guidance counselors who were a little too eager to push them into Psych-related fields.

Unfortunately, his parents and grandparents were the only other sets of initials we'd managed to work out.

Them, and Alex Warwick. Yes, his initials were there, like the Sarge promised—crossed out with a single line, and a date of death beside them—but they told us nothing. And Jacob's appeared on an entirely different page.

Not only was making sense of those notes painstaking and unsatisfying research, but we were doing it all behind our boss's back.

Laura Kim might be pretty keen on me, but her relationship with Jacob was complicated. Jacob had accused her of murdering Roger Burke. And while she was probably better off knowing she'd been possessed than remaining blissfully unaware, when Jacob accused her, he'd demonstrated exactly how far he'll go when he thinks he's right.

At some point, we might very well need to concede that we'd hit a dead end and entrust the notebook to The Fixer, who could put her top cryptographers on building an algorithm to identify all the initials and have the Arabic translated by the end of the day. This book was Jacob's albatross, though, not mine—therefore, it was his call. I'd set aside the pursuit of my own permanent record for the time being, since the bits and pieces I'd managed to unearth were so redacted they were useless. But on his own history, Jacob was nowhere near ready to admit defeat.

The notebook had become the bane of our existence, so it was with some eagerness that we sat down to the pile of papers we'd brought back from Wisconsin instead. Since you never know who might drop by, we'd set up our war room in the basement. Now that I knew the whole story of my old apartment with the baby in the basement—that it was basically a tragic accident—I wasn't so spooked by basements anymore. Or, more accurately, I was more worried about the feds catching me sticking my nose where it didn't belong than I was about spending time underground.

There was a narrow room behind some long-retired canning equipment—we think it was originally used for storing fruit. A good once-over with a shop vac, a coat of white paint and a powerful space heater had left it tolerably comfortable, though it had no modern light fixtures, and long extension cords served in place of outlets.

This odd, whitewashed bunker housed all of our research. A dedicated laptop with no wifi. A backup hard drive. A safe full of notes. If FPMP National ever decided to see what we were up to, they'd uncover our secret hidey hole in no time flat. But the casual visitor would have no reason to stumble across it. Not unless they decided to work out in Jacob's basement home gym and then throw in a load of laundry.

Jacob hauled out the box he'd brought back from his parent's place. It seemed doubtful to me there was anything he could hope to find, but he was still smarting from the ATM ghost fiasco, so I figured I should keep my eyes open and my mouth shut.

There were report cards from as far back as first grade—apparently Jacob needed to "apply himself" but was otherwise bright. There was a local recipe book with unvarnished critiques of several recipes penciled in the margins by Shirley. And there was a photo of a pre-adolescent Jacob in a Boy Scout uniform. But no helpful photos with men in black creeping around in the background spying on Jacob for a secret government experiment.

I was flipping through a family photo album, marveling at how Jacob was the spitting image of his father thirty years ago, when I realized Jacob had stopped shuffling papers some while back. I glanced up and found him with his drugstore cheaters perched on his nose, scowling hard at a sheet of stationery. "What is it?" I asked. Because from where I was sitting, it looked like it was covered in cursive. "Is it something about Kamal?"

Jacob took off the glasses, folded the paper in half and slumped wearily against the back of his chair. "It's a letter. A bunch of letters." He gestured toward a bundle he'd dug out of an old tackle box, maybe a dozen pages in all, tied with twine. "To my dad."

My stomach sank. I *liked* Jacob's dad. And the thought of

him being privy to some kind of psychic experiment was a real punch to the gut. Tentatively, I slipped a letter from the pile, giving Jacob ample time to keep me from reading it. But he made no move to stop me. I unfolded the note, and read.

I still think about you all the time. I know it doesn't do me any good. It's just hard to forget how we used to talk about opening up our own little cafe. Living upstairs with a dog and a cat and as many kids as God gave us. I guess it was all pretty childish. And now I'm with Darren, and you're with Shirley. Maybe we'll be happier in the long run, I don't know. But when I close my eyes and my thoughts turn to you, I can still see our little cafe.

Love always,

Leah

I'd braced myself for evidence of experimentation. But if there'd been experimentation going on, it sure as heck wasn't of the psychic variety. "The paper looks pretty old," I said eventually. "And your dad having a life before he got together with your mom isn't exactly a crime."

Jacob tapped the pile of letters. "But he *saved* these."

"Remember, mister, I've seen your parents' basement. They save everything."

You can't mollify someone who doesn't want to feel better, and Jacob was still chewing on the idea that he was nothing more than a product of some mad scientist's idea of eugenics. When I thought about it that way, even a few innocent love letters took on a more sinister bent. Jerry'd had a sweetheart before Shirley—a girl who hadn't wanted things to end. What had prompted him to ditch her for Jacob's mom? Some normal reason (like the type of sticking points our Wedded Bliss handbook insisted we overanalyze)? Or the direct intervention of Dr. Kamal?

Jacob shoved the letters aside. "This is going nowhere, and Pastor Jill is calling in fifteen minutes. We'd better run through the exercise and get our answers straight."

CHAPTER NINE

If I were a more sentimental guy, I might worry that Jacob's only objective was to do enough of the work to make it look like we were planning a wedding and not investigating a mad scientist. But I'm a pragmatist. And I was relieved he didn't actually expect me to explore my "feelings." Still, I had to admit, I'd figured the sections I'd feel most uneasy about participating in would involve talking about my sex life to a Lutheran minister.

I'd never realized how prickly the subject of "family" would end up being.

Oh, I'd been prepared to come off like a total basket case with something to hide. People tend to think I'm exaggerating when I say my childhood memories were erased by a nefarious hypnotist—or at least I imagine they would, were I to actually confide in anyone. I'd figured I would be the one who'd need to prep my answers.

Not Jacob.

We parked ourselves in front of the computer and the jaunty little Skype connection song announced Pastor Jill's impending arrival. I'd scanned through the questions and come up with a reasonable answer for everything. I'd grown up in the foster care system, I didn't know my parents, that's all there really was to say. It may not be the world's most satisfying answer, but it did sound reasonably normal.

And yet, after a hearty Wisconsin greeting and a few sports-related pleasantries (which Jacob gladly fielded), Pastor Jill threw me a curveball by saying, "Since I already know Jacob's parents pretty well, I figured Vic could start us off this week. Will I be meeting your folks at the ceremony?"

Your guess is as good as mine.

Obviously I couldn't say that, so I forged ahead with my canned answer about foster care, and after an awkward pause, added, "And the people who raised me are dead."

If my answer made the pastor uncomfortable, she didn't show it. "Then they'll be there in your heart. For better or worse, the people who are there in our formative years carry on in the people we've become."

I'd rather have Momma Brill and Harold at the ceremony than in my heart. Her in a color-clashing modern day hippie dress, him stoic in a suit. Last I saw Harold, he'd been graying at the temples. Maybe he'd be full on gray.

"Vic?" Pastor Jill said, and Jacob nudged me with his knee.

"Sorry, what?"

"Would you say you had a relatively positive experience with these foster parents?"

Until the men in black took me away. "Sure."

"And did you ever get the chance to thank them for the part they played in raising you? As an adult?" The Pastor *knew* about Darla's data plan to the other side? I must've looked confused, because she added, "Everyone's got their own idea of heaven. But I've always believed that our loved ones really can see and hear us. Not all the time. But when we talk to them directly, they hear us."

Would a normal person have found that notion soothing? Who the hell knows. As for me, I was busy tamping down the growing horror that Jennifer Chance was lurking around and listening in from the afterlife, still smarting about her kidnapping debacle and planning her revenge.

Silence stretched between us all, and eventually Pastor Jill took pity on me and filled it. "Whatever it is you believe—we'll delve deeper into that in our chapter on Faith—there are plenty of studies in Positive Psychology that show what a salubrious affect gratitude has in our happiness."

I realized she'd been looking at me expectantly for some while. "Uh...okay."

"Salubrious!" She grinned. I stared back. "It's my word of the day. It means healthy and beneficial."

"Oh. Right, yeah. Great."

I was scrambling to come up with a better compliment when Jacob shot up out of his seat and stormed off to the bathroom with nothing but a quick, "Excuse me," leaving the office chair he'd been sitting in spinning in a lazy circle.

"Sorry," I said. "We, uh. There's...a lot going on."

"Pre-marital counseling can be an emotional experience. Tell me about your dynamic. If I weren't here, what would you normally do in this situation?"

I wasn't sure I had a "normal" way to handle the fact that Jacob's whole childhood was nothing like we thought it was. Mine? Sure. It had "sketchy" written all over it. But Jacob really had seemed to live the perfect Normal Rockwell, small-town, nuclear family life.

And he'd just found potential evidence that it was all a lie.

There was still a good half-hour left on our meeting, but I cobbled together some BS about the way Jacob and I talk through our problems, which Pastor Jill seemed to buy. She said, "This would all be so much easier in person. I could give you both a big hug."

I was about to agree with her—in that half-hearted way I do when I'm really just trying to disengage—when it occurred to me that Jacob and I needed more than an afternoon visit in Wisconsin to get to the bottom of things. "Say, if the two of us could swing some vacation time, would we be able to do that? Switch our Skype meetings to in-person?"

Pastor Jill brightened. "Absolutely! I normally recommend my couples take at least a few months to go through the exercises and really give everything a chance to sink in. But we've already had two remote sessions, so I think we can pick the most relevant subjects and massage them into, say, a week?"

We'd never spent more than couple of days up there. I couldn't imagine a better way to snoop. "Yeah. We can probably do a week."

"Fantastic. Just let me know when you have the dates and I'll make time in my calendar." She gave me a broad smile. "This is bound to be quite the salubrious experience!"

I signed out and went off to let Jacob in on my latest stroke of genius. Our upstairs hall is squeaky, but I called out to him as if he hadn't heard me coming a mile away. "Everything's cool. I got rid of the priest."

Jacob shifted—I could see the shadows of his feet in the light beneath the door—and after a moment, he opened it. "Minister." He gave me a wan smile. His eyes were red.

I could count the number of times either of us has cried (in front of each other, anyhow) on one hand. It's not just a guy-thing. It's a cop-thing. You don't burst into tears when an assault victim is giving you the gruesome details or show up at a murder scene and start blubbering. Jacob and I were old pros as tamping down our feelings. And the fact that he hadn't managed to keep his distress contained just goes to show how deep his upset ran.

There was literally nowhere to sit other than the toilet in our afterthought of an upstairs bathroom, so I caught Jacob by the wrist and tugged him toward the bedroom. I perched on the foot of the bed and gave the mattress beside me a few clunky pats.

"Listen," I said. "My empathy is for shit. Seriously—all the tests say so. But if anyone can relate to what you're going through right now, it's me."

Jacob sat down wearily beside me and scrubbed at his face with both hands. "What if my parents were complicit in this whole mess?"

Yeah, that was my worry too—but it wouldn't help anything to admit it. "Think about it, Jacob. Your initials were in that book and you had zero clue. Who's to say it wasn't the same with them? Plus, even if there's more to the story of their get-together than they told you, they're still the same people who endured your boring-assed wrestling matches."

I tried to take his hand but ended up whapping him in the leg with my cast.

He took pity on me and enfolded my fingertips in his hand. He smiled sadly, and said, "My wrestling matches were anything but boring."

CHAPTER TEN

The next couple of weeks were a scramble of logistics. With all the extra hours we'd been putting in since Memorial Day, Laura Kim could hardly deny us time off for our freaking wedding. Still, she was pretty darn fretful about the prospect of being without her star medium for any amount of time. I may have joked about bringing Richie out of retirement...and I may have obliterated any future chance at a new Lexus. But sometimes sarcasm is its own reward.

Work hadn't been the only place we were busy. I could see how wedding planning would be stressful for anyone with a particular vision of their special day. Which wasn't to say Jacob and I didn't have a vision. Just that our vision was pretty basic: have all the typical wedding elements in place so no one would suspect that we were there for an investigation, and the wedding was more of a bonus. We grabbed the first available DJ, the first caterer to return our call, and the first "supper club" we found with a banquet room big enough seat two dozen of our closest loved ones.

And even that took a lot of legwork.

I was under no illusion that normal people spent months planning the sorts of details I was leaving to chance. Luckily, if anyone noticed my half-assery, I could play the guy-card and blame the fact that I was male.

But before we could lock up the cannery and say goodbye to our common-law partnership, there was one last thing I had to take care of—something I'd never entrust to the first person who showed up...and that was getting rid of the burden I'd been lugging around since I slammed my hand in a car door. Deliberately.

Dr. Ella Gillmore is the stern, no-nonsense ER doctor who heads up the night shift at LaSalle General Hospital. She sees ODs and GSWs, burst appendixes and busted heads. And ever since I'd encountered a roomful of habit demons in The Clinic, she's seen me. Even when it's not an emergency.

Given that the FPMP must be leaning on somebody important to make that happen, I did my best not to take advantage.

It was coming up on midnight by the time Dr. Gillmore got to me, though if she was tired, she didn't show it. I'd kept myself busy wandering the medical bays, once I'd flashed my F-Pimp ID to everyone who seemed bound and determined to keep me in my own curtained-off cubby. I had already exorcised LaSalle more thoroughly than I'd perused the men's underwear catalog in our last pile of junk mail (and not because I needed a new pair of briefs). Even so, medical buildings have big potential for ghost action. Habit demons, too. And I wasn't about to let any non-physical entities catch me with my pants down.

Gillmore strode into my cubby reading my chart with a frown of disapproval. Then again, that's pretty much how she always looks.

I took great comfort in her consistency.

"All right, Agent. I'll bite. You're a week and a half overdue to get your cast off, and it couldn't wait till your hand specialist could see you?"

"I'm going out of town...and he seems to think two more weeks in the thing would do more harm than good." The guy's exact words were more like, *If you're not going to follow my orders there's only so much I can do for you.* Hopefully he hadn't put that in my chart verbatim. "Besides, I was hoping you could write me a scrip for something that'll take the edge off."

Her only reply was a raised eyebrow.

"Wedding jitters," I explained. "Not me. Jacob. This whole thing's been a lot more, uh, trying than we could've anticipated."

I'd damn near said *traumatic* instead of *trying*. But before I could pat my back on the smooth save, Gillmore said, "And you think I'm about to write a benzodiazepine prescription for a third party on your say-so? You may be exempt from certain rules. But the pharmacy is not a free-for-all—for you or anyone."

Fantastic. After my personal habit demon incident, I'd scoured the cannery and disposed of every last benzo...and now I was paying the price.

That'll teach me to be conscientious.

Gillmore said, "I can point to some compelling studies that show meditation can be as effective as medication, but I'm thinking I'd be wasting my breath."

"That's okay." Jacob probably wouldn't have gone for a nice Valium anyhow. "I've got access to all that research and more. I've even read some of it."

Gillmore wheeled over a cart and draped it with a paper pad. "Wisconsin, right? So where are you staying?"

"With family."

"For your honeymoon?"

"Not exactly. We haven't gotten around to planning that quite yet." Because if it turned out our investigation led us anywhere unusual, an impromptu honeymoon would make such a plausible excuse for going out of town. "We get all kinds of alone-time—heck, we live together. We figured this would be a great chance to catch up with Jacob's folks."

"Take my advice. Unless you like strangers getting all up in your business, steer clear of a bed and breakfast. This was before Yelp, so maybe things are different nowadays. But the first and only B&B I ever stayed at, the owners acted like they wanted to be my new best friends. Everywhere I went, there they were." She shuddered. "It was unnatural, all that friendliness. Plus the room reeked of lilacs."

Once I was all situated with a very intense light shining directly on my cast (since when was it so filthy?) it occurred to me that maybe Jacob wasn't the only one with good reason for his anxiety to spike. The handheld cast-cutter Gillmore was brandishing was just the sort of thing you'd use to open up a cranium. I told myself they probably weren't exactly the same—and, in fact, it also bore a striking resemblance to an immersion blender. But my medical anxiety kicked into high gear as my subconscious refused to be convinced that she was making me a smoothie.

Calm your mind. A phrase tossed around all the time by the yoga lady. It seemed like it should've had the same effect on me that most phrases do. *Hope for the best. Cultivate an attitude of gratitude. Eat more fiber.* But there was something about Bethany that allowed her to reach me in a way most self-satisfied advice-givers never did. Was she speaking to me not only with her physical body, but her etheric form? Or was the fact that I was hooked up to a bunch of electrodes when we yoga'd focusing me in a way that led to some sort of crude biofeedback?

While the cast-cutter whined, I thought back to our umpteen yoga sessions and slowed my breathing. I kept a brainwave app on my phone nowadays...okay, technically it was a toddler video game, but I couldn't argue with the results. People can get funny when you pop in earbuds while they're talking to you. But I'd done the games often enough that I could imagine what the binaural pulses sounded like without having to hook myself up. I'd never done binaural pulses on electrodes. But I'll bet if I had, the imagined whub-whub-whub might've been almost as effective as the real ones.

The calming techniques helped, sure, but they were no magic bullet. I was still in a medical setting with a saw blade whirring so close to my flesh I could feel the vibrations in my newly-healed bones. I'm sure it only took a few minutes, but like all torture, it felt like forever.

Soon, my armpits prickled and my back felt clammy, and the mineral smell of airborne plaster was making it impossible to keep breathing deep. I thought about how much Jacob would appreciate not getting clonked with a cast all night. I reminded myself there's usually a price to pay for freedom. But before I could say, Never mind, I'll just live the rest of my life with a hunk of plaster at the end of my arm, I felt something I hadn't felt in weeks: the cool touch of air on my wrist.

I sighed with relief...and then I wished I hadn't breathed quite so deeply—and not because of the plaster dust. "What *is* that smell?" It sure as hell wasn't lilacs.

"A certain amount of odor isn't uncommon. Did you keep it dry?"

"I did my best." Given the amount of sweat currently trickling down my spine, I'd say I was incapable of keeping anything dry without a personality transplant.

"Well, Agent Bayne, that's a nasty rash. It looks like you'll end up with a prescription from me after all."

CHAPTER ELEVEN

My cast was the last bit of business that couldn't wait until after the wedding, and now that it was safely moldering in some biohazard bag at LaSalle General, there was nothing stopping us from heading up to Wisconsin bright and early the next morning.

The countryside we drive through to get to Jacob's folks' house is riddled with dead zones, and cell service is patchy at best. I'd been scouring the couples workbook in hopes of coming off even remotely like a normal human in front of Pastor Jill, and it occurred to me that my cell service should be cutting out anytime soon. It didn't, though. Which probably meant it was talking to its own special satellite.

So they could spy on me.

And yet, even I had to admit, its reception was awfully good.

Despite the fact that I was free from random pop-up "roaming" messages, the Wedded Bliss PDF was still fairly inscrutable. I was supposed to map my family relationships on two axes: closeness and flexibility. I'd settled on Mama Brill and Harold as my "family" even though my memory of them was fairly spotty.

Either I was with them longer than any other foster parents, or the tweens and early teens were just a formative time.

Or maybe it was their parenting styles. Harold was strict, though not entirely rigid. I'd successfully bargained with him for a reduction in punishment by acting phenomenally contrite...and why I'd dug up the backyard to begin with, I'll never know. And Mama Brill might be somewhat unpredictable, but she was full of helpful advice, like, "When you want to understand someone, try putting yourself in their shoes."

Unfortunately, I'd walked a mile or two in the shoes currently paining Jacob. And I knew what it felt like to wonder—with good cause—if your whole life was a lie.

Jacob's folks lived on a tree-lined street of unassuming split-level homes. Lawns were broad, basketball hoops hung from most every garage, and the lawn furniture never got stolen. We pulled up in front about fifteen minutes earlier that we should have, so Jacob must've had the pedal to the metal the whole trip. And when we climbed out of the car, he popped the trunk and began unpacking with such ruthless single-mindedness that half our bags were on the lawn by the time his parents came out to greet us.

He shoved a small suitcase into my arms, which I took without thinking—and then promptly dropped when my left hand cramped. It was a soft-sided vinyl case that should've survived a drop to the lawn. But apparently the zipper had other ideas. It split open, spewing socks and underwear and pajamas.

"I got it," I said hastily, with a spike of panic as I worried a bottle of lube might burst forth for all to see...followed by a wash of disappointment when I realized we hadn't even bothered to pack any. Not that I planned on getting hot and heavy just down the hall from Jacob's parents. But this was our wedding—it was the principle of the thing.

"Go get the laundry basket," Shirley told Jerry, then attempted to help us by carrying a tiny valise made to stack on top of a bigger bag. "So many bags—I guess you've never stayed over more than a day or two."

"Is that a problem?" Jacob said.

"Of course not, you know we love having you. You'll just be cramped in that little room, is all."

"It'll be fine," I said. "I'm used to sleeping on the barest sliver of mattress."

"Are you sure we can't put you up at the B&B? Our treat. And Marilee does a real nice breakfast with fresh scones and blackberry jam she cans herself—"

"Mom," Jacob said. "Remember the B&B incident."

I only realized this wasn't code for some Marks family vacation debacle when Shirley gave a little gasp and said, "I'm so sorry Vic. I should've realized."

Jacob read my blank look and said, "The B&B in Missouri. Roger Burke."

Oh...*that* incident. Chances of me getting kidnapped again were hopefully pretty slim. I hadn't even bothered to add B&B's to my repertoire of things to freak out about, and frankly, Dr. Gillmore's recent story about the nosy owners and the lavender were a lot more disturbing. Or maybe it was lilac. "Don't worry about it. We didn't want to squander the chance to spend quality time with you guys. That's all."

There was a lot of fretting followed by even more ineffective helping. "Where is your father with that basket?" Shirley said, and bustled inside with another tiny bag.

We glanced up at the big bay window on the front of the house. Jerry and Shirley were framed by white lace curtains.

Jerry was on the phone—a cordless landline handset—and he was stooping down to let Shirley listen in.

Jacob didn't seem to notice. His laser focus was turned inward, trained on that damn journal. "I think I'm getting cold feet." I must've looked a little panicked, because he hastened to add, "About the journal. Vic...what if it turns out they were actively involved?"

"Maybe we should just ask them and get it over with." We'd managed to scrounge a photo of Kamal from The Clinic—a photo of the photo from the wall in the Director's office, but it was good enough. Those cameras on our federal-issue cell phones were pretty darn good. "Show them the picture of Kamal and ask."

Jacob worked his jaw a few times. His dentist had been making noises about him wearing a night guard, but I could see that now was not the time to suggest that maybe he should take the plunge. "Do we really want to play that card right now? Then we have nothing to fall back on."

"It's either that or pretend we're just here for the wedding, then drop it on them later. Look at how betrayed you feel over the thought that someone might have had an ulterior motive, once, way back before you were even born. Your folks are good people. You know they are. And if they find out this whole trip was basically an investigation...?"

Jacob flexed his jaw muscles a few more times, then sighed. "Maybe I *should* just level with them."

There was no "maybe" about it. You'd have to be completely oblivious not to notice Jacob was utterly miserable. There's only so far the "wedding jitters" excuse would fly.

His gaze had turned inward again, hugging a piece of luggage to his chest. I eased it away from him—mostly with my right hand—set it on the lawn, and took his hand in mine. "Your parents love you. It couldn't be more obvious. It's easy to take it for granted."

"What makes you say that?"

"I must've read it in the PDF. Anyhow, let's stop torturing ourselves and hear their side of the story."

"Okay. And, Vic?" He squeezed my fingers gingerly, as if he wasn't quite sure which hand I'd broken now that the cast was off, then lavished a look on me that was poignant enough to flatten an empath. "You know how much I love you, right?"

"Oh, so you're keeping up with the PDF after all. Chapter three: verbal expressions of affection."

"Vic...."

I squeezed back. "Of course I know. Why else would I suggest making it official?"

Seeing him suffer took a toll on me. It wasn't even noon yet, and already I was exhausted. Playing Spy vs. Spy was bad enough at work. I didn't want to do it with my family and friends. I hated manipulating Crash to get to Dreyfuss, and I hated spying on Jacob's parents even more. I'm not a manipulative person.

Passive-aggressive? Sure. But that's a totally different thing.

Coming clean would be a huge relief. We'd just have a little sit-down with the parents, voice our concerns in a non-confrontational way, and listen to their side of the story. If we were lucky, it could turn into a bonding moment that left everyone feeling closer.

I squatted down to pick up our stuff while Jacob tried to convince the suitcase zipper that it wasn't really broken after all. My attention was on my underwear when Shirley came back outside. When I looked up, it was to see if she'd brought the laundry basket. What I noticed instead was that she was fidgeting weirdly with the hem of her top and that her voice sounded strained when she said, "Jacob? Come sit down. There's something I need to tell you."

A fresh cascade of socks hit the grass.

Shirley retreated to the narrow front porch where a trio of white resin chairs looked out onto the lawn. Jacob sat down in a daze while I hastily scooped up a stray pair of underpants and jammed it into the pocket of my windbreaker as I hurried over to join them.

Shirley sat and fidgeted some more, plucking at nonexistent lint, then sighed and said, "Don't be mad—we were waiting to see how things panned out before we said something—"

"Oh God," Jacob muttered, while dire notions fell out of my mind like socks from a wrecked suitcase, each one worse than the last.

But before I got down to the scenario where everything I knew and loved was nothing but a nefarious experiment, Shirley steeled herself and said, "It's Grandma Marks. We moved her to a nursing home last week."

Jacob sagged into the chair so hard the resin creaked and scrubbed a hand across his face. Most people would read it as concern for his grandmother. But I knew he was thinking, *Thank God it's something normal*. Because I was thinking the exact same thing. He said, "What happened—and why couldn't she just stay in her apartment? I thought she had plenty of help."

"She fell."

"Is she okay?"

"Nothing's broken—and that's a relief. She's been getting shots for osteoporosis and I guess they worked, but—"

"Did she sprain anything? Hit her head?"

"No, Jacob. Physically, she's fine."

That didn't sound good. Nursing homes are expensive, and you don't put someone there for nothing. Jacob met my eyes, and I asked what he couldn't. "And mentally?"

Shirley glanced toward the house, where a glimpse of Jerry could be seen through the picture window, still fielding the phone call. "She's an old woman," Shirley non-answered.

Pushing ninety-one, to be exact, but everyone figured she'd make it to a hundred on sheer spite. Grandma Marks was Jerry's mother, and she'd outlived all the other grandparents by over a decade. According to the stories I'd heard, Shirley's late mother was the sort of grandma who knit afghans and baked cookies. Jerry's mom was the one who complained that no one ever visited...after she drove everyone away with her negativity and criticism.

It was after one of Clayton's soccer games, half a year into my relationship with Jacob, that I slipped up and told Shirley I thought Grandma was giving me the evil eye. I'd expected to hear I was imagining things, so it surprised me when instead, Shirley shrugged and said, "She never much liked me, either."

Here, now, sitting on a porch beside a lawn riddled with socks, I could tell it wasn't Grandma that Shirley was worried about—it was Jacob's dad. She said, "I don't know if Grandma will be in any state to come to your ceremony. I'm sorry, Jacob. Because I think it was something she needed to see. You, Vic, a real church wedding...."

Jacob gave his head a rueful shake. "I doubt it would've mattered. Just more evidence that Lutherans are basically heathens."

"I don't get it," I said. "Isn't that what she is?"

"She's Catholic," Shirley said.

"Very Catholic," Jacob added.

Shirley shook her head in disgust. "And the old woman's never forgiven me for refusing to convert. How could I, what with the way they view women, and the priests with their weird celibacy rules—uh...you're not Catholic, Vic, are you?"

"I'm open-minded," I said. It was better than admitting that the more dead people I encountered, the less I understood anything.

CHAPTER TWELVE

Evidently, I'd been under the impression that all flavors of Christianity were essentially the same. It was an understandable assumption. None of my foster families had been churchy. And while Mama Brill kept a bathtub Madonna in the backyard, it was flanked by a Ganesh and a couple of Buddhas. At Camp Hell, I'd learned about a whole spectrum of religious practices, from Vodun curses to speaking in tongues, so most middle-of-the-road Christians seemed pretty tame in comparison.

Once we got our bags inside—though I can't say for sure all our socks made it—we lingered around awkwardly while Jerry fielded phone calls, until eventually we were able to duck out for our appointment with Pastor Jill. Who would've thought going to premarital counseling would actually be a relief? But at least now I understood why Shirley kept pushing the B&B option. Not because they had anything to hide, but because they were stressed out from dealing with Jacob's grandmother and didn't want us underfoot.

On our way to the church, we passed a gas station that sold cheese curds and bait. Someday I'll get used to that. Plus the fact that there wouldn't be winos dozing in the church pews. Steeping in the easy, small-town atmosphere, I wondered if maybe our conspiracy theories were a touch paranoid. As we parked, I floated the thought, "Maybe we should go to the B&B." Jacob shot me a look, and I said, "Unless the wallpaper is covered in trout and there's a massive TV console in the room, it won't remind me of my little vacation with Roger Burke and Jennifer Chance. We'll just need to make sure the owner doesn't get too clingy."

Jacob's shook his head sadly. "I don't know what's worse anymore—knowing, or not knowing."

I was so busy scrambling for a way to console him that the tap on the passenger window nearly shot me through the windshield. I pulled my neck twisting around, only to find Pastor Jill waving at me. The window framed her like a computer monitor—one we couldn't shut off with the click of a mouse. Not without flooring it and driving away.

I powered down the window and said, "Uh...hey."

"If it isn't my favorite Chicago couple," she said brightly. "What a beautiful spring day for our antepenultimate meeting!"

I must've looked like I had no idea what to do with my face, because the pastor took pity on me and said, "Third from last. You'd be surprised at how often you can sneak that into common conversation."

"We've been looking forward to finally getting to meet with you in person," Jacob lied.

Pastor Jill's grin widened. "Me too. Don't get me wrong—online meetings are super convenient. God's really outdoing Himself with all the amazing technology these days. Well, Him and the inventors. There's just something about a good, old-fashioned, face-to-face meeting, though. You can pick up so much more in person than you can through the computer."

Oh crap. Was this woman an empath?

She didn't seem to be reacting to my sudden gut-twisting spike of anxiety...so, hopefully not. Even I, with zero psychic empathy, agreed that there was a certain something to be gained from physical proximity. But that was due to the sorts of clues and impressions I picked up doing homicide investigations. Which, I'm sure, was nothing at all like marital counseling.

Hopefully.

Another thing about meeting in person—just dealing with the physicality can be unexpectedly weird. When I climbed out of the car, I realized that Pastor Jill was barely five feet tall. I towered over her awkwardly, willing my spine to compress and bring me down to a feasible human height, but I probably just looked like my posture was lousy. And then I reminded myself that in her line of work, she read people just as much as I did, and she'd probably make something out of the fact that Jacob was nearly as tall as I was, and he always held his head high.

No doubt, that "something" would be entirely correct. Which only made it worse.

Was it too late to jump into the car and high-tail it back to Chicago? Maybe I'd been able to bury my true feelings and present a normal face to the world—okay, normal-*ish*—but now? Hell, the more I trained with the FPMP, the more I learned about psychology and body language, the more I realized I wasn't fooling anyone. We'd sacrificed any hope for a normal wedding to dig up family dirt, and now I was going to blow our one and only chance to do it by acting like a headcase.

Then again...I pretty much *am* a headcase.

I squared my shoulders as best I could and followed the pastor inside.

I felt like I was doing pretty well. At least until I shoved my hand in my pocket and encountered a wad of fabric that felt way too big to be a sock.

The church building was fairly plain, with lots of stone outside and lots of wood inside. The pastor's office was in the lower level, which was even more modest than the main floor, with linoleum underfoot and walls of painted cinderblock. I recognized the wall behind her with its basement-gray paint job and harsh fluorescent lighting, but a fuller view of the room revealed that it was hung all over with snapshots and mementos. The photos—parishioners, I guess—featured happy, smiling people doing all sorts of things together, from singing to soft-ball. And there were enough children's drawings to decorate a whole fleet of refrigerators.

Instead of lecturing us across a desk like a couple of kids facing off with the principal, Pastor Jill led us to a cluster of more comfortable-looking seating, a love seat and a few chairs. It looked pretty cozy. At least until Jacob parked himself on the love seat and looked at me expectantly, and I realized that our gauntlet of scrutiny had already begun...starting with where I opted to sit.

I'd normally pick the chair with the best view of the door. It's a cop thing. But instead, I plunked down beside Jacob and gave his knee an awkward pat.

The pastor smiled. Evidently, I'd chosen right. And, bonus... it would camouflage the bulge in my pocket that I highly suspected was a pair of underwear.

Pastor Jill said, "I thought we'd go through the exercises on family today. That way, if Jacob has any questions, he'll have direct access to the people he needs to talk to while you're up here."

At my side, Jacob shifted. I could practically feel the queasy anticipation thrumming through couch cushions as his gears started turning.

Pastor Jill then turned to me and her bright smile softened. "And, Vic, I did see your answers on the initial questionnaire, so I know exercises like this—questions that presume you even had a stable family unit at all—can seem pretty pointless. But keep an open mind. Someone taught you adulting, even if it's not obvious who that might have been. Teachers, counselors, even characters in TV shows or books. When you answer the questions, just tell me whatever's on your mind, even if whatever comes up seems like a total non-sequitur."

I realized she was trying to suppress a grin. I said, "I know what that means." She leaned forward and raised an eyebrow, and I said, "A remark that's got nothing to do with anything."

"Very good! You'd be surprised at how many people think they understand something and it turns out they've got it totally wrong."

I highly doubted that.

The pastor settled more firmly into her chair and tapped open a tablet. "Wherever your influences might have originated, what's important now is the family unit the two of you are forming together. So let's start with the closeness quiz."

We'd filled out a bunch of stuff at the start of this whole process. Mainly what I remembered was cranking through everything as fast as possible—sounding as normal as I could—while I tried not to worry about how much time Jacob was spending in our war room. And also wondering if it was a crappy decision to tell him about Kamal's journal to begin with.

Pastor Jill said, "Remember the matrix of closeness and flexibility you filled out?"

How could I forget? When Jacob rated himself as "flexible," I'd had to restrain myself from saying, "In your dreams, mister."

I nodded.

"For the most part, it looks like you both feel the relationship is a good balance of intimacy and independence, with equal give-and-take. Does that sound about right?"

"Absolutely," Jacob said with great assurance...while my alerts pinged over the fact that she'd led with *for the most part*. "What we have is a truly solid partnership."

The pastor smiled. "I always love hearing that." Wait, was she humoring him? "But, Vic, I did notice that you rated yourself as *somewhat connected* rather than *connected*. That's pretty brave, don't you think?"

Brave wasn't the word I'd currently choose. I tried for damage control. "I'd been single for an awfully long time before I met Jacob. So I'm just used to doing my own thing."

"We both value our independence," Jacob added. "Our jobs are demanding and they impinge on our schedules and plans. It's just a matter of practicality."

Pastor Jill said, "I'd really like to hear more from Vic."

I swallowed hard. "About...what?"

"How you only feel 'somewhat' connected."

How ridiculous would I look if I admitted that I checked that box at random so as not to make it look like I was covering something up by rating our every last dynamic as ideal. "It's work-related," I said vaguely.

Jacob chimed in. "If Vic needs time alone, I respect that. Sometimes it's best we don't relive our day at work."

"How do you feel about that, Vic?"

"Uh...fine?"

Pastor Jill fixed me with a look that was just a smidge too

long, then said, "I'd like to do an exercise with you—a few simple questions to help me get a better picture of what makes you tick." I shifted uncomfortably and she said, "There are no wrong answers. Just say whatever comes to mind and finish the sentence."

"O...kay."

"Great! My favorite meal is...?"

"Uh...pizza?"

The pastor rewarded me with an encouraging smile, then said, "One of my favorite books is...?"

"I'm not much of a reader." I thought back to high school and named the only book I could remember. "*Lord of the Flies* was okay."

"I get really embarrassed when...?"

"I'm supposed to make small-talk."

"If I had more time, I would...?"

Drop everything and hunt down the guy whose experiments turned our world upside down. Because consciousness existed on the other side of death, even a consciousness as corrupted and degraded as Dr. Kamal's. I was the strongest medium I knew—off the charts. If anyone could interrogate him from this side of the veil—if anyone could put an end to Jacob's suffering by getting some straight answers—it should be me. But apparently all the talent in the world wasn't worth shit if you didn't know how to work it.

Pastor Jill blinked expectantly and I said, "If I had time? Maybe I'd work out."

I think she bought it.

"Okay, guys, I can tell you're both pretty goal-oriented, and I'd really love for you to connect over an activity that's not so serious." She thumbed through some papers and handed me a printout. "Here's a list of local activities and classes. I know you've got a million and one things to do leading up to your wedding, so chances of the two of you taking up ballroom dancing or macrame over the next week are pretty slim. But just invest an hour connecting over something low-stakes, something playful, and I guarantee you'll each discover some new and interesting things about your better half. In fact, you might even find the experience *meritorious*."

Jacob leaned into me and peered down at the page. "Scrapbooking Your Family History," he read. "That would definitely give us something to talk to my parents about."

Pastor Jill said, "Vic, how does that sound to you?"

"Fine." An awkward silence followed the answer, putting me on the spot to elaborate. "Jacob's folks have a basement full of memories. I think it would give us a good excuse to go through it all."

At the sound of the truth, Jacob's thigh tensed against mine—but the pastor must've taken my answer at face value. She said, "Old photos and mementos can be a real treasure trove. But I will warn you...go easy on the glitter. That stuff ends up everywhere."

CHAPTER THIRTEEN

Jacob climbed into the car, slammed the door, and sagged into the seat. "Why did I think this would be a good idea?"

"Because doing something feels better than doing nothing?" I reached for him carefully so as not to whack him with my cast, then remembered my bulky plaster burden was no longer there. I wasn't as adept at threading our fingers together as I might have liked, but at least my arm could breathe again. And the prescription salve had done a really good job. "Nothing we find out is gonna change the way I feel about *you*. Nothing."

We drove the rest of the way back in silence, though that actually wasn't saying much, since you could drive from one end of town to the other in fifteen minutes flat. Back home it sometimes took me that long to get from one stoplight to the next. As Jacob turned down his parents' street, he took his foot off the gas and just coasted in a way that you'd never get away with in Chicago without some road-rage douchebag ramming you from behind. But there was no one else on the street, which gave him a moment to collect his thoughts, then say, "I thought I could compartmentalize the damn notebook and all its ramifications. I really did. But then I look at my parents and I wonder if my whole life was a lie, and...."

He pulled over and took my hand—gingerly, like he wasn't used to the cast being gone either, and ran his thumb along my knuckles. "I'm sorry," he said. "I'm ruining everything."

"Give me at least some credit. Look how long you've had to put up with all my bullshit—half of which I can't even freaking remember. Not only can I handle the fact that you need some answers, but I'd feel like a grade-A asshole if I didn't help you find them."

Despite the protest of the seatbelts, we leaned in and stole a kiss. I can't say for sure that sadness has a flavor...or if it does, maybe I'd been inured to it, once upon a time. But it had been a while, at least for me. And I can't say I recommend it.

When we came up for air, I freed myself from the seatbelt so I could take his face between my hands and make him look me in the eye, though I softened it by bonking our foreheads together so we were too close to really focus. "Us. That's what's important. And if either of us ever loses sight of that, it's up to the other one to remember. Sometimes that's you—and sometimes that's me. And that's why we're good together. Because it only takes one of us to set things right."

We weren't kissing, exactly—more like breathing each other's breath and staring at the blur of one another's eyes—when another voice intruded. A distinctly annoyed voice saying, "Seriously? You're half a block from Mom and Dad's house and you've gotta pull over and make out?"

Jacob's sister Barbara stood in the middle of the street in a green and yellow Packers sweatshirt with her hands planted on her hips. If this were Chicago, someone would have mowed her down by now. But, as we'd already established, this was definitely not Chicago.

Jacob powered down his window and said, "Nice to see you too, Barb."

In the way of siblings, she was entirely unaffected by his sarcasm. "I've been waiting for half an hour. We need to go see Grandma before visiting hours are over."

Jacob popped open the locks and said, "Come on, we'll go right now."

"Maybe we should just wait till tomorrow," I said. "When we have more time."

While I had more time to weasel out of going along was more like it—but Barbara climbed into the back seat, gave her purse a very decisive settle, and said, "I didn't want to say anything in front of Mom, but I think sooner is better than later."

She gave Jacob directions, more like a series of cryptic landmarks like, "...that breakfast place—no, the other one," but he seemed to know what she was talking about. And as we pulled up not twelve feet from the front door, she said, "Don't get mad if Grandma doesn't know you. Ever since the fall, she's been confused."

I guess that's not something most people would want to hear—but I'd be perfectly fine if she mistook me for a random passerby. Judging by the muscles working in Jacob's jaw, though, he wouldn't be nearly as calm if it happened to him.

Nursing homes are potential hot zones for ghosts, what with the concentration of death being abnormally high. But I was better at handling myself these days, and no longer had a free pass to get out of potentially haunted situations...even ones I'd really love to sit out. But I could hardly toot my horn about being there for Jacob and then stay in the car, so I called down some white light, wrapped it around me, and headed in.

The place was nothing like the home where Richie Duff whiled away his days watching TV, playing cribbage and arguing with old Jewish ladies. It was smaller and plainer, and way more clinical. Sure, there was a nod to making things look homey, with plants and posters and the occasional stuffed animal. But underpinning the whole place were the particulars of institutions: fluorescent lights, rubbery flooring, and the chemical reek of disinfectant.

Every corridor looked the same to me and I quickly got all turned around, but Barbara had been there before, and she knew the way. We found the elevator and piled in, and when the doors closed, she said, "Grandma's timing stinks."

Jacob shrugged uneasily. "It would never be a good time, would it?"

"I guess not. But your wedding is enough to worry about without all of this." She gestured vaguely—at the elevator, the nursing home, the world.

I kept my mouth shut. It was longest Barbara had gone without criticizing either of us, probably because her chronic dissatisfaction was now aimed at their grandmother. And I wasn't about to say or do anything to swing her focus off that target.

We passed a nurses' station where the staff gave Barbara a nod, me a once-over, and Jacob a lingering stare. TV chatter drifted out from doors up and down the hall, but the room Barbara led us to was silent.

Unease crept down my spine and I automatically pulled down more white light. I doubted it would do me much good, though, since the cause of all my dread wasn't even dead yet.

Barbara poked her head in the door. "Grandma? It's Barb." She managed to come off pretty cheerful, if you ignored the frown line between her eyebrows. "Look who's here."

I followed Jacob into the dim room, where his grandmother sat in a lounger wedged between the bed and the wall, staring out the window while she wrung her hands. She looked smaller than I remembered. But her intimidation factor had never had anything to do with size.

The old woman peered at us through hazy bifocals as we filed into the room. It was a double, though the second half was empty. I instinctively backed up toward that half to put as much distance between me and them as possible. Maybe Pastor Jill would have insisted that this family was now mine as well as Jacob's...but in this case, I was perfectly content to stay on the outside.

"Hi, Grandma," Jacob said, and went down on one knee beside her so she could get a better look at him. "It's good to see you."

He took her hand. There was a clatter of beads, and I realized she hadn't just been sitting around lost in her own jumbled thoughts. She'd been praying the rosary.

She seemed surprised to see Jacob. At least, I thought she was...until she said, "Freddie?"

No one had mentioned a Freddie to me before, but I figured they'd fill me in later.

Jacob squeezed her hand. "No, Grandma. It's Jacob."

"What are you doing here?"

"He's visiting." Barbara said. "He's getting married next week."

Grandma jerked her hand out of his grasp. "Well, he'd make a terrible husband."

Jacob flinched like she'd just slapped him. "How could you say that?"

Grandma turned her head away and refused to even look at him, let alone apologize.

Jacob is usually pretty good at keeping his emotions to

himself, so it really sucked to see his heart breaking. And as much as I wanted nothing more than to blend into the institutional wallpaper, I couldn't just stand by and do nothing. I angled my way around the beds, slipped past Barbara, and put a hand on Jacob's shoulder. "Come on, let's give her some time to digest the news. We can come back in the morning."

Grandma Marks might not have been willing to look at Jacob, but she was sure eager to get a load of me. Her gaze snapped up to take me in, and I steeled myself for an earful of recrimination. But instead of pelting me with insults for getting hitched with her grandson, she looked at me in shock and said, "Father Paul? What are you doing here?"

Jacob and Barbara both cut their eyes to me, and Jacob cringed.

"Yeah, I can see it," Barbara said—whatever that meant. "Vic is right, let's let Grandma get some rest. We'll try again tomorrow."

Barbara tried to give her grandmother a kiss on the cheek, but she squirmed out of the way. Jacob was too hurt to even make the attempt. Hopefully the old woman wouldn't kick the bucket and leave him with a sour memory of their final encounter. Though I guess if she did, I could always concoct a different parting message—one where she left him with a less awful goodbye.

We walked to the car in silence, which Barbara broke with a gusty sigh. "Well, I don't know about you guys, but I could sure use some pie."

Even pie would have a pretty hard time cutting through the pall that had been cast over our mood, but since our only other option was to go back home to Jacob's parents and paw through their basement, I figured it was in our best interest to try and shovel down a few slices.

We stopped at a diner. It was small and dingy in a way some hipster in Chicago would spend big bucks trying to replicate. But it was relatively quiet, with just a few old-timers at the opposite side of the joint having a loud discussion about whether someone's great-grandson was named Taylor or Tyler.

We slid into a booth with Barbara across from both of us. Neither Jacob nor his sister seemed very interested in the menu, which led me to believe that "pie" was code for "talking." Which made it a hell of a lot less appealing.

The waitress came by and we got coffee all around. It was so late they only had apple pie left, which was better than nothing. I ordered myself a slice so the trip didn't turn out to be a total loss.

While Jacob was shredding the paper wrapper from his drinking straw, Barbara finally worked up the wherewithal to speak. "I didn't realize she'd be so bad. We'll try again. Tomorrow's Saturday and I can come by nice and early."

Jacob sighed. "If she's declining, I don't know that I can handle going back for another round."

"The nurses said it gets worse after dark. I guess it's a common thing with dementia."

"That's what's wrong with her?" Jacob said—almost as if he thought it was Barbara's fault. "Dementia?"

"That, or maybe some kind of delirium. Brought on by the trauma."

"And once she gets over the fall, what are the chances of it getting better?"

Barbara shrugged. "At her age? Not good." She reached across the table and took Jacob's hand. "I really didn't know she would be that bad tonight. Just yesterday she knew exactly who I was, and even asked about Clayton."

Jacob took his hand back. "Big surprise. You were always her favorite."

"Me?" Barbara seemed genuinely confused. "Since when?"

"Since always. The two of you were always doing church things together."

"I guess...but she never seemed too happy about it. And the way Mom was always making little digs about me going, I figure it all balanced out. But speaking of church...?"

Both of them turned to me with identical looks of appraisal. I busied myself with my bland coffee.

"There's not *that* big of a resemblance," Jacob said.

"Father Paul was tall...he had dark hair...and you know Grandma can barely see three feet in front of her own face. I'll bet she just saw Vic as a tall blur. Same reason she took you for Uncle Fred."

I said, "No one's ever mentioned Uncle Fred. Is he coming to the wedding?"

In the awkward silence that ensued, I wondered if maybe Uncle Fred was six feet under. Which technically wouldn't mean he'd miss out on the festivities. Just that it would be harder for him to RSVP.

It was Barbara who finally answered. "We don't have anything to do with Uncle Fred. I guess I met him once—"

"You did," Jacob said. "You were little. But I was maybe ten, so I remember. He brought us these giant Hershey bars. And Mom got really mad, yelled at him, and threw them in the garbage."

That didn't sound like the Shirley I knew. "Anti-sugar phase?"

Jacob shook his head sadly. "*You think you can buy them with candy?* That's what she said. At the time, I didn't know what to make of it. But over the years I pieced together that he had money."

"Lots of money," Barbara said. "He was loaded."

"Grandma put him through college—even grad school. But she refused to give our dad any help at all—not a single cent."

This was a prime example of how biological families aren't all they're cracked up to be. I'd always figured Jacob was descended from generations of healthy, well-adjusted, loving people. Turned out they were just as screwy as everyone else.

Jacob said that since his uncle was estranged, he hadn't even thought about tracking Fred down for the sake of a wedding invite. But now that Grandma was declining?

Barbara shrugged. "I wouldn't know how to get ahold of Uncle Fred even if I wanted to. After all, if he wanted a relationship, he should've made some effort to reach out."

Effort was right. Being part of a family was a heck of a lot more work than I'd ever imagined.

CHAPTER FOURTEEN

While Jacob's grandmother was no fun to be around—even at the best of times—seeing her out of her gourd truly sucked. I wished I could say something to comfort Jacob, but empty platitudes would do more harm than good. All night long, we were crammed together on a mattress a lot smaller than we were used to. And though I felt valiant about not complaining that he'd mashed me into the wall so hard I was practically flat, in the grand scheme of things, I wasn't particularly helpful.

As I was climbing over him the next morning, attempting to unflatten myself, my gaze fell on a folded sheet of paper on the dresser—the "fun" date assignment from Pastor Jill. You know things are dire when an assigned date sounds good. But did it really need to be scrapbooking?

As a rule, I don't engage in anything one would call a hobby. They seem awkward and pointless, and the opposite of relaxing. "Say, Jacob...maybe there's another option on this list that's not quite so...soccer mom. This workshop on taking better pictures with your phone that might not be too bad—I'm told I shoot pictures like I'm documenting a crime scene."

"But that wouldn't give us an excuse to go through the basement."

True.

We parked ourselves at the kitchen table with our coffees and Jacob smoothed out the paper between us. He scanned the list with a frown and said, "Basket weaving? That's really a thing?"

"I've always wanted to try basket weaving!" Jacob's mother said as she scuffed into the kitchen, adorable in a pink terry-cloth robe.

I didn't know how I'd ever deal with it if she turned out to be anything other than a normal Midwestern mom.

Shirley joined us at the table and exclaimed over all the "fun" activities. I think she was wishing she could come with us—and while I would've gladly given her my spot, I suspected that wouldn't fly with the pastor.

Eventually we came back around to the scrapbooking class. Not only did it sound better than basket weaving...it was the only thing that gave us a good reason to paw through the basement and scare up an old photo album to use.

I envied people who got to do things like scrapbooking just for the sake of doing them, and not to dig up dirt on their future in-laws. I hated being cagey around Jacob's parents, and it was a relief to finally head over to the class.

Happy Crafts was a massive hangar of a building filled with inexplicable goods, from pom-poms to pool noodles. There were paints to make old things look new, and new things look old. There was an entire wall dedicated to scissors. And there was a gaggle of middle-aged, blonde-haired Wisconsin women staring at Jacob and me as if we'd just parked a flying saucer beside their SUVs and minivans.

Once I got a load of the place, I'd just as soon have turned around and walked right back out. Too bad Jacob was in my way—though when he said, "We're here for the scrapbooking class," even he sounded vaguely intimidated.

The women fluttered apart like a startled flock of blonde sparrows and made room for us smack dab in the middle of the table. So much for my usual M.O.—lurk around the fringes and leave early when no one's looking. Not only would we be directly across from the teacher, but all the other students were way more interested in us than they were in their glue sticks and gel pens.

"We don't see fresh faces in our group that often," the instructor said. She seemed pleased, I think...or maybe she was just humoring us. "Let's all go around and introduce ourselves. My name is Sue."

We introduced ourselves, and the rest of women all said their names, which I promptly forgot. There were a couple of Heathers, though the group was so homogenous that within moments I couldn't tell you which ones they were.

Sue eyed a photo album tucked under Jacob's arm and said, "And I see you brought some family photos along to work on your family tree?"

The album in question had been prized form a teetering stack that smelled like mothballs. Jacob had gone for an old one, hoping that a few frozen moments might help him make sense of things.

Sue looked to me. Specifically, to the way I was standing there empty-handed. "And what about you, Vic? Are the two of you...related?"

"We will be, as of next week."

A couple of the women looked scandalized at that, but the rest of them were just relieved to know what our deal was. Sue seemed fine about sharing her passion for scrapbooking with a couple of gay guys, but it looked like she wasn't about to let me coast by on Jacob's work. "The tree is more meaningful when it's your own roots. If you've got some pictures on your phone we can print them up on our photo printer."

"I don't think anything I've got on here would work."

"You'd be surprised at what kinds of pictures make for the best layouts. Let's see your camera roll—I'll help you pick out some good ones."

Most guys would worry about flashing good ol' Sue a dick pic. But I've never shot one, myself, since anything I put in my phone goes straight into the FPMP database. The majority of my shots were of locales where I'd spent time funneling white light and throwing salt. Not that my camera lens could pick up on a ghost, even if one were still there to see...but I felt like I should keep some kind of record.

I could show her that my photo albums were filled with a bunch of empty rooms, but it would be a lot easier to just produce some random people. "I've got my pictures in the cloud," I said. I'm not a hundred percent sure what that means, but she seemed to buy it. Sticking my phone under the table so none of the Heathers could see, I sent a quick text to a co-worker who owed me a favor.

Veronica Lipton was an undercover specialist at the FPMP. She was also the owner of three spoiled cats. And on the rare occasion when she was out on assignment and her sister couldn't come stay with them, their care fell to Jacob and me. The cats had actually grown pretty fond of us, and they hardly ever clawed our furniture anymore (now that we knew to cover anything important in bubble wrap and double-stick tape). Still, they made for pretty good leverage when I wanted something.

I thumbed in a quick text: *Need a dozen plausible family photos ASAP.*

She replied, *5 min.*

Either that meant someone in her department was really on the ball, or she already had a contingency plan for this and just needed to dig up the folder. That was kind of creepy. But also pretty darn convenient.

"They'll take a few minutes to download," I said.

"That's just fine," Sue said. "It'll give me time to show you the new papers we have in stock."

She rolled out a sheaf of papers, an armload of pens, a wad of ink pads and, yes, several pots of glitter. I'd been wondering why the class was free, but now it was pretty clear that the whole point of it was to sell us a bunch of ridiculous stationery.

Jacob picked out his background pretty quickly. Either he really liked it or he'd chosen at random. I did the same. In keeping with the "family tree" theme, everything was some variety of woodgrain or leaf—basically the same—but the Heather on my right made a big deal out of helping me pick different "scales" of print for my accents, while the one across from me tried to educate me on complementary colors.

By the time I had my pile of supplies assembled, my phone dinged, and I found a new folder in my files marked *family*. Inside was a variety of shots, from portraits to candids. Some were digital. Some were older.

I tried not to think too hard about the kid who appeared in a few of them—the kid who was clearly supposed to be me. Had they hired a model and styled the scene to look three decades old, or just usurped some other person's past for me to claim as my own? I wasn't sure I was comfortable with either scenario... but at least it would get Sue off my back.

Once she helped me print out my pictures—that kid was really eerie—I found my seat and let my Heather help me cut things out.

Sue was already going on about how to divide up the page and where to put the lettering, but Jacob was obviously way more interested in the photo album than he was in the lesson. He tried to pry a shot from the acetate sleeve, and his Heather said, "Don't force it out if it's stuck. You'll peel off the emulsion."

Jacob was so focused on the photo, I'm not sure he even heard her.

I forgot about the strangers standing in for my family and craned my neck to get a look at what Jacob was peering at. My first impression was that it felt a lot like the pictures Veronica had sent me—oddly colored and old-fashioned, from a decade where men side-parted their hair with brilliantine and women allowed it. The focus of the photo was the car, which took up most of the frame, though the guy beside it stole the show.

"Is that your dad?" I said. "He looks just like you." Albeit a heck of a lot younger, though I didn't mention that.

"That's him—and the Cutlass Supreme. He loved that car."

"And your mom?" Off to one side, a sassy looking girl with a snub nose and waist-length, honey-brown hair had a cigarette in one hand and a toddler on her opposite hip. "Holy crap, that's you."

I'd seen plenty of Jacob's baby pictures, but there was something about this one—unposed, unscripted, a slice of life that felt so natural and real—that my heart hurt to think that a few initials in some quack's journal was making Jacob wonder if his whole history was a lie.

He tried again to peel up the plastic overlay, but no dice.

His Heather said, "Ope, don't tear it—just put the whole page on the copier. The color copies come out real nice."

But it wasn't what we could see that Jacob was focused on... but what we couldn't. "It's folded in half."

"That's funny," his Heather said. "There's plenty of room on the page for the whole thing."

All the Heathers stopped inking their stamps, sticking their glue dots and scalloping their edges...and turned their eyes to Jacob. Their leader, Sue, had been doing her best to not make a big deal out of two gay guys crashing the scrapbook party, but even she couldn't resist the intrigue. "Hang on there," she said. "If it's stuck, warm it up with the heat gun first."

All the Heathers held their breath while Sue carefully wielded the mini blowdryer, and the scent of warming plastic mingled with the pervasive smell of markers. Someone produced a scraper with a rounded edge, and Jacob worked it underneath the sheet protector. There was a brief sound of something tearing, a shocked intake of breath, and then all at once, the photo peeled free.

On the back? Two more guys—just teenagers, really—with side-parted hair.

I'm not sure what the Heathers expected to see, but whatever it was, they seemed pretty disappointed that it wasn't anything more lurid. They went back to their sticking and stamping and scalloping while I leaned in to get a closer look at the photo. One guy looked even more like Jacob than his dad did. "Is that your uncle Fred?"

"Must be."

"And the other kid?"

"No idea."

"Turn it over," my Heather said. "People use-ta write names on the back."

And sure enough, there it was, in faded cursive.

> *Jerry*
> *Shirley*
> *Baby Jacob* (snerk)
> *Freddie*
> *Norman K*

I was connecting dots before I fully realized what was going on. The logic ran something like this....

Even the handwriting looks old. You don't see too many guys named Norman anymore. Since they put his last initial, he must not be related. Have I ever met a Norman before? It seems like I might have.

By this time, I'd flipped the photograph front side up and zeroed in on the kid next to Jacob's uncle. While teenaged Fred was smirking, arms akimbo, the picture of confidence bordering on arrogance, his buddy had his arms crossed and a scowl on his face that belonged on a guy twice his age. In fact, he'd already developed some impressive frown lines.

Impressively familiar.

My stomach churned as if realization dawned on my body first before it fully hit my brain. I knew what the *K* in "Norman K." stood for. Why? Because he'd been at Camp Hell.

Not as a fellow inmate...but as the director.

The rest of the scrapbooking class was a blur in which I used every last technique in my arsenal to stave off a raging, full-on panic attack. I visualized a tranquil sunset. I counted my breaths. I even slipped in a set of earbuds, claimed I was just getting into the scrapbooking groove, and cranked some binaural pulses to try and calm myself the fuck down.

It worked, kind of...in that I was able to cut out photos of strangers who looked vaguely like me, stick them on a page and douse them with glitter without making a complete spectacle of myself.

Meanwhile, I struggled to find a reason why the guy in the photo couldn't be Director Krimski. The Krimski I knew back then was in his late forties—so he'd be what, sixty-something now? A few years younger than Jacob's folks.

No matter how I tried to second-guess myself, it still fit.

And there was no mistaking those piercing, deep-set eyes.

Under any typical circumstance, Norman Krimski would intimidate the hell out of me. He was the one who locked us in our rooms like inmates—who fired the instructors, replaced the normal orderlies with savage bullies, and used us all as guinea pigs. Any one of those things would leave a mark. But it was the ghost in his office that really scared me.

Krimski's official story was that Director Sanchez had retired. I knew different.

There was only one instance where I'd seen what was left of Sanchez, but once was plenty—face red, eyes bulging, clawing at the garrote around his neck. Back then, I hadn't known a repeater was nothing more than trapped energy, an etheric stain. Then again, I guess it's hard to tell whether you're dealing with a mindless repeater or a potential possession until it's way too late.

I did my best not to spiral down a loop of experimentation and possession, to just focus on the task in front of me and stop stray rhinestones from sticking themselves to the hairs on the back of my hand—but the class seemed to stretch on forever. Apparently, though, it wasn't just my perception of time dragging on. The hour-long class was half an hour past its scheduled stopping point with no end in sight. It was actually a relief when Jacob got an irate text from Barbara reminding him we were supposed to be at the nursing home.

Fifty bucks later, dragging along a sparkly trail of glitter, we headed out to the car. I fully expected Jacob to call me on the panic attack, and I'd been trying to figure out how to break the Camp Hell connection to him without him completely disowning his parents. Was it possible Jacob didn't notice my panic? I guess I forget that he isn't actually empathic. While I'd been quelling my freak-out, he'd been busy ruminating on his own concerns.

He frowned and said, "Why would my dad have been in that journal, and not Uncle Fred? Unless the milkman is my grandfather's spitting image, it's pretty plain they're from the same genetic stock."

"No idea." I unlocked the glovebox and pulled out the journal. We'd both worried over it so many times it fell right open to the critical page. I scanned the penciled letters as if I was looking for Fred's initials, but what I was really searching for? NK.

And there it was.

I already knew Norman Krimski was a True Stiff—Stefan had told me so. But seeing it there in black and white was still a major jolt to my reality. There were no siblings or children listed, but who knew if the list was even complete, since Barbara wasn't on it—Uncle Fred, either. Try as I might to forget about Krimski—to leave him in the past where he belonged—I was starting to suspect he wouldn't stay put forever.

Another thing that bothered me was the total lack of context. We knew "who" was part of Kamal's experiment...but we didn't know "why." Were they breeding Human Shields? What purpose could there possibly be, if telepathy hadn't been officially discovered yet? That thing Jacob did when he went red and veiny in the etheric plane—when the lights flickered and the habit demons quaked—maybe that was the whole point of whatever it was Kamal was trying to achieve.

But without wringing an answer out of him, we might never know.

CHAPTER FIFTEEN

I was still scanning and re-scanning the initials on the page when Jacob said, "Maybe at the nursing home, you could distract Barbara."

"What do you mean?"

"Get her out of the room. Just for a few minutes."

"Whoa, hold on. You want some privacy to put the thumbscrews to your *grandmother*?"

Jacob glared at the dash. "I might not get another chance." When I was too stunned to answer right away, he soft-pedaled with, "I just want to ask her a few questions that Barb doesn't need to worry about."

I'd have to concede, Barbara was already twitchy about my mediumship. I'm guessing a conversation about a psychic breeding program wouldn't go over too well. And if his grandmother had anything to complain about once he'd finished with her, everyone would just chalk it up to dementia.

"Be nice," I said. Jacob gave me a look. "Or at least be gentle."

We pulled up in front of Barbara's house, a brick ranch with a finished basement and a manicured lawn. Barbara was a single working mother, and in Chicago, the property would've been way out of her reach. But small-town Wisconsin wasn't inner-city Chicago, and real estate here was not nearly as precious a commodity. Up here, I regularly marveled at the abandoned properties we'd pass on the highway (or the two-lane, as the oldsters called the winding country roads). But a lot of these places were dauntingly far from civilization as I defined it, which meant there were precious few jobs to be had nearby. And without an expanding population clamoring for somewhere to live, the buildings eventually fell in on themselves.

Barb's place was definitely not in danger of falling in. In fact, her shrubs were trimmed with such precision they looked fake. Jacob's sister was a real stickler for the rules, and not just in terms of her home maintenance. As we pulled up, we found her standing at the end of her drive, checking her phone as if to underscore the fact that we were nearly fifteen minutes late.

The mere sight of her made me question whether I was on-board with this harebrained idea of Jacob's. "I don't know if I'm up for this," I whispered as she strode up to the car, already annoyed. "Your sister is weirdly intimidating."

"Keep in mind, you can always outrun her."

Based on stride length, maybe. But given my endurance levels, I wasn't eager to put it to the test.

Barbara climbed into the back seat and slammed the door like an accusation, but before she could start complaining, Jacob distracted her with a question. "Where's Clayton?"

"You didn't expect him to come, did you? He shouldn't have to see Grandma like that."

Neither should we, but since she was the last remaining grandparent we could question about Kamal, I'd need to pull up my big boy pants and tough it out.

Jacob cut his eyes to hers in the rearview. "You left him alone?"

"Yes. He's thirteen years old, Jacob."

"We could have dropped him off at Mom and Dad's."

"Their TV is too old to hook up his video games. Don't worry, he's fine. He spends hours building Minecrafts, him and all his friends online. He only gets up when he needs to pee. I'll bet when I get back I find him sitting in the exact same spot."

Sounded like a win-win to me. Clayton got to do exactly what he wanted while Barbara got a nice break from being a mom.

Jacob still wasn't sold on the idea. "There are predators out there—"

"If you want to be a parent, Jacob, then have kids of your own. Don't dump all your baggage on me and act like you know best. You don't live here anymore—you haven't lived here for years—so you're not the judge of what's safe and what isn't. There are no 'predators' lurking around this neighborhood. And I want Clayton to be able to stand on his own two feet someday, which starts with me leaving him alone now and then. Was it scary the first time? Sure. But I figured out that if I keep enough Hot Pockets in the freezer, he might spoil his dinner, but he's not gonna burn the house down."

If I wanted to distract Barbara somehow, I'd need to figure out my strategy now, since we were already pulling up outside the nursing home. As we all climbed out of the car, I grabbed the only prop available to me: the photo album that had fallen to the passenger side floor. "Say, Barbara." I shoved it toward her and her arms reflexively flapped up to accept the book.

While she might have registered that Jacob was already walking away, she was more curious about the photo album. She juggled it awkwardly, then blew off some glitter. "Ope—what's this for?"

"To help jog your grandmother's memory." We'd shoved in our glittery scrapbooking efforts, as well. It was tempting to lob them in the trash on the way out of Happy Crafts, but we weren't sure if Pastor Jill would demand evidence of our date, so we decided to hold onto them. And good thing. "Oh, crap, I got glitter all over you."

Barbara was not nearly as alarmed by this as I might have been, but she did attempt to bat off some of the sparkle. "That's glitter for ya."

I deliberately fumbled the album as I turned it the right way around in her hands, dousing her with even more glitter. "Sorry—"

"It's fine."

"You've got some on your—" I whapped at her shoulder a few times.

She shook out both her arms as if she was trying to take flight. "Vic—it's fine. It'll come out in the wash."

"No, hold on." I brushed vigorously at her shoulder blades until she relented and stood still for my de-glittering process. How long would Jacob need to question his grandmother? No idea. But probably longer than I could manhandle Barbara before she got suspicious.

"Aw, jeez."

"Just a little bit more."

"Really, it's...fine." Barbara said this without much conviction, since she was thumbing through the album as best she could while awkwardly holding it aloft and open. "I've never seen this. These first pictures have gotta be a good dozen years older than me." She set the album down on the hood of the car, and I stopped swatting glitter and came up beside her to look, figuring the best stalling tactic was to not annoy her too much.

The photos were roughly chronological, with Baby Jacob appearing about halfway through and Little Barbie about ten pages later. Back when you had to actually buy film and pay for developing, most people took only a small fraction of the photos they did today. Kids always seem to merit a few shots, though. Especially birthdays and Christmas.

Jacob's birthday is at the height of summer, when July makes way for August and the humidity's thick enough to eat with a fork. There was a whole page devoted to a series of birthday shots, judging by the banana bike with the big red bow on it, and Jacob grinning like he could hardly wait to hop on and go cause trouble. Barbara was a tiny thing with a wild mop of dark hair, maybe three or so, which would make Jacob nine or ten. Jerry looked about the same, though his hair was more poofy without the Bryl Cream. Shirley had started to pack on weight—maybe she'd quit smoking. And Uncle Leon was young and vigorous, even without his right arm.

I wondered if Leon's mill accident had actually been an accident. And then I told myself that even if I proved otherwise, it would hardly bring his physical arm back.

"Look at my grandmother." Barbara pointed to her and I barely stifled a flinch. Grandma Marks was lurking in the shadow of the garage like she was about to lure a few unsuspecting kids out of the forest with some gingerbread. Doing the math, I realized she wasn't too much older in that photo than Jacob was now. But even in her fifties, she looked old and brittle.

"Was she always so...?"

"Miserable?" I'm glad Barbara said it, not me. "I didn't notice it when I was a kid—that's just how she was. But now, thinking back on it? I dunno. Maybe she was struggling with depression, or some other issue you could talk to your doctor about nowadays. Not back then, though. Too much stigma."

There was still plenty of stigma attached to mental health. I wasn't about to volunteer about the time I'd done in a nuthouse, for instance. Even though the doctors eventually figured out I wasn't schizophrenic, I knew that piece of my history made people look at me different anyhow.

I said, "But you were close to her, right? That's what your parents said."

"I spent time with her, I guess. But I never saw us as close. Not like I was with Grammy Joyce—my mom's mom. She was always covering me with slobbery grandma-kisses." She found a very 70's fishing photo of the Larsons. Her nice grandmother was proudly brandishing a catfish while her grandpa grinned around a cigarette. Barbara sighed sadly. "Grammy died when I was in college, and Grandpa Gus was gone a month later. I miss them so much."

When most people tell me stories like this, they're followed by a hopeful look. I don't think they even realize they're doing it. But the allure of getting one final message from a loved one is strong. At least, from what I gather, it would be—if you didn't know how gory, grabby, or just plain freaky ghosts usually were.

Not Barbara, though. She wasn't fishing for a visit from beyond the grave. She was just conveying information: she missed her dead grandparents. In fact, if anything, Barbara *avoided* talking Psych with me. She related to me not as the guy who slimed her brother with ectoplasm (or even the guy who slimed him with other things) but the guy he'd made a home with. As future sister-in-laws went, I could do worse.

"We shouldn't leave Jacob dealing with Grandma by himself," Barbara said...in the way I might say, "I shouldn't eat so many gas station burritos." Instead of heading inside, she propped the photo album on the hood of the car and started paging through it. "She's not in very many of the pictures, is she? I remember her being there for most things—like, look, here's Jacob starting high school." Wow, his teeth were ginormous before his head grew into them. "Makes you wonder if your memory really is all it's cracked up to be."

"Maybe she just didn't like to be photographed."

"Yah, maybe not." She flipped through the next few pages, then paused. Her brow furrowed, and she looked an awful lot like her big brother. Then again, he'd been making that face a lot lately. I peered over her shoulder.

The photos appeared to have been taken at regular intervals—a year apart—but other than that, they were all the same. A carnival, with Jacob and Barbara standing beside a cutout sign of a painted pelican that read, "Riders must be this tall," with the pelican's wing stretched up to indicate 48 inches.

Barbara stared at the page for a long moment, and eventually said, "Is this weird?"

The pelican was not only pointing out the four-foot mark, but holding a long ruler—which reminded me of the sort of thing you see in mugshots, or mounted beside the door of a bank or convenience store. But people liked to track their kids' progress. Didn't they? "I dunno. Weird...how?"

"That Grandma insisted we go to this carnival every year."

"Maybe she wanted to spend time with you."

"Maybe." Barbara didn't sound particularly convinced. "But we didn't even like it—look at our faces."

I had to admit, no one looked particularly happy to be there.

"Plus, it was a really long drive. There must be a reason she dragged us there year after year. People don't just do things for no reason."

That's true. Even the most random and senseless acts of violence I'd seen in all my years on the force had some logic behind them. Far-fetched and screwed up? Yes. But still, a reason.

If it weren't for Kamal's notes, I would presume the reason Grandma Marks tracked her grandkids' growth was purely sentimental. But having seen that branching tree of initials, I couldn't help but wonder....

"What else do you remember about the carnival?"

Barbara's gaze turned inward. "It was a fundraiser for Sacred Heart Hospital—I don't know if that place is even around anymore. It was way off in the middle of nowhere." Funny, this was how I viewed the majority of Wisconsin. "I guess you'd just call it our tradition. There was a big field behind the hospital where they'd set it up every year. Grandma took Jacob and me out there, and we'd spend the day playing carnival games."

"No rides?"

Barbara looked puzzled. "Grandma always steered us away from the rides."

Which made the pelican even more suspect.

Barbara said, "I guess the whole point was to make money with the games."

"Is that something hospitals typically do?"

"Catholic churches have bingo—so why not? They sure made enough off us. I remember Grandma would get this big load of tickets, split them in half, give them to us, and tell us to go win a prize."

"That sounds...fun."

Barbara shrugged. "Does it? She wouldn't let us stop until all the tickets were gone."

She closed the photo album decisively, and a puff of glitter sprayed out. "Anyways. Maybe this will help Grandma get her bearings."

By the time we joined Jacob, Barbara was pretty darn annoyed—but since that's par for the course, I doubt anyone thought much of it. "Look what Jacob brought," she said testily as she held up the photo album.

If I wasn't watching Grandma so closely for her reaction, I might not have seen it, but she glanced up just long enough to take it in, then looked away just as quickly.

"It's pictures," Barbara said. Rather loudly, at that. "From when we were little."

Grandma was propped up in bed with a tray table beside her. Oddments of institutional pre-package food littered the tabletop: a Jell-O cup, a small plastic juice with a foil lid, a packet of untouched saltines. Barb shoved them aside with her glittery forearm and parked the photo album in their place. She opened it to a random page and said, "Look, there's dad on his bowling league."

No response.

Barbara tried again. "Remember this? The Christmas we tried to go caroling but we got snowed in?" I craned my neck and glimpsed a group of mostly dark-haired Markses laughing in outrageously big parkas. Barbara took in Grandma's non-acknowledgement, then flipped to the page of the kids and the pelican sign...which definitely did look weird once you compared it to all the other normal photos. "How about this, Grandma? Sacred Heart Carnival. Remember that?"

Jacob hadn't kenned to the fact that anything was wrong. But something told me Grandma had. She jerked her head away as if something on the page offended her, which only made Barb try harder to make her acknowledge it. "Remember? We went every year. You and me and Jacob. Every. Year."

Grandma blew out a whuff through her nose—but hard to say if she was trying to communicate something, or just breathing.

"You made us play games till we cried."

"I did not cry," Jacob said firmly.

Barbara ignored him. "All day long, even after dark sometimes—and it was summer, too, so the days were real long."

Grandma huffed and shook her head, glaring.

"You forced us. Every darn year. Why? So you could get your grandma duties over with and act like you loved us?"

Grandma's gaze snapped to Barbara's, and she said, "You have no idea how much I sacrificed for you kids."

I wasn't expecting an actual answer—I don't think any of us were. Barbara jumped like she'd grabbed the wrong end of a hot glue gun. "Well. At least you recognize us today."

CHAPTER SIXTEEN

I'm not sure what was worse—Grandma babbling at Jacob and calling him Freddie, or Grandma giving Jacob the cold shoulder and refusing to speak to him at all. Our plan to visit her while she was lucid hadn't exactly panned out. And this time, no one suggested pie.

Barbara glared out the backseat window. "What is with that woman?"

"We'll try again tomorrow," Jacob said. "If her mental condition changes throughout the day, maybe we need to catch her first thing in the morning."

Barbara said, "She knew full well what was going on. Stubborn. That's what she is. Just plain stubborn."

I wisely refrained from any comment about it running in the family.

Barbara flipped open the photo album. "You remember Sacred Heart, right? The dumb carnival? The pelican? How she always bought us that big wad of tickets?"

"Yeah. So?"

"I don't know. It just seems weird." She fell silent again, and

I figured that was that...until she piped up with, "I can't find Sacred Heart."

I turned around so fast I nearly got whiplash, but the damage was already done. Barbara was swiping away at her phone, where a search on the old hospital had pinged through the cloud, alerting every governmental agency keeping track of peoples' curiosity that someone was poking their nose where it didn't belong. I wanted to grab that phone out of her hand and snap, "What, are you stupid?" But of course she wasn't. She just had no idea that she had more than one big brother—and the one she was unaware of was really big on surveillance.

Once I was sure my voice would be normal, I said, "Can I see?"

She handed me her phone. It was nowhere near as slick as mine and clumsier to navigate. You don't realize how good you have it with top secret government tech until you're forced to fumble around with a civilian phone. Then again, maybe civilian phones weren't quite so easy to monitor. I poked back through her search and looked at the results for Sacred Heart Hospital. One in Eau Claire—hardly out in the middle of nowhere—and another "up north."

"That isn't the one?" I asked.

"Vic...that's four hours away." The "What, are you stupid?" came through loud and clear in Barbara's tone, which made me feel pretty virtuous for holding my tongue.

Jacob said, "It would've been somewhere south. Toward Platteville."

My clumsy searching turned up nothing. I gave the phone back to Barbara.

Jacob said, "It probably merged with something else twenty years ago."

"I guess." Barbara swiped around without much enthusiasm,

then pocketed her phone and sighed. "There's nothing out there but dairy farms and trees."

Jacob cut his eyes to me. I gave him a subtle nod. Hopefully, between the civilian phone and the fact that she'd given up so easily, no one back at HQ (or worse, F-Pimp National) would be pawing through Barbara's browsing history.

Then again, maybe she'd just given the whole thing a rest because we were practically home already. Jacob made the final turn onto her street, and she scooted across the seat to mash her face into the opposite window and said, "What on earth is Clayton doing outside?"

While, intellectually, I knew kids grew up, I was always fairly baffled that he looked so much older, every darn time. He stood on the lawn in a T-shirt, cutoffs and flip-flops, working some kind of handheld gizmo with his thumbs while an odd mechanical sound buzzed in the distance. We'd just seen him a few weeks ago. Yet somehow, he seemed practically adult-sized now. A smallish adult, maybe—but still, it was weird, because I'd never stopped thinking of him as the snot-nosed brat who parroted random homophobic remarks to try and get a rise out of me.

Barbara powered down the window and barked, "Clayton Joseph!"

I flinched. Her kid didn't. She was out of the car like a shot before Jacob even cut the engine.

"I told you to stay inside with the door locked. And why in the heck would you need to stand in the middle of the lawn to play your video game?"

"It's not a *game*—it's a drone."

We all looked up as we joined her on the edge of the lawn. So that's where that buzzing noise was coming from.

I wondered if it was only civilian drones that were so loud.

Barbara was not impressed. "And where did that drone come from?"

"Dad."

"Figures," Barbara muttered under her breath. "I swear Derrick lives to make me look bad. I told Clayton no drone. And what does he go and do? Buys him a frickin' drone. And now, if I take it away, I'm the bad guy."

The whining grew louder as the drone floated down to earth. "Did you see that landing?" Clayton turned to Jacob, and his careless tween attitude slipped. "Uncle Jacob, did you see?"

"Awesome," Jacob said. I think the enthusiasm was genuine, too, despite everything he'd been through. He's always had a soft spot for Clayton.

Jacob and Clayton wandered toward the sidewalk, trailing after the drone. Once they were out of earshot, I dropped my voice and told Barbara, "You can always use it for leverage. Take it away when he does something wrong."

"Oh, I will. Believe you me. Even so...it pisses me off." She whispered the curse word as if she was afraid God might hear her and put a black mark on her permanent record. "I never wanted to be the only disciplinarian in Clayton's life. But now I'm stuck being the strict parent."

I wasn't sure how much or how little Barbara wanted to tell me—and to be honest, other folks' personal details tended to leave me feeling uncomfortable and strange—but for whatever reason, people seem to think they want my advice. "He'll thank you for it later," I said vaguely.

"I wouldn't be so sure about that. Derrick is always showering him with money and toys. How can I compete with that?"

"By being there for him."

Barb pressed her lips together and gazed off into the middle distance. Her eyes looked a little bit wet. "Sometimes I wonder if that's enough."

The conversation was hitting uncomfortably close to the bone, and I saw Barbara's attention swing back to her phone, as if locating Sacred Heart would save her from having to think about how thankless it was to be a single parent. It was bad enough to shield ourselves from the prying eyes of the FPMP. I had no idea how to extend the protection to her. If she knew how far we went to avoid surveillance, she might think we were being paranoid. Or she might believe us, and jump on the paranoia bandwagon herself. Either way, I'd hate to be responsible for her ending up under the microscope.

"You should probably act interested in Clayton's new gizmo," I said, way more decisively than I felt. "Reverse psychology. The more you act like you're cool with Derrick's bribes, the less Clayton can play the two of you off each other."

She put her phone away. "You're right. Kids can be incredibly manipulative—and even when you know darn well that they're doing it, there's no avoiding the guilt."

Funny...Jacob's sister and I seemed to be getting along awfully well these days. You'd think the stress of her grandmother's fall would've made her even more prickly and domineering. But instead, she just seemed vulnerable.

We crossed the lawn to join them, and Barbara proceeded to ooh and ahh over the drone. She was pretty darn convincing. Clayton seemed surprised that his mother was interested in his new toy, but since he was unwilling to relinquish his newfound teenaged ennui, he managed to downplay his reaction.

When I was his age, I flew airplanes made of balsa wood

with propellers powered by rubber bands. They sold them at the corner store for a buck-nineteen. But as flying toys went, this drone was in an entirely different league. Clayton demoed the controllers—forward, backward, hover. It even interfaced with his cell phone.

Frankly, I'd never given drones much thought. And now, of course, I'd need to look up into the sky every time Jacob and I attempted a private conversation. We were being treated to a dizzying camera view of the roof of his house when Crash's ringtone sounded, and I gratefully disengaged from the group to take his call.

"Hello?"

"So—what kind of stripper did you want for your bachelor party?"

"First of all, none. And second—there is no bachelor party."

"Sexy cop answering a noise complaint is the standard. But I figured that would only give you work flashbacks. Plus, I'm none too fond of pigs. Even fake ones with tearaway pants."

"There is no bachelor party."

"We could go with a fireman—a talented dancer can really put a pole through its paces. But again, is that too expected? You know how I loathe cliché."

"No. Bachelor. Party."

"Maybe we could do something meta. A stripper shows up as an off-duty stripper—"

I sighed gustily.

Crash said, "Clearly, you're convinced I'm yanking your chain. But take a look on the calendar and you'll see—"

"What calendar?"

"Wednesday night is all blocked out for the bachelor party."

"*What calendar?*"

My phone dinged and a link appeared. I poked it and a calendar opened up. I might have figured it for some elaborate gag (since Crash truly did love to yank my chain) but then I noticed it had been authored by Barbara...and a variety of real obligations were already plugged in.

"This was supposed to be simple," I groaned.

"If you really wanted simple, you should've just gone downtown and had a judge do the deed. But don't worry. I promise not to pipe up with any objections during the ceremony...as long as *you* promise to be super nice to *me*."

"Are you done?"

"Just one more question...sushi, or taco bar?"

"I'm not so sure I trust Wisconsin fish unless it's beer-battered and deep fried."

"Taco bar it is. *Hasta luego.*"

Crash hung up and left me staring at the calendar, wondering if the whole stripper thing was a legitimate threat. A few yards away, the drone plunked down onto the lawn again—apparently they don't have much fly time—and Clayton showed off how to swap out the battery. While Jacob was enthusing over his nephew, he'd forgotten all about those rows of initials...and was just Jacob again, enjoying his healthy, normal family. It would've been a heartwarming scene, except I knew it wouldn't last.

I wished I could reach through the veil and throttle Kamal for turning Jacob's normal family life into a big, fat lie. Out on the lawn, Barbara finally lost her cool and exploded about Clayton wandering outside while she wasn't home, threatening to donate that "gosh-darned drone" to needy children who listened to their parents...and even that made me nostalgic for the illusion that Jacob's upbringing was normal and good.

I edged over toward Jacob and gesture with my phone. "Did you see this calendar?"

Barbara stopped haranguing Clayton and turned her attention to Jacob. "Are you telling me you didn't send it to Vic?" That thing about her not being so prickly lately? I took it back. "Jeez, Jacob—I can't do everything around here."

Before she could tear him a new one, I said, "It's fine. I've got it now. But this bachelor party—"

"Are you going to be late for that too?"

Jacob pulled out his own phone. "What bachelor party?"

Then Clayton piped up with, "How does that work, since you're both guys? Do you each get a separate party, or do you have to share?"

"Is Crash really in charge," I asked, "or was he just trying to get a rise out of me?"

Barb said, "Well, I don't have time, and who else would do it? My parents? Fine—if you wanna play euchre all night." Euchre was a card game, I knew that much. But since cards typically involved counting, strategy and luck, I've never been a fan. "I figured one of your Chicago friends would be more fun anyhow, so I went through the guest list and found a volunteer."

Yeah, well. That depended on your idea of *fun*.

"So you're sure you have the calendar now?" she asked me, in a tone that implied, I'd better.

I dutifully called up the link Crash had just sent to demonstrate that she had nothing to worry about. She angled my phone so she could see it better and scowled at it so hard I was surprised she didn't call up the operating system. Belatedly, I wondered if Crash had sent me the actual calendar, or something filled with inappropriate innuendoes.

"Jeez, it's ten to twelve already?" Barbara said. "You're supposed to meet with the photographer by noon."

Oh great. Just what I needed. A photo shoot.

CHAPTER SEVENTEEN

Since Barb wasn't about to let Clayton out of her sight—or us, for that matter—we all bundled into the car and headed off to the park. "Did you really need to do that scrapbooking today?" she asked Jacob. Clayton snorted. "You knew we had a packed schedule."

Jacob said, "What are these pictures even for? Won't we have plenty from the wedding?"

"Normal couples do engagement shoots, so they have plenty of shots to put up on the projector wall at church. But since you guys didn't bother—"

"It's fine," I cut in. "Let's just do this and cross it off the list." Judging by the calendar, our whole week was basically one gigantic to-do list. We were better off just getting our obligations over with.

We showed up at the location with no time to spare. "Park over by the pergola," Barbara said. The word *pergola* wasn't in my vocabulary—Pastor Jill probably knew it—but Jacob managed to figure out where to go.

He pulled up by a wooden structure that looked like the unfinished frame of a garden shed, one that had been abandoned so long ago that vines were now crawling up its wooden skeleton. Underneath was a wooden swing-seat. Some of the vines were starting to bloom. All in all, not a bad place to take a picture. And despite all the rushing around, it looked like we'd managed to beat the photographer there, too. The only other person in sight was a chubby guy walking half a dozen yippy little dogs.

We climbed out of the car and Barbara assessed us critically. "Look at what you're wearing. We should've stopped by Mom and Dad's for your suits."

Her complaining was starting to get annoying—but it was drowned out but the cacophony of the little dogs, which were easily twice as loud. The guy holding the leashes trundled along behind the group of them, red-faced and sweating as they dragged him relentlessly toward a nearby shrub. While individually, none of the yipping furballs could've outweighed Clayton's drone, together they seemed to wield some collective muscle.

"We don't need suits." I wasn't sure if Jacob was raising his voice over all the barking, or if he was starting to get pissed off.

"But you're wearing *cargo shorts*."

"It's fine."

As the dog walker reached down with a baggie-covered hand to pick up a dog turd, he piped in, "I agree. Casual couples' shots are the big thing nowadays."

We all looked at him like he'd sprouted a listening device from the top of his head while his dog pack snuffled around the bush.

"Abner Stroud," he said as he tied off the bag, then offered me his hand in greeting. Given that it was probably still warm from touching the poo through the thin plastic, I shoved my hands in my pockets and took a half-step back.

"You're Abner Stroud?" Barbara demanded, as if surely he must be full of dog shit.

"And you must be Barbara. Your mother told me all about you." Stroud veered her way and tried to aim his handshake in her direction, but she was no more eager to experience it than I was. "I can't tell you how excited I was to get the opportunity to document your family's big day!" He then tried for Jacob's hand, which clearly wasn't gonna happen either. "You must be Jacob. I've heard so many great things about you, too."

Jacob was looking at the dogs with bewilderment. "You're the photographer?"

"Maybe you've heard of me. Abner Stroud. Portraits-by-Abner.com."

The smallest dog—a scruffy, whitish thing—lifted a leg and peed on the side of the pergola.

Clayton smirked, then pulled out his phone, thumbs flying, and turned his back to ignore us boring grown-ups.

"Where's your camera?" Barbara demanded like she thought she was being punked.

Stroud patted himself down with his free hand while the dogs yanked at the one holding six leashes and the turd, threatening to send the plastic bag flying God-knows-where. He brightened and pulled out a tiny point-and-shoot. "It's amazing how much firepower they can pack into such a tiny footprint nowadays!"

He staggered off toward a trashcan, being pulled every which way by the pack of yipping dogs. Once he was out of earshot, Jacob said, "Where did you find this guy?"

"I don't know. Mom picked him out. She said he had glowing reviews." They both watched with identical looks of disgust as a grayish living dustmop wound through Stroud's legs and very nearly sent him sprawling.

Clayton turned his phone to flash us a portrait of a chihuahua in sunglasses. "Look—he's a *dog* photographer."

It was tempting to double-check that the site he'd found really was Portraits-by-Abner…but I had the sinking feeling it couldn't possibly be anything else.

"Mom's gonna hear about this," Barb muttered.

Stroud aimed his dog pack in our direction and they dragged him back toward the pergola. While he tied off their leashes to a nearby signpost, I leaned into Jacob and said in his ear, "Look, you've seen the schedule. The photo shoot will be over soon. So do your best to grin and bear it, and I'll make an effort to stop wincing over the sheer badness."

Some of the tension went out of Jacob's shoulders and he shot me a grateful look.

"Maybe we'll even laugh about it someday," I offered.

"That's pushing it," he said…but his annoyance was softening.

Barbara was annoyed enough for all of us. She parked herself on a nearby park bench, fuming, while Clayton half-sat, half-leaned on the bench's arm, once again engrossed in his phone. Stroud gave each of his yip-dogs a treat, which shut them up—for maybe ten seconds. And then the barking started up again, even louder.

Stroud didn't seem to hear it. I guess there's no telling what a person can get used to given enough exposure. With the miniature camera dangling from his wrist by a tiny strap, he pulled some folded papers out of his pocket and shoved them toward Jacob and me, followed by a pen. "All righty, then. All I'll need is a signature from each of the grooms and we'll get started."

I scanned my page, noting it was thick with legalese. "What is this?" Jacob asked.

"Just your standard models' waiver."

"What do we need a waiver for?" I asked.

"My website, obviously. So I can post it in my photo gallery."

"With the dogs," Clayton chuckled, eyes still on his phone.

Jacob pulled out his wallet and showed Stroud his identification. "That won't be possible. My contract with the government precludes my appearance on the web without a lengthy vetting process...and there's no time to go through all the channels now." He delivered the news calmly, but with his usual utmost certainty. "I'd hate to have to find another photographer on such short notice...."

And I'd be perfectly fine with skipping the shoot altogether. But the more wedding details we glossed over, the more obvious it would be that we were just here to snoop around.

Stroud stood no chance against Jacob's authoritative-voice, and he agreed that not only would we not appear on his website, but he'd delete the master photos from his backup drive.

We dutifully positioned ourselves under the pergola. "Okay guys," Stroud told us. "Look happy!"

I never knew what to do with my face at the best of times. I looked to Jacob for reassurance, but all he could manage was a subtle head-shake, like he couldn't quite wrap his head around how we'd arrived at this point either.

"Okay, great. Now, closer together. Relax your shoulders. Maybe something where the two of you are actually touching would be nice."

When we moved to slip our arms around each other, we each vied clumsily for the top-arm position.

"Kibbles does that too!" Stroud announced. "We call it pat-a-cake. Wanna see?"

"Just take the pictures," Barbara snapped. "We're on a tight enough schedule as it is."

Stroud unsuccessfully tried to bite back a wince. Since we couldn't manage to arrange our own limbs, he came over and did it for us. "There you go. Now look at me—normally I'd be holding up a piece of cheese for you to look at, heh heh."

I couldn't even imagine the expression I must be wearing. Stroud snapped some pictures, then said, "Okay, now look at each other." Even Jacob looked somewhat chagrined. "That's great, just perfect—uh, hold on. There's something on your jackets."

Jacob and I both looked down...and saw we were covered in glitter. Jacob batted at his sleeve, but I didn't bother, since I already knew from whacking at his sister that the tactic was useless. Stroud produced a lint brush from his pocket. "Never fear! I'm a trained professional!"

Jacob grabbed the roller from him, and we dispensed with the majority of the glitter.

"Okey-doke, let's try that again. Look at me. Good. Now look at each other. And now turn toward me with just your shoulders...hold on, there's a weird bulge in Vic's pocket."

I had a momentary flashback to junior high portrait day when my friends and I all put the fear in one another of "popping a boner" during our sittings, never mind the fact that the photos were only shoulders-up. It wasn't my jeans pocket he was talking about, though. It was my jacket.

Cripes. "Never mind," I said—I sound especially belligerent when I'm embarrassed—and palmed the wad of fabric as best I could to switch it to the other side. Nothing about it should especially register as "underwear" from this distance, but I strongly suspected I'd now be blushing in the remainder of the photos.

We went through the same rigmarole again. Look at each other. Look at Stroud and his imaginary cube of cheese. Swivel our shoulders. Tilt our heads. And for heaven's sake, stop scowling, this is a wedding and not a funeral.

I dunno, maybe a funeral would be preferable. At least no one would expect me to smile.

Stroud must have given up on my face. With forced enthusiasm, he said, "If you've got your wedding bands with you, I can do a shot of your hands. Everyone loves to see the rings."

Jacob grabbed them from the car and I took solace in the fact that he had to run out of things to take pictures of soon. But my optimism was short-lived. When the rings came out and Stroud moved in for the close-up, he said, "What's wrong with your hand?"

I like to think I'm not particularly pasty for a white guy, but sealing my limb in plaster for so many weeks had left it a whiter shade of pale. I'm not sure if it was an optical illusion, or if all that time in the dark had done something to my follicles, because the hairs on the back of my hand looked abnormally thick and black.

"We can skip the hand shot," Jacob said.

"How's your other hand?" Stroud asked, and I held them up side-by-side. My right hand was just as long-fingered and knuckly, but was lacking the morgue-like appearance of the one I'd deliberately broken. "I'll shoot the photos with your right hands and flip them around in Photoshop."

Huh. Maybe he knew a little something about photography after all.

He did some shots of us slipping the rings on each other while the dogs in the background yipped and whined, Clayton played on his phone, and Barbara fretfully checked and re-checked her watch.

"That's great," Stroud said. "Now how about a hug?"

I'd heard of small-town friendliness, but this was getting ridiculous.

"Each other," he added hastily, backing away.

I sighed as I put my arms around Jacob. Did he feel as awkward I did? If you'd asked me before, I would have said my better half didn't know the meaning of the word. But now, I was starting to suspect that he just hid it better than the rest of us. Our bodies normally clicked together like a jigsaw puzzle, but now they were fitting like pieces from two different boxes.

My stomach sank as I realized we'd have to kiss for the camera. It was the logical next step. My mouth went dry and I wet my lips nervously. How many kisses had Jacob and I shared since that first fateful tongue-lashing in Maurice's basement? I couldn't even begin to count. But now it seemed as if I would undoubtedly manage to do it wrong—and that moment would not only be preserved for all posterity, but splayed on the wall at our wedding itself, larger than life, for everyone we knew to see.

Awkward stretched into unbearable, and I almost pulled away to take a breath, to collect myself and pull on the neutral mask I hid behind when my emotions cut way deeper than I expected. But Jacob sensed the motion before it picked up any momentum. Under the unflinching gaze of the dinky point-and-shoot, he pulled me up against him and pressed his mouth to mine.

Maybe it was the knowledge that other people were watching. Maybe it was the memory of our very first kiss, when he teased the aftertaste of Auracel from my tongue—in particular, my disbelief that my hot PsyCop colleague from the Twelfth Precinct was actually putting the moves on me. As much of a pain in the ass as our to-do list might be, the fact was, never in my wildest dreams would I have pictured us ending up together in the long run. And not only was I banging this guy—I was marrying him.

This G-rated kiss would've been enough to check this whole

photography business off our list and move on. But instead of pulling away once expectations were met, Jacob leaned in, pressed his temple to my cheek and whispered, "You seem hesitant. Not having second thoughts...are you?"

"The only thought going through my head is how lucky I am."

Something unhitched inside Jacob. When he tightened his arms around me—to the serenade of a half-dozen yipping dogs—we finally, truly clicked into place.

CHAPTER EIGHTEEN

We ticked a few more things off our to-do list before we finally dropped off Jacob's sister and her kid. All in all, it wasn't a particularly long day—we were both used to working lengthy shifts—but no one had trained me for dealing with nursing homes and dog photographers and wayward glitter. I was so out of my element, I found our errands surprisingly draining. And as we pulled up to his folks' house, I realized our day was far from over.

As grueling as the day was, Jacob seemed in high enough spirits when Jerry and Leon looped him into helping them fix the lawn mower. I was in the kitchen with Shirley, trying to convince her that it was perfectly fine to open a bottle of wine (even though the other guys all drank beer and I didn't want any). She cocked her head, looked at me, and said, "Is that glitter?"

Apparently the sticky-roller wasn't as good as I'd hoped. Oh well. Maybe the sparkles would make our dog portraits look more like glamor shots. Naturally, I didn't want to be the one to criticize her choice of photographer, so I went for the logical change of subject. "Yeah, that craft store was full of sparkle. This mandatory date idea of Pastor Jill's.... I hadn't realized there'd be so many hoops to jump through to get married in the church."

"Oh yeah? Try marrying a Catholic!"

"No thanks, my heart's set on Jacob."

Shirley poured me the glass of chardonnay I'd told her I didn't want, but it least it was a small one. She said, "Let's see what you made. I went to a scrapbooking party once, but I really didn't have the patience for it—so I'm sure anything you came up with would be better than my attempt."

We adjourned to the backyard to keep the sparkle-contamination to a minimum. It was a coolish evening, but it was worth putting on a jacket to enjoy the spark of fireflies against the dimming sky. I wished I could just enjoy the moment, but Kamal's notebook had ruined that for me. And if I was feeling robbed, I could only imagine how Jacob must feel.

She spread out the pages on the picnic table. "Is that your mom?"

"Oh, uh...no. It's complicated."

Usually, when family resemblance strikes, it's about how much Jacob looks like his dad. But when Shirley met my eyes in that moment, I totally saw where Jacob got his spark of shrewdness. Shirley might come off easygoing, but she didn't miss a trick.

I felt like I'd better explain so she didn't draw conclusions any weirder than they really were. "The thing about being a high-level Psych...it makes you a target. And sometimes that means glossing over certain things and leaving my past in the past."

"But when you really think about it...." Shirley dropped her hand to mine. There was a twinge of protest where it hadn't quite recovered from the car door, but mild enough that I didn't flinch too visibly. "So does everybody."

I dry-swallowed. While I hadn't been fishing for an opening to interrogate her—I could hardly pass it up. "Like...how?"

With a sigh, Shirley settled back into the patio chair, fortified herself with a long sip of wine, then said, "We weren't always so understanding, Jerry and me. When Jacob came out, I mean. But you have to realize, in our generation—it wasn't something people really talked about. Not around here, anyways. We get it now. In fact, I think it's kind of sad so many couples had to pass themselves off as roommates. Some still do. Like the two ladies in the old farmhouse out by the creek. They've gotta be pushing eighty by now."

My stomach was still doing queasy somersaults—because I'd been poised for some big confession. And I suppose I'd gotten one. Just not the one I'd expected. I fanned out the glittery, clumsily-assembled scrapbook pages and took in my pages, with their photos of my white, homogenized fake family. "My foster parents—well, Harold in particular—I don't think he would have taken it well. My coming out."

"And there's no way to settle things now?"

In all this time, I realized, Shirley had never once mentioned my mediumship. Not to lure me out ghost-hunting, like Jerry and Leon, or to try and deny it even existed, like Barbara.

I thought about Darla reaching beyond the veil, with the dead folks struggling to get away from the contact like they were being waterboarded. I wouldn't wish that on anyone I loved.

"No. Not really. Some things, the best you can do is let it be."

As replies went, it was vague, but it seemed to satisfy Shirley well enough.

We turned our eyes back to the photos. Shirley slid mine aside since they were full of strangers and looked instead at

Jacob's pages. I'm not sure how much actual thought he'd put into his page. It was haphazard and minimal, with three random photos and the word "family" stamped crookedly across the top. She said, "Jacob's no better at this than I was."

"At...what?"

"Scrapbooking." Her eyes went shrewd again. "What did you think I meant?"

"Uh, say, we noticed something odd while we were looking through the album." I flipped through the pages until I found the one with the pelican. "Jacob said his grandmother took these."

Shirley dragged the album toward her and took a closer look. "Oh, that awful carnival at Sacred Heart. She insisted on dragging them there year after year."

I pointed toward a picture in the lower corner. Jacob looked older than Clayton, but not by much. "Was that the last year? Why did they stop going?"

"Well, the whole hospital shut down. Some big malpractice scandal. It was so bad, their head administrator killed himself rather than go to trial."

"What year was this?"

"I suppose Jacob would've been fourteen, fifteen." Shirley pulled out her phone and poked around. "Huh. That's funny. I can't find any articles about it online."

A thread of unease crept down my spine. "That's okay. Doesn't matter."

"What was his name? It's been so long" Shirley snapped her fingers a few times. "Dr. Mann—that's it." She continued to search. "You think there'd be *something*. It was a really big deal at the time."

"Old records are funny that way. Depends who's gotten

around to digitizing them." Did my voice sound normal? It must have, because Shirley continued to flip through the album, blissfully unaware that I was freaking out over the fact that Jacob had apparently survived his own personal Camp Hell.

CHAPTER NINETEEN

Anyone whose life has been touched by suicide knows it's a tragedy of the highest proportions.

And then there's me, whose first thought is how I can turn it to my advantage. Because murders and suicides aren't likely to cross over without a hitch.

When Jacob finally came in from the garage with old grass stuck to his T-shirt and a smudge of shop grime on his cheekbone, I covertly motioned him into the bedroom and told him about the administrator offing himself.

He was halfway out the door again to go find the guy before I even finished getting the words out. I hurried along behind him. As we passed his startled family on our way outside, his dad said, "Where ya going?"

"Wedding stuff," I said, then realized they'd all be eager to help. "Another assignment from Pastor Jill."

Shirley, Jerry and Leon all deflated a little bit. Imagine how disappointed they'd be if they knew we were looking for a ghost.

As we climbed into the car, Shirley poked her head out the door and called out, "What about the shopping trip?"

"What shopping trip?" Jacob called back.

"The one on your sister's calendar."

"It's fine," Jacob non-answered, and then we were off.

"Is it really fine?" I said, as we pulled away from the curb.

Jacob made a *forget-it* gesture. "How is this the first I'm hearing about a suicide?"

"I don't know—your mom didn't make it out to be any big secret. How old were you at the time? Clayton's age? Plus, there was Barbara. If they told you, no way could you have resisted telling her."

Jacob couldn't deny it—I knew him too well.

I said, "Maybe your parents didn't want to scare you. Heck, maybe they just weren't prepared to have the conversation. But either way, I don't think it necessarily means anything more than the simple fact that they didn't want to talk about it."

We pulled onto the highway. Crown Vics have beefy engines, and when Jacob really floored it, he went from zero to eighty so fast he left my stomach somewhere back at the last intersection. "Ease up," I said. "If I've gotta talk to a suicide, I wanna do it from this side of the veil."

If there's one thing all men absolutely love, it's being told how to drive. But before Jacob could tell me exactly what to do with my suggestion, his phone rang in its dashboard holder, and Barbara's name and number lit up on the screen. If it were me, I'd just let it go to voicemail. But it wasn't in Jacob's nature to avoid something when he could butt heads instead.

He jabbed the speaker on. "I'm in the car."

"Good. I was starting to worry. The party store closes at nine."

"We'll have to postpone the store." Jacob said in his most authoritative tone of voice.

Apparently that tone meant nothing to his sister.

"We can't postpone—this is the time I blocked out, and I'm not using my vacation time next week just to help you pick out your favors—"

"You're right," I blurted out. "Send me the list and I'll take care of it."

There was a silence in which I figured the call had dropped—hilly Wisconsin backroads are infamous for their lousy reception—but then I realized Barbara just didn't know how to react to anyone agreeing with her right off the bat. "Don't cheap out on the candy," she warned. "You don't want it to be stale."

"Right. No stale candy."

"And make sure you don't get the plastic bud vases. They just fall over."

"Okay, got it."

"You're sure we can't just go the party store quick? The reception's at a nice enough supper club, but people still expect you to jazz it up a little."

"Barb," Jacob said testily.

I cut in with, "We would, but Pastor Jill gave us this huge thing to go through."

I'd hardly call a 20-page PDF a "huge thing" compared to some of the documentation they saddled me with at the office... but Barbara didn't need to know that. "No," she said, "that works. It gives me time to follow up on some of the last-minute things. Just make sure you're not late for your manicure tomorrow."

Ugh...the manicure. "Will do," I said, then prodded Jacob until he added, "Okay, Barb, thanks," and disconnected.

A few seconds later, a list pinged my phone. I considered asking Jacob what tulle circles even were, but judging by the laser beam look in his eyes, the wedding was the farthest thing from his mind.

Shopping is nowhere near as big a deal as most people make it out to be. If you honestly don't have a preference, it goes pretty fast, and with two-day shipping, I didn't need to worry about whether the party store would be open when all our schedules eventually aligned. Candies, vases, balloons and ribbons. Even tulle circles—yeah, apparently that's a thing. Into the cart and onto the credit card they went. I went down the list, checked it twice, and even made sure they were shipping it up here and not to the cannery. But before I could gloat about my efficiency, I found myself bracing against the glove box as Jacob took a hairpin turn on two wheels.

Okay, not really. But the tires did squeal a little. "Look," I said, "I know you're eager to get there. But the traffic sign with the wiggly road on it says we should slow down to forty—"

He wanted to grumble, I could tell, but wouldn't give me the satisfaction. We passed more signs you'd never see in Chicago. Falling rocks. Narrow bridge. Loose gravel. But nothing that alerted us to the presence of a long-gone hospital.

"Grab me the map," Jacob finally said.

"A printed map?"

"Obviously—"

A flash in the darkness as our headlights bounced off something reflective—the eyes of a massive deer in the middle of the road. Jacob braked so hard my seatbelt almost strangled me, but Bambi managed to trundle off without a scratch...followed by several of his closest friends and relatives. Where was a deer crossing sign when you needed it? Not that Jacob would've been paying it any attention.

Once my heart was done trying to pound through my throat, as calmly as possible, I said, "You don't know where we are?"

"I do. Basically." Jacob flipped on the hazards and pulled over.

"It's been a few years."

As far as I'm concerned, maps are for practicing your folding skills, since I can't make heads or tails of them. But plugging the defunct Sacred Heart Hospital into the phone wouldn't do us much good. Not only would it alert F-Pimp to our snooping, but it wouldn't show up on the GPS anyhow, since they'd likely wiped it from the cloud years ago.

If the map wasn't inscrutable enough, it was full dark now. Out here in the country, streetlights didn't exist. Our surroundings felt surprisingly isolated and profoundly dark, and the meager light of the overhead dome was swallowed right up. Jacob insisted he could read the map, though, following the twisting, turning routes with his finger. "Okay, we crossed the river about three miles back, and we haven't seen an intersection since then. Were we on AB or Business AB?"

"Look, maybe we should just ask our phones where we are."

"And while we're at it, maybe we should call work and fill them in on exactly why we're out here."

The last thing I wanted to do was argue. I took his pointer finger in my hand and worked the rest of his fist open so I could weave my fingers through his. "Listen. We're on the same side. And I really do get what you're going through."

Jacob stared at our hands a long while, then squeezed my fingers gently and sighed. "I need to know so bad, it hurts. And yet I'm dreading whatever it is I'll find, and somehow, that only makes me more determined."

Say what you will about being avoidant—at least hiding from your problems allows you to give something a rest. But Jacob wasn't wired like me, and he was simply unable to let anything go. Not until he dug up the ugly truth—one that everyone would rather stay buried. "I don't know what you're going to find, but I can tell you this: no matter what, I still love you."

"Vic—"

"Let me finish. Even knowing that I'd been committed and experimented on, you gave me a chance. Even when we found out Big Brother had erased my memory and was still keeping tabs on me, you stood by my side. Whatever skeletons are buried in your family's closet—how could I possibly care? You're still you, and that's all that matters."

I gave his hand a squeeze.

"Me and you, Jacob. We're a team. We're a *family*. I know you're supposed to enjoy the journey and not focus on the destination—maybe I read it in our workbook—but I think the destination's pretty damn important, too. Our individual histories, however it was we got to this point...maybe it doesn't matter. Not nearly as much as how we ended up."

I'm not really what you'd call a hugger—but I'm not a total asshole, either. While I can't fathom how anyone would find me particularly comforting, I'm willing to go through the motions. At first Jacob didn't move, and it was like putting my arms around a crash test dummy. But then he cut the engine and let the tension go out of his body. The *click* that had been conspicuously absent for most of our ridiculous photo shoot? There it was...just waiting for both of us to stop clenching.

Kissing Jacob wasn't my main objective, I just wanted to relieve him of the need to answer. Thanks to our premarital sessions, we'd done so damn much talking about our feelings lately. His answers? Glib, patent responses that he thought his pastor wanted to hear.

Maybe I liked it that way.

Maybe I was the one who was relieved when I didn't need to respond to his inner hurt. I sensed it though, and I was under no illusions I could kiss it and make it all better.

But hopefully I could make it at least *somewhat* better.

First tongue? My fault. Nervous that maybe the chink in Jacob's armor was now poised directly over his heart. I prodded the hard edge of his teeth before I even realized I'd done it, then took it back just as quickly. It was an awkward volley. Maybe he would have ignored it, if not for my breath catching as I realized what I'd done. But instead of pretending this maladroit come-on hadn't happened...Jacob threw himself into it full tilt.

When I made to back off, he came at me so fast his seatbelt snapped like we were facing down another deer. He grunted his frustration as he fumbled himself free, then flattened me against the passenger door. Good thing the arm rests folded up, otherwise one of us would end up with serious bruises. But no. The Crown Vic was an early-model beast with a front seat roomy enough for two grown men to grapple. Not that we did it often, mind you. Chicago's just got too many people around.

Here, though? In the middle of nowhere with the impossibly dark night wrapped around us? It felt like we were the only two people in the world—and without anyone else to care, our baggage was easy enough to set down. Or at least set aside for the moment.

Jacob had my fly down before I could even dig the seatbelt clasp out of my back. I wasn't quite hard when he crammed his hand down my underwear, but a few quick strokes took care of that. I bit back the word, *Wait*. Because I mostly didn't want him to wait. And the small part of me that was worried some small-town deputy would come along and cause a big scene... well, it wasn't putting up much of a fight, so I'd say it was willing to be convinced.

When our mouths found each other in the darkness, restraint

had gone right out the window. Jacob crammed me full of tongue, and damn, it was hot. Because I'd come right out and told him I dug it when he was forceful? Maybe. Or maybe he just needed to think about something other than that damn notebook.

His kiss slid off my mouth, trailing wetness to my jaw. I grabbed what I could of his hair to stop him from laying into my throat and leaving me with a necklace of bites in our wedding pictures. My neck is one of my biggest hot-spots, and the mere threat of him clamping down wrenched out a needy sound I was trying my damnedest to keep quiet.

Me, squirming like prey beneath his solid bulk? That's what got Jacob off. Not forcing me...but the satisfaction of getting me so hot my embarrassment slipped through my fingers. When he shoved his shorts down, he was rock hard and leaking.

The hot slick of pre-come chilled fast on my hip, like an echo of the kiss he'd slid from my mouth. I had my hand wrapped around his hardness before I even realized why it felt so strange. It was my broken hand—or should I say, my healed hand. Whichever, it was awkward and weak and ached a little when I squeezed. That, combined with the both of us pawing and fumbling in the darkness, gave a precarious edge to the jacking that made Jacob's thighs tremble.

He was close already. So was I.

Obviously, given the circumstance, it was stupid to nut all over each other—I knew it. He knew it. Yet somehow, neither of us seemed to care. His beard played across the sensitive spot below my jaw, and his hand was working me fast and hard, just shy of painful, and the hottest little huffs of effort were escaping him....

"Fuck yeah...." I groaned in Jacob's ear as my back arched and my floodgates let loose.

I shot—God knows where. He puffed a hot breath against my throat as his cock pulsed in my awkward grasp. His jizz ended up mainly on my bare belly. Though it was unlikely my jeans or T-shirt went completely unscathed.

After Jacob was done shooting, he stilled. His forehead pressed into the crook of my neck. His cock softened in my grasp. His breathing slowed, though it was still damp against my collarbone. I wondered if I should say anything. Maybe there was nothing that needed saying.

It was almost romantic, sprawled across the seat together in the thick blackness of night. I could just about make out our hands by the tiny glow of the hazard light button, fingers loosely woven together—my right hand, Jacob's left. The romantic sap in me suspected this was the last time we'd do it without me finding a ring there. It felt dangerous, in a way, to look forward to anything. But, hell, if we could find a pocket of safety in the midst of the shit show of our histories, maybe we were strong enough to handle anything.

I was busy patting myself on the back when light flooded the car. Not dashboard lights, but something from outside—something *bright*. Too bright for a cop flashlight, even one that could double as a weapon. We bolted upright and turned to see what the hell was blazing through the rear window—and even though I shielded my eyes, my pupils were so acclimated to the deep, dark night, my eyes watered from the glare.

It wasn't headlights—there were too many of them, a whole row. I hitched my jeans, yanked my shirt down and said, "Prime spot for alien abduction if ever there was one."

"Too slow for aliens." Jacob scrambled for napkins from the glovebox. There were none. "Farm equipment."

"At this time of night?"

"Farmers work long hours."

And here I thought being a ghost hunter was demanding.

I patted myself down in search of napkins and—lo and behold: the random pair of underwear in my pocket was good for something other than shaming me in polite company…though once I was done de-splooging myself, it would do Jacob more harm than good.

If I were a farmer and I came across a random car after dark in the middle of nowhere, I'd presume it was some kind of setup. Maybe it's the cop in me that thinks that way. Or maybe my hard-earned paranoia. But the big machine pulled up behind us, filling the cab with light.

We'd reassembled ourselves by the time the farmer came up and motioned for us to roll down the window. He was maybe our age, though the sun hadn't been kind to him, and he was wearing the sort of brown canvas overalls you only see on guys who do serious labor. "Car trouble?" he asked.

"Thanks for stopping," Jacob said, "but we're fine. Just…getting our bearings."

The farmer gave the car a once-over. Though the partially unfolded map on the dash made for a pretty good prop, the passenger window was a little steamed up. He frowned. Maybe he wasn't necessarily as gullible as I'd thought. Probably just braver.

"Cell service can be a little iffy out here. Where ya headed?"

Before Jacob could trot out some knee-jerk lie, I leaned toward the driver side window and asked, "How long have you lived around here?"

Cautiously, he said, "All my life."

"You wouldn't happen to remember Sacred Heart Hospital, would you?"

That got the farmer's attention. Polite interest turned to actual interest, and he jammed his hands in his overall pockets like he was settling in for a nice chat. "Sure. Spent a few days there when I was a kid. They kept my appendix."

I found myself vaguely surprised any actual medicine transpired there, and not just clandestine psychic experimentation. "Are we close?"

"Fifteen minutes, maybe twenty? But you can't really get there from here. There was talk a few years back about the county knocking it down to keep kids from getting up to trouble inside. But the bridge washed out and the road grew over, and it's just too much trouble for 'em to even bother."

If the only way to reach the abandoned hospital was on foot, I sure as hell wasn't about to do it after dark. Once Jacob coaxed an inscrutable series of directions from the farmer, we said our goodbyes...which concluded with him saying, "But I wouldn't go there if I were you." Which wasn't creepy at all.

As his brightly-lit farm implement rolled away and our eyes readjusted to the dark, Jacob said, "Are we sure that was a living person?"

Aside from the fact that Jacob could see him too? "Definitely alive. He smelled too much like diesel to be a ghost."

CHAPTER TWENTY

It was a long drive, but we manage to get back to Jacob's folks' house just shy of midnight, and without hitting any deer. We brought the map inside and pinpointed the most likely spot Sacred Heart would have been, and then we found a decoy nearby we could track on our phones without setting off any alarms. Although Big Brother might wonder why we were so interested in Historical Marker 21: Site of the great walleye tournament of 1932.

We could always claim we were taking up fishing for one of our mandatory dates.

It wasn't exactly the crack of dawn, but it was pretty early when we peeled ourselves off the sofa-bed and started strategizing about our trip. We had flashlights, but it couldn't hurt to bring a few more. A burner phone to take pictures with. And plenty of salt.

All that was left to do was print out some recent satellite photos of "Historical Marker 21" and we'd be all set. Thanks to my adventures in scrapbooking, I theoretically knew how to print photos from my phone. Unfortunately, before the old printer churned its way through its starting sequence, Jacob's parents woke up.

Shirley bustled over in her pink terrycloth robe to see what we were up to. "You need to print a picture? The yellow ink is low."

"Print it in black and white," Jerry called from the kitchen.

"You'd think that would do the trick. But the printer can be so gosh-darned stubborn. And why don't you just use our computer? The password is *touchdown*. It'll be a lot easier than trying to go through the wifi on the printer."

"That never worked right," Jerry called out.

"We wouldn't just hop onto your computer," Jacob told them.

His mother made a never-mind gesture. "Don't be ridiculous. It's not like we have anything to hide."

Well, shit. Let's hope not.

For all our sakes.

I can't claim to fully understand the more sophisticated methods of surveillance, but I do know that these days, everything you do leaves a trail. The trick is to do enough random, mundane things that no one picks up on your shenanigans until it's too late for them to do anything about it. Hopefully our sudden interest in historic walleye would be chalked up to "boring stuff Wisconsinites do" by whoever it was that monitored our goings-on.

Once the map was printed, Jacob grabbed us a couple of waters for the road. But when he closed the refrigerator door, Shirley was there, hands on hips. "You're not going to visit that historical marker now, I hope."

"Why not?" Jacob asked.

"Well, we've got church in twenty minutes." She patted her hair self-consciously. "Actually, I'd better go get ready."

Once she scurried off, Jacob and I exchanged a look. We'd never been expected to accompany his parents to church before. But now that we were marrying each other in that church, there was no good way to bow out.

I wasn't sure what to expect from a Lutheran service. It was pretty much like the non-denominational generic Christian things I'd been exposed to at Camp Hell, but with more talk about love and inclusivity. Probably because Pastor Jill was gearing up to do a gay wedding—*our* gay wedding—and wanted to reassure the congregation that God wasn't going to smite us with a lightning bolt.

Which wasn't to say the entire congregation was thrilled to see us. Some folks were friendly, sure. Most were curious. But a few of them were giving us the stink-eye. Especially when, after the service, Shirley made sure her voice really projected when she announced to one of her acquaintances, "You remember my son Jacob? And this is his fiancé, Victor."

The acoustics were startlingly good.

Pastor Jill had been standing by the door, touching base with her parishioners on their way out, but once the crowd had dwindled to small clusters lingering behind to chat, she came over and gave me a companionable shoulder-bump. Instead of her usual button-down oxford shirt and chinos, she had on a navy pantsuit for service. Stuffy. But still a far cry from my mental image of clergy.

"I envy you," she said.

Clearly, I was doing a good job at camouflaging my actual life during our little counseling sessions. "How's that?"

"Your height, obviously. I've got a great view of the room from the pulpit, but put me in a crowd and I'm invariably stuck looking at the back of someone's head. You should take advantage of it."

"At least people have stopped asking me if I play basketball."

Pastor Jill might be pint-sized, but there was something authoritative about her. A charisma born of confidence. When she strolled away from the crowd, I followed along like I'd been caught by her gravitational pull. "How tall are you, anyhow. Six-five?"

"Not...quite."

"I hadn't realized, since we met online. But seeing you now, standing head and shoulders above the crowd, it got me to thinking about how I fell in love with vocabulary."

"Really?"

"You know how people mishear song lyrics—like, all the time? That's called a mondegreen. But *mondegreen* wasn't the word that got me. It was *excelsis*. I was Christmas caroling with my fourth-grade class, and the kid sitting next to me belted out the words, *In egg selfish day-oh*. And I couldn't for the life of me figure out what eggs had to do with Christmas. But even worse, who was being selfish? Obviously, I couldn't just look it up on the internet. Can you imagine what it would've been like if we had access to all the answers to all the questions at our fingertips back when we were kids? Luckily, though, my curiosity was strong enough that the next time I had a hymnal in my hands, I paged through until I found it. *Gloria in excelsis deo*. Glory to God on high. But it sounds a lot more magical in Latin."

So did exorcisms, but that didn't make them any more effective.

She said, "You're wondering why I'm telling you all this."

"Maybe a little."

"God made you six-four."

"Six-three." And a half.

"God made you gay, too. So if anyone gets snitty with you

about your wedding, that's just too darn bad. Because God doesn't make mistakes."

I wasn't so sure about that. Granting psychic powers to some folks but not others seemed like a surefire route to chaos.

As soon as it was possible to extricate ourselves, Jacob and I hit the road to Sacred Heart...manicure be damned. We'd lost a couple hours of daylight, but that shouldn't make that big a difference.

Right?

The roads didn't seem anywhere near as treacherous during the day. There were no deer. No tractors or falling rocks, either. And Historical Marker 21, a plaque on the side of the road with a couple paragraphs about walleye, was just where it was supposed to be.

But we couldn't say the same for the hospital.

We'd been fully prepared to follow a neglected road and even wade across a creek bed. But the road wasn't just in disrepair... it was completely gone. Instead, there was just an impenetrable wall of trees. We coasted back and forth between the two perpendicular roads that bookended the wooded area, about a half-mile stretch where there, according to our calculations, a road used to be. Then we drove around some more to see if we'd figured wrong. But between the farmer's directions and the landmarks Jacob remembered, we were looking in the right spot. There was just nothing to see.

I can't say I was actually all that surprised. Someone had made Camp Hell disappear. And that was nowhere near as secluded.

We pulled over where the shoulder was widest and headed into the trees. Jacob paused beside me in our tromp through the woods and planted his hands on his hips. Shoving through undergrowth and stepping over branches was hard work, and he was glistening with sweat, with a tiny cut on his cheekbone (which would hopefully heal up by the wedding). He pulled the satellite picture from his pocket and consulted it again, as if maybe our new perspective from the thick of things would shed some light on the old hospital's location. The paper was limp and wilted now. And the image was less than helpful.

We didn't speak—what would we say? But it was far from quiet.

Woods have a sound that's all their own. Trees creak in the wind, and the tall ones are especially loud. Birds make all kinds of racket. And things rustle in the undergrowth. Probably squirrels. That's what I was telling myself. I made noise, too— startling cracks and pops as I brushed past twiggy bushes or stomped on old, dried branches. Even when I tried being quiet, I was still loud enough to startle sparrows from the trees as I passed, so eventually I stopped trying. I needed my whole attention for the old hospital...or whatever might be left of it.

We searched for hours—and if it were my problem, my past, I would have given up already. But it wasn't me, it was Jacob. And even though it was pretty obvious we weren't going to find anything, doing something, even something totally fruitless, was better than doing nothing.

But even Jacob wasn't about to comb through the same ten acres of woods forever. We paused again by the creek, soaked through with sweat, with mosquitoes whining in our ears. The satellite printout was soggy now and the ink had bloomed through the back of the page. He jammed it back in his pocket and said, "This is getting us nowhere."

I didn't know about that. Maybe we'd learned that whoever hid their traces, they were really damn good at their job. Either that, or I wasn't the only one who'd had his memory wiped. How fucked up that that was an actual possibility. But it was some consolation that the farmer remembered the hospital too.

"Damn it." Jacob bent down and picked at his ankle. "Tick."

It took me a second to wrap my head around the word—I'm a city kid through and through, and my knowledge of ticks comes from TV commercials for flea collars.

Jacob peered at it. "It's fine. I got the head."

I threw up a little in my mouth.

He flicked the bug into the creek. "One more pass, and we'll call it a day." I must've looked a little green, because he added, "Don't worry, you're wearing jeans. Next time, we'll double down on the bug spray."

Next time. My heart sank. I was about to put on a brave face and soldier on when I realized the insect sound had a slightly different character where we were standing. Not just the whine of mosquitoes, but the distinct buzz of flies. I'm no entomologist, but I've chased my share of annoying houseflies around the cannery with a rolled-up newspaper.

This was no single fly.

When I registered that thought, I became aware of the smell: the sweet-decay hint of decomp.

White light.

It thundered down from the heavens so fast I staggered. I'd reacted so quickly to the thought of some rotten old ghost shoving its way into my body like the tick burying its head in Jacob's ankle, it took my conscious mind half a second to catch up.

My visual field flashed white from the turbocharge. Like lightning, but softer, and with no afterimages.

This is what it would feel like to come into my power. Me, so amped up on white light that I glowed. No psyactives. No

Mood Blaster app. No yoga. Just me, in the zone.

Unfortunately, that zone was more of a blip, and no sooner did the white light spike than it ebbed again, followed by a sickening stab of pain somewhere between my eyeballs and my skull.

Jacob massaged the back of his neck. "What is it?" Apparently, I had a look.

"Don't you smell it?" Thanks to my time in homicide, I must've been more finely attuned. "Decomp."

I could practically see Jacob's adrenaline spike as much as I did my own. His demeanor shifted from weary defeat to sharp interest. No one *likes* stumbling across a dead body. But he'd take his answers any way he could get them.

No clue what we'd be walking into. Images of charnel pits churned up from a recent rain flashed past my mind's eye, and the bag of salt weighing down each pocket suddenly felt way too small. Hell, given how many times we'd fumbled through this stretch of woods, I was lucky I wasn't possessed already. (I wasn't, was I? No...if I had enough awareness left to ask that question, I wasn't. Probably.)

Jacob tilted his head—listening, or feeling?—then picked a direction and gestured for me to follow.

White light. White light. White light.

"What is it, Vic? See something?"

"No. But I just got another whiff of rot."

If there was a ghost still attached, it wouldn't necessarily be as decomposed as its physical body. But given the way our day had been going, a rotting ghost was a distinct probability. The buzzing intensified, and I felt the feathery touch of a fly lighting briefly on my cheek. Normally, I'd think it was tracking something from a mound of dog shit across my face. The thought that it had erupted from the soupy abdominal cavity of a corpse was way worse.

I held my forearm to my face to breathe through the filter of my sleeve, which also put my bag of salt at the ready. Funneling white light into the salt while trying not to step in a dead body was like walking and trying to chew some really unpleasant gum, but I managed.

Probably because I let Jacob take the lead.

It wasn't easy—especially after the incident with the ATM ghost. But while Jacob couldn't see any potential hauntings, he knew how to navigate the woods a heck of a lot better than I did. Yet, although I knew he was spirit-Teflon, I hated the thought of using him as a human shield...even if that was exactly what he'd been bred for.

I shuddered. And not from the thought of stumbling over a body, either.

The wind shifted, and we lost the scent—and for a moment I thought that maybe we'd go home empty-handed after all. But then a branch cracked beneath Jacob's foot, and a cloud of flies erupted with a buzz that sent gooseflesh racing up my arms. I squinted my eyes and hunched my shoulders while just ahead of me, Jacob went very still. I figured, like me, he was imagining them laying eggs in his mucous membranes. But then his shoulders sagged, and I realized he'd found something.

I made my way up beside him and looked for myself—and with a mixture of disappointment and relief, discovered it wasn't a Camp Hellish casualty after all.

But it would be a long time before I purged the stench of decaying deer from my nostrils.

CHAPTER TWENTY-ONE

"Where in the heck were you two yesterday?" Mild words, but I could tell by the way her neck tendons were starting to pop, Barbara was seriously pissed.

"We had something to do," Jacob said vaguely, which only made her blood boil more.

"For Pastor Jill," I added. "You know. The workbook."

Barbara was a devout woman who'd never go against her pastor...but she'd been so invested in being angry. She even showed up at their folks' house to berate us on her way to work on a damp Monday morning, so clearly she meant business. "I don't remember going through all this with Derrick."

Jacob said, "I'm sure it just seems that way because our lead time is more condensed."

"Still, we have a schedule. We have a calendar. And when do you expect to do your manicure now?"

"It's fine, Barb, we'll fit everything in." Jacob was using his confident voice. It was pretty convincing. Even though I knew it was all an act, I still bought into it myself.

Barbara didn't. "You say that now, but believe you me—even

with all the planning in the world, a bunch of stuff is bound to crop up. You've gotta leave yourself time to put out all the last-minute fires."

Jacob said (in his calm-down-already voice), "It's a simple ceremony and a small reception. We have the venues, the pastor, the vows and the rings. Even if everything else fell apart—"

"Don't go tempting fate," I muttered.

"—we'd be fine. So you don't need to worry on our account."

Jacob's sister pulled the mulish expression I was accustomed to seeing on him—the one that meant it shouldn't much matter whether or not she was actually right. I was okay with that face of his. It usually preceded a grudging agreement...and Barb's was no different.

"Well, if you're not worried, I'm not gonna lose any sleep over it. Just don't forget we need to meet with the manager at the supper club after work to sort out all the final details."

"We'll be there," Jacob said with only a minor amount of condescension.

As Barbara stomped off toward her car, I said, "We should probably be paying more attention to the calendar. There's only so much mileage we can get out of Pastor Jill's PDF."

Jacob gave me a look, and I answered with a sigh. Because only a real knucklehead would expect him to prioritize the manicure over digging up dirt on his own past.

Breakfast with his parents would normally have been convivial—despite Shirley getting me to try some appalling flax meal concoction—if not for Kamal's goddamned notebook. Afterward, I found Jacob in our room, glaring at the satellite photo, which was creased with folds and had blooms of inkjet ink on the back. "How likely is it that the entire tree canopy would regrow over the course of twenty-five years?" he asked.

I suspected that if you knew what you were doing, you could make it happen.

Then again, the same could be said for doctoring a satellite image and putting it online.

"The hospital was there," he insisted, as if I somehow didn't believe him.

"I know it was. But we looked all day and found nothing but ticks and a dead deer." I shuddered. "So maybe there's nothing to find."

"You found something at Camp Hell. Not much. But something."

I *had* found something. With Jacob right there by my side. "Look, obviously Sacred Heart existed—your sister, your mom, even the random guy on the tractor—everyone remembers the place. But it's a lot easier to bury something out in the woods than it is in the middle of a city. It was a whole lot of ground to cover, and it all looked pretty much the same. For all we know, whatever we were looking for might've been right around the next tree." I took the paper from him and folded it up. "But we'll need more to go on than that."

I could practically hear the gears turning. Jacob stood so fast the sofa bed nearly folded itself up behind him, looked me square in the eye, and said, "The basement."

Evidently, there was still mileage to be had from Pastor Jill's PDF after all. Claiming we weren't done scrapbooking just yet, Jacob and I were able to retreat downstairs and sift through decades of old detritus without his parents thinking anything of it. And while some F-Pimp specialist might be able to Photoshop tree canopy over any incriminating bald patches on a satellite photo, I doubt they'd have as much luck navigating the Markses' basement.

Unfortunately, the search didn't turn up much. We found a few more carnival photos in another album and a flyer for a blood drive, but nothing that provided any more landmarks we could use. And while I thought I hit the jackpot with a stack of phone books almost as old as me, it turned out that because the hospital was in a different county, it wasn't even listed.

I was toying with suggesting to Jacob that we give Sacred Heart a rest—let things simmer in our subconscious until we came up with an actual plan—when I found myself shoving a teetering stack of books upright to keep it from tumbling down on his head. The main culprit was the top book, which was thicker and heavier than the ones beneath it. I pulled it off the top of the pile and brushed off a few cobwebs.

Huh. A library book.

What's New in Fondue was a weighty, colorful tome picturing a woman whose waist was no bigger than my thigh hovering over a fondue pot, exhibiting a maniacal enthusiasm for melted cheese. Or maybe she was just starving. I opened the cover and found the due date was in 1997. Someone was racking up one hell of a fine.

"Jacob," I said, as an idea began to take shape, "you know who'd have some pre-digital information on Sacred Heart?"

He looked at the book in my hands and mouthed the word, *fondue?*

"The library."

I'd hardly consider myself an old-school investigator, but I did know my way around a microfilm reader. You don't realize how lucky we have it nowadays with searchable text until you need to go through years of information manually. It's mind-numbing work flipping through old newspapers and scanning headlines, but it was our best shot.

The library we wanted—the one that was most likely to consider Sacred Heart part of its local history—was two counties over. It was shorts weather...for those of us who'd ever be caught dead in shorts, anyhow. Even so, I noted Jacob wore jeans this time around. Hopefully we weren't in danger of picking up ticks at the library.

We briefly considered trying to cover our tracks somehow—leave our phones behind, borrow Jerry's car and navigate by paper maps. Maybe it was paranoia fatigue, or maybe we just figured that if anyone questioned our movements, the couples assignments from Pastor Jill would be a good enough excuse.

The closest library to the old hospital was a dumpy municipal building in an even dumpier small town. When we first pulled up, I thought it was closed. Permanently. Good thing we'd driven all that way, too far to turn around without at least trying the door. Turned out it wasn't closed. Just totally devoid of customers.

The inside of the building was equally as depressing as the outside, with dingy carpets and dark paneling. Whatever daylight managed to struggle through the windows was instantly sucked away by all the relentless drabness.

It was warm inside, too warm, and the air tasted like dust. Despite the stuffy atmosphere, Jacob chafed his upper arms.

"Yeah," I said, "I'm not a big fan of the decor, myself."

"This place is depressing."

"No argument on my part. Let's get to work so we can get out of here."

A quick scan showed no signs of a microfilm reader, so I found the empty circulation desk and tapped the bell. It rang disproportionately loudly, and Jacob and I both flinched. But given how quick the staff room door banged open, I'd say it had done its job.

A middle-aged Caucasian woman with graying hair and a sour

look on her face strode out to greet us. She clipped an engraved name tag to her blouse that read *Helen, Reference Librarian.* "Were you interested in a library card?"

Jacob said, "Actually, we were hoping to take a look at some of your local history."

"Oh. Can't say I've ever had that request from anyone other than school kids doing mandatory projects. I'll just need to set you up with a library card first."

I said, "We weren't planning on checking out any books. We just wanted to see—"

"Doesn't matter. Library materials are for patrons only."

Jacob and I both looked around as if to see whether there were other "patrons" around competing for such limited resources. Nope. Just us.

Jacob said, "We'll be happy to pay whatever fee is associated with—"

"There is no fee," Helen snapped. "This is a public library."

"Fine," I said. "How do I become a patron?"

"I'll just need a valid I.D. with a current address."

I almost hesitated, since I'm loathe to leave a paper trail if I can help it. But given that we'd already pulled up a map to the library, it would be no big surprise to anyone who was eyeballing my surveillance. I opted for my driver's license so as not to freak her out with my F-Pimp I.D...and as soon as the plastic hit the countertop, Helen pulled a face. "You're from Illinois."

"Yeah. And?"

"I'm sorry. Libraries are funded with local taxes. We have a reciprocal agreement with Vernon county. But not Illinois."

What the hell did she expect us to do? Move? "Look, we were just hoping to—"

"Do you realize how precarious our situation is? Our local

population has been in steady decline. Nobody needs a reference librarian's help anymore, not when it's easier to just pull up a search engine. What difference does it make that most people can't tell a legitimate website from a parody? It's so *convenient*."

Clearly, we'd managed to strike a nerve. But if anyone could smooth things over, it was Jacob. Not only is he so handsome that everyone wants to bend over backwards to please him—the guy oozes charm. I turned to him, fully expecting him to say something that would save the day...only to find him itching at the back of his neck and scowling at a chipped spot in the formica countertop.

"We're staying in Wisconsin through the end of the week," I offered lamely.

Helen frowned harder, and I found myself feeling nostalgic for the days when the worst you could hope for was a good shooshing. But maybe it was more of a thinking-frown, because instead of showing us the door, she said, "If that's the case, we can issue a temporary card. But you can only check out one item at a time. No exceptions."

"No problem," I said. "Unless you check out microfilm readers." Helen squinted at me and I added, "That's a joke."

"No one ever asks to see the microfilm."

"Aside from the schoolkids," I offered.

The librarian squinted harder. Tough audience. She put an application in front of each of us, then stamped a big red "temporary" across the top of each one. "I'll go open up the archive room while you fill those out. But just remember—I'll be following up on your information. Thoroughly. If you try to pass off some fake address, I'll know."

Once she was out of earshot, I muttered to Jacob, "If a

vacancy opens up in Internal Affairs, you know where to start your headhunting."

Jacob rolled his shoulders and something cracked. I guess the hours of driving were beginning to take a toll. He said, "After all this, I'll be seriously pissed if we don't find anything."

Oh, he was already seriously pissed. I could tell by the way the little muscle in his jaw was pulsing.

Helen returned just as I was scrawling my name on the signature line. "Fair warning, guys. It's a little musty back there."

She wasn't kidding. If the main part of the building was drab and inhospitable, the archives were downright forbidding. The area was about the size of the Markses' basement, but broken up by floor-to-ceiling shelves. While the shelving definitely made the space a lot more organized, it cast pretty deep shadows, and turned the room into more of a maze. A funk hovered in the air that I couldn't quite place. Maybe dry rot. Maybe despair. Helen showed us to the microfilm reader, then left us to our research with a stern parting look.

Jacob took in the drawer of microfilm arranged in tidy rows. "If we were at work, I'd have these scanned for optical character recognition and we could search it for even the smallest mention of the hospital in seconds."

Maybe so. But if we were at work, undoubtedly someone would have shut us down by now. In this dusty back room, we did have a couple of things going for us. At least the local rag only published weekly, so we had less film to look through. And at least we could narrow it down to a rough date based on the year his grandmother stopped taking him to the creepy carnival.

We fired up the reader and loaded the most likely film roll. "We'll scan headlines first," Jacob said. "The closing of the only local hospital would've been big news."

Given that the first headline to pop up had to do with the County Fair, I suspected he was right.

Even though we were focusing only on front-page headlines, there were still fifty-two newspapers a year to scan, and no way to jump from one to the next without spooling through the whole damn thing. Unlike Jacob, I have no glutes—and after a couple of hours on a hard wooden chair, my sit-bones were starting to complain. Loudly.

The tiny library might be low on natural light, but there were plenty of chairs. I stepped away to go grab one with some padding and nearly collided with Helen in the dim hallway.

"Listen," she said, "sorry about giving you folks a hard time."

Somewhere in the stacks beyond, the shadows shifted. It was subtle enough that I might not have noticed if Helen hadn't stopped me to talk to her. And it could be something as innocuous as a potted plant by an air vent casting a shadow.

But given the overall sense of discomfort I'd been experiencing, I highly doubted I was dealing with a plant.

Helen must've been blissfully unaware. Either that or she was just used to it. "This morning I got a nastygram from the county threatening to merge us with another branch if we don't get our numbers up."

"That sucks," I said carefully, searching for movement.

"Mightily. The nearest branch is over half an hour away, and my patrons will lose valuable work time traveling an hour just for a trip to the library. A lot of them will stop going at all, especially the older ones who depend on us for their large-print books and magazines. You know what the funny thing is? All my regulars tell me I'm a heck of a lot nicer than their last librarian. But no matter how I try to keep luring people in, our usage keeps dropping at a higher rate than anywhere else in the state."

"The last librarian...." I couldn't just come out and ask, *She's dead, right?* "Maybe she could give you some advice."

"Not without a Ouija board."

The hair on the back of my neck prickled.

"Sorry, that was a pretty tasteless thing to say. I didn't really know her well."

"No, it's fine...." A shiver raced down my spine.

"When she interviewed me for the job, she made some weird remark about the 'big-city scarf' I was wearing. What does that even mean?"

I forced out an uneasy laugh. The bookshelves formed tall narrow corridors casting way too many shadows. I did my best to scan them without being obvious.

"Frieda Berkenkopf," Helen said. "Haven't thought about her in ages."

Movement? Maybe. Maybe not. I was about to get back to the microfilm when, at the far end of the narrow aisle of book-shelves, a figure crossed from one side to the other. And it was most definitely not Jacob.

Helen said, "When you think about it, I guess, Frieda was a real character."

Yeah. That was putting it mildly.

CHAPTER TWENTY-TWO

White light came rushing down, and my visual perception went glowy around the edges. The telltale spot behind my eyeball that tells me I'm totally topped off gave a little twinge—but I couldn't get a bead on the ghost. Hard to say if she was deliberately camouflaging herself or just following her own ghostly agenda. Either way, I'm especially leery of non-corporeal stuff I can't quite track. I wanted to grab Helen by the elbow and hustle her out of there, but I couldn't risk the off-chance that she was some sort of undocumented Psych and my light would bounce over to her. To buy myself some time to think, I tried to get her talking about herself. "This is quite a place, how long have you been here again?"

My interest surprised Helen, but like most people, she was happy enough to talk about herself, given the chance. I barely listened as she spun out a mundane story about transferring from a big, well-funded library with the intention of helping people who really needed it. I was busy surreptitiously wiping sweat from my upper lip while keeping my eyes peeled for another flicker.

Maybe there was some sort of Bloody Mary effect in play—a magical summons achieved by the speaking of the ghost's name. To test that theory, when there was a gap in Helen's story, I said, "So you didn't work with Frieda at all."

"No, she was already in hospice by the time the Library Board gave me a job offer."

I scanned the shelves. No dead Frieda.

Maybe she was bound by time and could only pop in at the hour of her death. Or maybe she was nothing more than a mindless repeater. But judging by the ick-feeling creeping down my back, I suspected Frieda's consciousness was still with us.

"I just thought of something I need to tell Jacob," I blurted out, and back-pedaled into the archives for all I was worth. Helen must not have thought my abrupt departure was too weird—or if she did, at least she didn't follow to see what the hell my problem was.

A glance over my shoulder showed Jacob hard at work scanning headlines. "Ghost," I whispered, and the gentle whir of the microfilm reel went silent.

He was up and out of his seat immediately, but despite moving fast, he was careful not to touch me this time. "Where?"

"Out there." I gestured vaguely. "It's the old librarian. We haven't had a chat yet, so I can't tell if she knows she's dead." I pulled a bag of salt from my pocket and opened myself to the white light, shoving the energy toward the salt. Jacob watched. These things never got old for him.

So it surprised me when he wasn't on board. "Was she threatening?"

"Not...exactly."

"Then aren't you going to try reasoning with her first?"

"Just wanna make sure I'm not walking into a gunfight with nothing but my dubious charm to back me up." Okay, maybe that wasn't my original intent. But now that Jacob had pointed out the fact that I'd been willing to "shoot first, ask questions later," I knew in my gut that he was right, and I should be leading with my powers of persuasion.

Fantastic.

With Jacob following an arm's length away, I eased out into the spot where I'd last seen Frieda. Non-Fiction, with its outdated textbooks and its Dewey decimals. Elsewhere in the library a phone rang, followed by the faint murmur of Helen speaking to the caller. Hopefully she'd be occupied long enough to stay out of my hair.

"Frieda?" I whispered. "I just want to talk. You're here...somewhere. And this would all be a lot easier if you showed yourself."

A flicker...which I strongly suspected was sunlight bouncing off the chrome of a passing car. Even so, the sight of it made that tender spot in my brain throb. Since I was full of adrenaline (and therefore, mojo) I gave the place another scan. Again, nothing.

It's bad enough talking to ghosts while someone else is listening in...I couldn't even be sure Frieda was there.

But where else would she be?

"Look, you don't want to have a discussion with me, that's fine. But what if you just listened? Because I might not know all of your particulars, but I've dealt with a lot of folks in your, uh, situation." Was that a flicker, over by the magazine racks? I eased closer. Found nothing. "You're not physical anymore. Not...alive. Not anymore."

"Tell her not to be afraid of the veil," Jacob prompted. "Tell her there's nothing to be scared of—that it's a relief to finally cross over."

It was tempting to ask him who was the medium here—him or me? But given that his past was apparently as shrouded in fucked-up machinations as mine, I wasn't about to go there. "He's right," I said to the empty air. "The physical world is for the living, but that doesn't mean you stop existing once your time here is up. There's something else waiting for you beyond the veil. And whatever it might be, it's a heck of a lot better than haunting your library to the point that no one can stand being here. You care about this place, right? I'm sure you don't want to drive it into the ground."

White light fatigue was setting in—it was taking more effort to try and hold it, and no matter how hard I clenched, I could feel it starting to ebb. I hated it when there was no clear answer. Do I leave dead Frieda roaming around where she might someday hop into a body that wasn't hers? Or do I hunt her down and salt her like a mindless repeater and get on with my day?

Hell, maybe by failing to act when I first saw her, I'd made my choice. Because now I couldn't even tell if she was still lurking around, or if the goosebumps prickling along my forearms were a result of my own vivid imagination.

From the front desk came Helen's voice telling her caller to have a good day, followed by the click of a phone hitting the cradle. No doubt pretty soon she'd wonder why I'd wandered away from the microfilm, and she'd come over to check on me. If I sent Jacob to run interference, would he take that as me benching him—again? Probably. Plus, I was the one Helen had inexplicably warmed up to.

"I'll be right back," I told Jacob. "Stay quiet." Frieda would probably prefer that he keep his voice down, anyway.

I headed off Helen somewhere by the DVD collection. "Did

you find what you were looking for?" she asked.

Oh, we'd found something all right...but it had nothing to do with the hospital. As much as I probably could've used her help digging up dirt on Sacred Heart, now that we had a ghost situation, it was more important to keep her out of the possession zone.

And so I did what I do best, and lied through my teeth. "It's going great."

"Good. But we're closing in fifteen minutes, so if you need to print anything out, you'll want to get started now. The micro-film printer is phenomenally slow."

"Will do."

She must've bought it, because she headed back to the main room and started turning off the reading lamps and tidying up the newspapers. It wasn't exactly a huge place, and pretty soon she'd start to hover. I shook myself off and sucked down a fresh volley of white light, then headed back to shelve that librarian ghost once and for all.

I found Jacob more or less where I'd left him, staring at a sad little display of gardening books. I was about to point out that neither of us had a green thumb when I saw Freida was standing right beside him.

"Three o'clock," I told Jacob. He gave a little start, then back-pedaled away.

Freida was so close I could describe her to a sketch artist. The stern set of the mouth, the slightly crooked glasses...and the fact that she was looking back at me with some glimmer of consciousness. We had a full-blown ghost on our hands, then—not just an empty repeater.

I slipped my hand into my pocket and squeezed the com-forting heft of the salt-filled baggie. "Look, Frieda, I'd love to continue lecturing you on the pros and cons of digging in your heels on the wrong side of the veil, but we're running out of time. Fact is, you don't belong here, and you're not doing this place any favors by sticking around. So leave the library in the capable hands of the person *you* hired—"

Freida moved. Not like a living person moves. More like a series of still photos. One, standing there, staring me in the face. The next, still looking directly at me—but pointing at the wall. Before I could even blink, she was gone, as if maybe it was really costing her to stay in the physical plane. Hopefully so. I'd rather face off with a weak spirit than a strong one.

The spot she'd indicated was just about where Jacob had been looking, only a couple of feet higher. "What's over here?" I said, and edged closer to the display. There was a framed poster on the wall above.

No, not a poster....

"A plat map," Jacob said.

"A what?"

"A real estate map that shows the boundaries of all the land parcels." The two of us peered at it more closely.

This particular map was old—decades old. Not because the library couldn't afford to replace it, but because it celebrated the year the library was built. The parcel of land we were currently standing on had been decorated with vibrant strokes of paint, and the map all around it was covered with a variety of groovy 'we love our library' type slogans. But despite the psychedelic 1960's teenage paint job, the other parcels of land were visible enough.

"There." Jacob prodded something with his finger. "Sacred Heart is right there."

Since I doubted my ability to sweet-talk Helen into letting

us take the map home, even as much as she seemed to inexplicably like me, a picture would have to do. I grabbed some snapshots with a burner phone, double checked that, yes, I'd captured the old hospital, then tucked the phone away by the time Helen came to regretfully shoo us out the door.

We climbed into the car and sat together in silence. My heart was pounding. Not from the ghost—as far as I could tell, Frieda was harmless, just doing her job—but from the knowledge that we were one step closer to Sacred Heart.

Days are long at the cusp of summer, and there was enough daylight to go take another look, especially now that we had a better idea where to put our attention. Jacob pulled out the satellite photo to compare with our plat map while I flipped through our road atlas, a big, floppy book I could never seem to make heads or tails of. We were right on the verge of something big—I could feel it in my bones.

And then Jacob's phone rang. Barbara's ringtone.

He made no move to answer.

"Aren't you gonna get that?"

"She'll have to wait."

Eventually the ringing stopped. And then started again...on my phone.

The thing Jacob doesn't get about Barbara is that she's no good at being ignored. Maybe they're just too much alike. I decided it was better to face her now than to give her annoyance the opportunity to really ratchet up. I took the call and cautiously said, "What's up?"

"Where are you? We're supposed to be at the supper club."

"Oh. We must've lost track of time...."

"Don't tell me you've got another assignment from Pastor Jill. Honestly, it's ridiculous how much homework she's giving you, what with your wedding in three days. Whatever it is, finish up and meet me at the club."

CHAPTER TWENTY-THREE

Apparently, "supper clubs" are a big Wisconsin thing. When I'd asked what the difference was between a supper club and a restaurant, my question was met with a vague shrug and speculation that supper clubs were more likely to put a relish tray on the table. (I didn't even bother asking what a relish tray was.) Whatever the finer distinction of restaurant vs. supper club might be, thanks to a cancellation, Kaiser's Downtown Inn had a banquet room available on the night we needed it. That's all that mattered to me.

Barbara had been less than thrilled to hear it would take us nearly an hour to get there, but short of teleportation, there wasn't a whole hell of a lot she could do about it. We found her at Kaiser's pacing back and forth in front of the door, likely scaring away customers.

"It's about time," she snapped. "They close at nine on weekdays."

"It's barely eight," Jacob said. I personally would have let it drop. But he had "that look" about him: the one that preceded the digging in of heels.

Unfortunately, so did Barbara.

"Look, Jacob, you can't just go around expecting everyone to pick up your slack. I get that planning a wedding is stressful, but the least you could do is deign to show up."

"It's barely eight," he grit out again. At which point I decided they should probably have this conversation without me.

As venues went, the supper club was old-fashioned to the point of being kitschy, which was fine. But it was filled with wood, wood...and more wood—which meant the whole place was also full of shifting shadows. We had researched the club before agreeing to host our reception within its wood-paneled walls, and according to all records, no one had died there. Even the original owner was still alive, though in terms of age, he'd give Grandma Marks a run for her money.

Ghosts usually end up in the spot where they died...but not always. Case in point: the library. But stepping through the door with all my feelers out, I didn't get that same sense of foreboding I had in the library. Oh, I'd still figure out some way to salt the corners so I didn't have to worry about anyone dead crashing the party, but I still thought I was getting off to a pretty good start.

At least until the current owner bustled up, a chunky white guy, roughly my age, in a suit that looked to be camouflaging one hell of a beer belly. "Jacob Marks?" he asked.

"No, Victor Bayne."

"Ah! The...*husband*."

He said the word with a half-laugh, as if it was something foreign he wasn't quite sure how to pronounce.

I quelled a sigh.

"I'm Bill Kaiser—named for my grandfather, Willhelm, who opened Kaiser's right after Prohibition was lifted. We're famous for our mahogany bar and smoked maple brandy old-fashioneds." He looked briefly puzzled, then said, "Should we wait for your—?"

I glanced out the window. Jacob and Barbara were really getting into it. "No, let's get started." With him and his sister each as stubborn as the other, no telling when World War Marks was going to reach its armistice. As long as no one made me sample any smoked maple brandy, I should be able to handle one or two minor details while I was stalling for Jacob.

"First of all the napkins," Kaiser said. "We could do a pocket fold with a printed menu inside. But maybe you'd prefer swans...."

"The pocket fold is fine," I said without even needing to fake any confidence. Because I might not know what a pocket fold was, but I was pretty damn sure Jacob wouldn't go for swans.

My quick thinking must have made me seem decisive. Kaiser pulled out a hefty book of fabric samples and said, "And the matter of color...."

"White. Just...white."

"Always an elegant choice. Would you prefer bright white, soft white, or antique white?"

Since I doubted the napkins came in my favorite color of all time, landlord white, I said, "The second one."

"Soft white it is. Now for the tablecloths."

While I may not have any strong opinions on table linens, I knew my future husband well enough to feel confident that neither did he. Kaiser had a mind-numbing list of decisions to run past me, but not one of them struck me as anything we might actually care about. Then again, when you've got an existential crisis of the magnitude Jacob was currently facing, it was pretty hard to get excited about chair sashes.

I might not be able to travel past the veil, grab Dr. Kamal, and force him to tell us what sort of experimentation he'd been running on Jacob, but I could at least shoulder some of the inconsequential BS on Jacob's behalf. And there was a *lot* of BS. I was starting to think that surely Kaiser would get to the important questions anytime now when he closed his three-ring binder and said, "And you're sure you don't need to run any of this by Mr. Marks?"

"Any of—?" I blinked stupidly at the binder. Was he pulling my leg? Didn't look like it. "No. It's fine."

"Well, then." Kaiser gave a stilted titter. "I guess we know who wears the pants in this marriage."

I couldn't decide if he was prejudiced, ignorant, or just your basic, all-around dumbass. Since I had no idea where to even begin schooling him, I settled for the facial expression that usually unlocks my phone.

He blanched and bid me a hasty goodnight.

Could I have given him the benefit of the doubt and patiently spelled out that neither one of us had been assigned the role of "the woman" in the relationship? I supposed. And without an explanation, I'd doubted he'd have any idea why I was scowling. Even so, he should really consider himself fortunate he hadn't been dealing with Jacob.

I headed back outside. While I was meeting with Kaiser, a moderate rain had rolled in—and heaven help me, I was relieved we were within range of our usual creature comforts, and not in the middle of a tick-infested forest. Barb and Jacob had moved their argument into our car. The windows were getting foggy.

Confrontation isn't my style, and I was none too eager to insert myself into their dynamic...especially since they'd been honing that dynamic for forty freaking years. But since I could hardly stand there in the rain and claim I was just getting some air, I took a fortifying breath and ventured into the back seat.

Whatever the two of them had been saying, they fell silent when I joined them. Jacob checked his watch. "I guess we'd better get started."

Barbara muttered, "Might as well, it's not like we're getting anywhere out here."

"It's all good," I said. They turned identical looks of suspicion on me, as if surely I was just making up a story to blow off our obligations and go get pie. "There were just a few questions to run through." The looks grew even more apprehensive over my ability to handle things myself, so I added, "Mostly about napkins."

Two sets of shoulders unhitched and Jacob let out a sigh. "Thanks for taking care of that."

Normally, I'd make a wisecrack about being good for something *other* than talking to ghosts, maybe with a salacious undertone—but not with Barbara in the car. "Look," I said, "we're all stressed out...about the wedding. There are bound to be some snags, and not everything will go to plan. But unless the church falls in on us, the wedding's gonna happen. Any screw-ups that crop up along the way, we'll be laughing about a year from now. So, everyone keep in mind that we're all on the same side and take a chill pill."

Jacob didn't have the decency to look chagrined, but then again, I'd be shocked if he did. The two of us locked eyes, and I tried to convey that he had to stop stressing about our investigation too, and that somehow we'd dredge up the clue that made everything fall into place.

But as the two of us exchanged our look, Barbara said, "What's this?"

Jacob's breath caught. "It's nothing."

Holy crap—it better not be a pair of jizz-crusted underpants.

I bonked my head on the roof scrambling see what she'd found. But instead of the evidence of our back-roads tryst, what Barbara had in her lap was Kamal's notebook.

Not only had Jacob's sister managed to lay her hands on the most damning piece of evidence in our possession, but we'd studied one particular page at such great length, the notebook fell open directly on it. Jacob went still. I went still. And the atmosphere in the car went fragile enough to shatter.

Barbara had always harbored a visceral aversion to psychic abilities. What would she make of the fact that her family had been somehow involved with a mysterious branch of Psych? Not just recently, but for generations?

"Is this your seating chart? I can't make heads or tails of it."

Jacob took the notebook from her unresisting hands. "It's just a rough draft."

"Jacob, Kaiser's doesn't even have long, skinny tables like that. They're round, and a lot smaller, with eight settings apiece. Vic, you saw the banquet room. Tell him."

I fumbled for a plausible reply. "Yeah, no...it's a really rough draft."

"Well, don't forget to finalize it. Otherwise your reception will be nothing but a big, crazy free-for-all."

Though telling people where to sit was the least of our worries, we dutifully pretended we would follow through with a final seating plan. Barbara must've been satisfied—or maybe she'd just run out of ways to express her disappointment—because she gave us each a parting "don't screw this up" look, went back to her own car, and left us to contemplate just how close we'd come to exposing her to the psychic underbelly that civilians really weren't prepared to deal with.

Once she was gone, I rifled around under the seat, scrounged up three bottle caps, an old french fry, and the dreaded underwear, and marched them out to a trash can.

Sometimes you've just gotta take comfort in averting the crises you can control.

When I got back to the car, Jacob shook his head and said, "That was way too close." And he wasn't talking about the briefs, either.

I took the notebook from his hands, tucked it into the glovebox, and locked it up. "Close only counts in horseshoes and scrapbooking. Your sister said herself that she didn't know what it was. Everything's fine."

Jacob pinched the bridge of his nose and sagged into the seat. "Juggling that damn notebook with our wedding is more stressful than breaking up a prostitution ring."

"Well sure, because you've got more skin in the game when it's personal." Especially when you're worried your whole life has been a lie. I worked my fingers into the seam of his fist, then squeezed his hand once he finally unclenched. "I know it doesn't feel like it, but we've made a lot of progress."

Or found a lot of nothing, judging by the way he cut his eyes to me, like he wasn't sure he wanted to be mollified.

I said, "First thing in the morning, we'll load up with salt and prayer candles, head out to Sacred Heart, and dig up some answers." But before we did, I figured I should double-check our calendar and make sure we weren't on the receiving end of any frantic phone calls...only to find that tomorrow was packed to the gills.

Well...damn.

CHAPTER TWENTY-FOUR

I waited until morning to tell Jacob we couldn't go hunting for the old hospital after all. If it were closer, or if we knew where, exactly, it used to be, maybe I could've pried him out of bed at the crack of dawn so we could poke around. But between the two-hour round trip and the fact that every tree looked pretty much the same as the next, chances of making any real progress were slim to none.

In other words, we'd likely miss our various appointments—for nothing—and piss off a whole lot of people in the process.

Funny how uncomfortable I was making unilateral decisions, given how many of them I'd managed to put up with over the years.

I thought Jacob took the news pretty well...until he gazed at me over his oatmeal from across the kitchen table and said, "We don't have time for Sacred Heart? Fine. Then we go have another chat with my grandmother."

I'd rather be swarmed by ticks. But it meant so much to Jacob, I could hardly bow out.

Grandma Marks had been moved to her lounger so she

could look out the window at the unmemorable manicured lawn. "You picked a great time to visit," the nurse told us. "She's pretty lucid today."

Grandma might not be so happy about that once Jacob was done interrogating her.

The nurse left us to our visit, but even after she was gone, there was an awkward silence. Eventually Jacob said, "Hi, Grandma."

And got no response at all.

I found myself feeling nostalgic for the ticks.

Jacob tried to engage her in conversation—we learn these things on the force, the sort of small-talk you'd use to determine if someone acting erratically is a real danger to themselves or others. "I see you're up and around today. How are you feeling?"

No answer.

Jacob peered out the window where a few oldsters were sunning themselves in their wheelchairs or tottering down the path on their walkers. "It seems nice outside. We could ask about going out, if you want. Get a little sun and fresh air."

He might as well have asked the fake plant in the corner for all the good it did him.

Jacob isn't exactly what I'd call patient, but when it suits him, he can fake it. He carried on with the pleasantries to try and wear her down, because we'd never get her to talk about that carnival if we couldn't get her to talk at all...which, unfortunately, was beginning to look like a distinct possibility.

Jacob chatted about the family. He reminisced about her famous pot roast. He even went so far as to offer to read aloud from her bible. But he'd inherited the trademark family stubbornness from somewhere—and attempting to get the old woman to talk was like trying to shake all the glitter off a sherpa-knit sweatshirt. No matter which angle you came at it from, it never did a damn bit of good.

It was painful to watch.

Jacob's resolve cracked first. Hands on hips, he turned to me and muttered, "This was a bust. Just like the hospital. Hell, just like the goddamn notebook."

"It's not over till you throw in the towel."

"That's not true, though, is it?" Jacob glanced at his grandmother, who was glaring resolutely out the window at the fine, sunny morning. "We can try till we're blue in the face but we can't force her to talk. She's obviously not gonna tell us anything—frankly, I'm starting to doubt she even can."

"We'll try a different time—"

"We have! And what good has it done? Maybe she'd be willing to come clean with you after her time is up...but knowing her, she'll hold on until we leave, just because."

"Leave!"

Jacob and I both jumped at the sudden, startling interjection. When we turned to Grandma, she was looking right at him.

"You heard me," she said. "You don't belong here anymore. No one *wants* you here. Get out—and don't come back!"

Everyone has their go-to stress reaction. Jacob? He hunkers down in his armor. I've seen it happen enough to know the signs. He goes still—oddly still—but just for a fraction of a heartbeat. And in that moment, the shields come up.

Now? I swore I could feel the metal plates click into place.

With a parting look as cold as steel, Jacob turned on his heel and strode out the door.

If she'd been yelling at me, I would've done the same. Avoidance is, after all, my forte. But she'd laid into Jacob. And

I was pissed. "Okay, old woman, I've had just about enough of your—"

"How dare you!" Crap. I hadn't realized she'd fight back. "You might think you can get away with corrupting him, but remember this: God sees you."

"So let 'God' look. There is nothing wrong with what we're doing. Nothing whatsoever."

"You can't possibly believe that. The sinful things you're doing pervert the natural order."

"Whoa, hold on. It's not sin to love someone."

"Don't get cute with me—you don't love him. You don't love any of them." Huh? Exactly how many guys did she think I was engaged to? "Oh, you might claim to have their best interests in mind, but you don't fool me. You're helping that doctor experiment on them. Plain and simple."

Whatever this rant was—and it was a hell of a lot more than I'd bargained for—I couldn't risk calling Jacob back in, since I had no clue who she'd mistaken him for. But I knew exactly who she saw when she was arguing with me: Father Paul.

"We're just playing a few carnival games," I said carefully, neither confirming nor denying her accusation.

"Do you think I'm stupid? You're testing them."

I knew the Marks family—and I knew the best way to get them to open up was to contradict them, so with false confidence, I said, "You have no idea what you're talking about."

"You told me it was just a routine follow-up, but that Arab wouldn't be there unless you'd finally found something."

Kamal? Must've been. "Testing...for what?"

"To put them in that government program! Only one child— that's what he promised—and leave the other one alone. But I can see what you're doing. You're after them both."

"Listen, I'm sure this is all just a big misunderstanding."

"Liar," she snarled, then looked pointedly out the window.

Evidently, Jacob wasn't the only one who retreated into his armor when the chips were down.

By this point, he'd cooled off enough to come back for round two. He strode back in and demanded, "What were you talking about?" And when his grandmother ignored him, he turned to me. "What did she say?"

I snagged him by the arm and pulled him out of the room, and out of earshot. My "cover" as Father Paul might come in handy at some point. Best not to blow it.

"It sounds like your grandmother wasn't on board with whatever was going on with Kamal. The best she could do was bargain for one of her kids to stay out of the mix."

"And that's why my father was in that journal, and not Uncle Fred." The same for Shirley and Uncle Leon. "So it was fine to throw Dad to the wolves—?"

"Hey." I grabbed Jacob by the biceps. Wow...he was really tense. "Listen. I'm not defending her. I'm just saying that she wasn't a willing accomplice. And that should count for something."

Jacob ground his jaw a few times then huffed out a sigh and said, "Maybe it's just easier if I have someone to blame."

I gave him a little shake. "You do—and that someone is Kamal."

We were so focused on each other, I nearly jumped out of my skin when Jacob's dad cheerfully called out, "Trying to shake some sense into him? Good luck—it never worked for me!"

Cripes. Hopefully we just looked startled and not totally blindsided. On the bright side, at least Jerry hadn't walked in on anything too incriminating.

Shirley was right behind him with a Tupperware so full she

needed two hands to carry it. "I made muffins," she said. "Want one? I made plenty. The staff deserve a treat for putting up with Jerry's mother."

She peeled open the lid. I hadn't really intended to deprive the nursing staff of their reward, but I wouldn't want Jacob's mom to feel her baking was unappreciated. Plus, the sight of the chocolate-chocolate chip muffins—and especially the sweet smell of fresh baked goodness that came wafting out—convinced me otherwise.

They were still warm.

I took a huge bite, right then and there...and realized it wasn't chocolate, but bran. And those dark things weren't chocolate chips.

They were raisins.

"Well?" Shirley asked brightly.

"Mmm," I said, more or less, around my gigantic mouthful of gluey bran.

Luckily, Jerry changed the subject. "How's Grandma doing?"

"Not good," Jacob said. "She's disoriented. If she says anything strange...I'm sure she's just confused. I wouldn't take it too seriously."

"Well, that's a shame," Shirley said with bland Midwestern pragmatism. "But it was sweet of you boys to visit." Her brow furrowed. "But weren't you supposed to be at the church?"

I tried to tell my phone to open our calendar, but what came out around the bran blob sounded more like Charlie Brown's teachers. It took a few jabs, but eventually I got the thing to open manually...and saw that we were due to meet Pastor Jill in ten minutes. I flashed the screen at Jacob, gave his parents a stilted wave, and said, "Gotta go," around the food-wad.

And though we were in a real hurry, I did manage to slip

into a men's room on our way out the door and spit out the travesty of a muffin.

"You could've just said no," Jacob told me.

"It's fine." There was bran stuck between my teeth and the raisins had left behind a shriveled-grape aftertaste—but I hated being late even more than I hated raisins. "Let's just focus on getting to our appointment."

CHAPTER TWENTY-FIVE

We peeled into the church parking lot with no time to spare and booked it down to the pastor's drab office.

"Sorry we're late," Jacob said. "We're having some issues with my grandmother."

I supposed that was true. Technically.

We settled ourselves on the loveseat. Belatedly, I realized we hadn't pre-scanned the PDF, and resigned myself to winging it. Which always worked out *so* well.

Pastor Jill said, "Since we're coming up on the wedding the day after tomorrow, I figured we should pull out the big guns today." Jacob and I both stiffened—because in our line of work, guns are literal. But the pastor was armed with nothing more daunting than a notebook. "Now, don't roll your eyes—but we need to talk about the languages of love."

I might not have rolled my eyes...but I did narrow them.

"I know, I know," she said, "kinda cheesy. But I can't tell you how many couples I've counseled that just don't know how to appreciate each other. Let's start with gifts. Vic, what was the last gift you gave Jacob?"

"Well, I, uh.... Christmas?"

The pastor's eyebrows hitched up in surprise.

Jacob said, "You did pick up that sunscreen for me the other day."

True. But I was at the drugstore and he wasn't. "In my defense, Jacob's birthday isn't until next month."

Pastor Jill said, "So, Vic, what you're saying is you only give gifts on special occasions? And how do you feel about receiving them?"

Jacob failed to stifle a humorless laugh.

I said, "I'm what you might call a minimalist."

Jacob nodded. "Gift-giving isn't really something we do."

"And, be honest now, Jacob—would you like Vic to present you with tokens of affection, or is it more that you're trying to adapt to his preferences?"

Like Jacob's ever adapted to a thing in his life...but I will admit, I was curious as to how he'd respond.

He considered the question for a moment, then said, "Maybe cooking dinner is the closest I come to gift-giving. But isn't that more for me than for him? I'm sure it sounds old-fashioned, but I like being the provider."

Pastor Jill nodded vigorously. "Interesting. A very perspicacious observation."

Okay, I may have rolled my eyes at that.

She cracked a grin. "That means insightful...but I just like the way all the letter p's and c's dance through the word. But the dinner thing also fits another category: acts of service." That sounded X-rated...but I doubted she was talking about the same kind of *service*. "In a partnership, it's important that both sides feel like they're shouldering a fair amount of the burden. And sometimes the best way to show someone you love them is to lighten their load. Jacob, aside from the sunscreen, what's the last thing Vic has done for you?"

Jack squat, I was tempted to say, but without missing a beat, Jacob said, "The supper club. I was busy and Vic took care of it. He handled it so I didn't have to."

"Don't thank me yet," I muttered. "Not until we've actually seen the napkins."

Pastor Jill turned to me. "Did you realize, at the time, how much your taking care of that task would mean to Jacob?"

I shrugged. "I can't say I gave it much thought." Mostly, I was trying to duck out of the argument between him and his sister. Wasn't I?

"And did he verbally thank you at the time?"

"No. Why should he? It's my wedding, too." Now Jacob was staring at me—I could feel the laser beam look aimed at the side of my head. I turned to him. "You don't need to thank me for being a grown-up, y'know."

"I know," he said gently.

"Because that would be pretty weird."

He nodded. "I get it."

"So long as we're on the same page."

"We are."

Pastor Jill said to me, "It sounds like verbal affirmations of gratitude make you uncomfortable."

"I just think it's ridiculous, is all."

"Really."

"It's important to me to carry my own weight. No thanks are required."

"I see."

"Am I being psychoanalyzed?"

"Just making observations."

Yeah, right. Nothing is just an observation—plus Pastor Jill was looking at me expectantly. Finally, I realized what she was getting at. I sighed and asked Jacob, "Do you need me to *thank* you more often?"

He shifted in his seat. "Not because I don't feel appreciated. More like letting me know I'm on the right track. You can be... hard to read sometimes."

Weird. I've always felt like an open book, at least where Jacob was concerned. "If that's what you want, I'll start thanking you."

"You don't need to go overboard or anything."

"It's fine."

Pastor Jill said, "Is that your fallback response? *It's fine?*"

Oh, I was being psychoanalyzed all right. "I don't know. Maybe."

"Don't worry, I'm not trying to put you on the spot. But your partner just said you're hard to read. And then you replied that something was fine, but your tone said otherwise. Think about it this way. We're here to communicate, and this is a great opportunity for you to tell Jacob how you really feel about the subject of gratitude and appreciation."

With everyone putting me on the spot, it was hard to collect my thoughts, but I did my best. "Jacob, you seriously don't need to thank me—in fact, I'd prefer you didn't. One of the things I like about us is that our personalities, our skills, seem so complementary. You're the one I lean on, and I'd like to think it's the same the other way around. No thank-yous required on my end." I jostled his knee with mine. "But since it means something to you, I'll make an effort to say it out loud."

Jacob was somewhat mollified. He asked Pastor Jill, "If Vic doesn't want gifts or thanks, then how am I supposed to let him know I appreciate him?"

The pastor nodded toward our knees, which were still touching. "Physical touch is a powerful language—and it's also one of the five ways to express your appreciation." Huh. Jacob and I both went very still, and she hastened to add, "I'm not just talking about sex, either. And I think, in your case, it's complicated by the fact that as a same-sex couple, in certain social situations it might feel safer *not* to touch. And, I'm sorry to say, that assessment is probably true sometimes. But even a casual touch—say, to the back of a hand—can speak volumes."

Maybe for your average couple. For us, though, it meant we thought surveillance was listening in.

Jacob said, "There's a certain image to maintain. At work."

"That must be stressful sometimes."

Jacob took my hand deliberately in his—luckily not the freshly healed hand—and gave it a bone-grinding squeeze. "It is."

"What about you, Vic? You don't strike me as a hugger, but you seem comfortable enough with physical contact."

Apparently I'd managed not to wince. "With Jacob. Sure."

"You say that like it's a given, but rest assured, it's not."

Well, when she put it that way, I supposed I should be grateful that my years of being poked and prodded at Camp Hell hadn't left more of a mark.

CHAPTER TWENTY-SIX

On our way out to the car, I turned over the idea that Jacob and I communicated best through touch. Maybe I shouldn't be surprised, since within moments of officially meeting him, I'd jammed my hand down his pants.

But Pastor Jill was right about one thing: it wasn't always practical to grab each other. The FPMP was way more liberal than the police department in its attitude about the gays—but work was work, and even the straight married couples didn't go around hugging and kissing. So, if Jacob was big on verbal acknowledgement, I'd need to start practicing.

"Thank you for driving."

Jacob gave me the side-eye. "Yeah, that's weird."

"But really—I'm not blowing smoke. Even though I hardly ever see repeaters around here, two minutes outside town, the roads turn into the hairpin turns of death. With deer popping out left and right. And zero streetlights. So even though you're a real leadfoot when you're pissed off, I'd still rather have you behind the wheel."

I pulled up our infamous calendar to see if we could grab

some lunch without missing something important. Maybe. If we were quick about it, we could sneak in a quick bite before we moved on to our next task, dropping off our suits to be pressed. As much as we claimed we were keeping everything small and simple, the to-do list was staggering. Or maybe it just seemed that way because our attention was so divided, thanks to Kamal's notebook.

We were just pulling into the restaurant parking lot when a monkey wrench fell into our schedule, thanks to a frantic phone call from our baker. We'd gone with a local up-and-comer for our wedding cake. Not because we were fancy. She was just the first one to answer our email.

For a millennial, Candy Myer was awfully intense. But so what? Once the cake was ordered, we'd figured our interactions with her were pretty much done.

And apparently, we'd been mistaken.

"We have a situation." Through the phone speaker, Candy's voice trembled like she was on the verge of tears. "Flip on your video. We need to chat as soon as possible, or else you'll end up with a supermarket sheet cake for your wedding."

"We're on the road at the moment," Jacob told her. "It would be easier just to swing by."

"From Chicago?"

"We're in town," I said patiently.

"Ohmigosh. Oh. My. Gosh. Maybe we can save this cake after all."

Once we'd hung up and mapped her location—a three-minute drive from where we currently were—I wondered aloud, "Would a sheet cake really be all that bad?"

When Jacob didn't answer right away, I thought maybe he was giving the sheet cake option some serious consideration.

But instead of redirecting us to the nearest grocery store, he said, "Imagine if our problems actually were this simple. Suits and napkins and cake."

Jacob is usually the optimist, so hearing him sound so defeated really hit home. "Maybe they *can* be our only problems—just for the afternoon." I grabbed him by the knee and squeezed until my hand bones complained. "I know we'll both be fully aware that we're trying to fool ourselves if we stop thinking about Kamal for a few hours. But take it from someone who's been fake-married. What I'm doing with you, here and now, feels a hell of a lot more real."

Jacob got a little misty as he stared down at my naked left hand…but then another call from Candy lit up the dash, and with a sigh, he ignored it and put the car in gear.

The cake shop looked a lot smaller in person than it did online—and twice as pretentious. And then there was the name: Crumb. Obviously, the owner was missing out on the golden opportunity to call it Candy's Cakes. Probably guilty of overthinking it.

We were "downtown," but instead of skyscrapers and a lakefront, there was a strip of quaint 1800's buildings and parking meters that accepted nickels. Crumb was a narrow storefront squeezed between a juice bar and a bar-bar, both of which were pimping ridiculously complicated cocktails. The building's Victorian details had been picked out in a dozen different colors of paint, and business names were gilded on the windows.

"I remember this place," Jacob said. "They used to sell cheap donuts, and half the shops around it were empty. They've really spruced up the neighborhood."

Given what we were paying for their second-smallest wedding cake, I wasn't surprised they could afford to be so fancy.

As we were sizing up the joint, Jacob's phone trilled yet again. "Let's get this over with," he said, sending it to voicemail, and we headed in to meet our fate.

Inside, the store was sparse and eclectic—everything wood, glass and metal—with exposed ductwork and old, scuffed floors that had been left deliberately unfinished. Three vintage cafe tables filled the front room, spindly metal things that looked none too comfortable. A glass counter offered cupcakes "iced to order." The only decorations on the walls were floating glass boxes with dramatic lighting, each of which contained a truly elaborate cake.

As desserts went...these cakes felt way too fancy for the likes of me. But the local go-to bakery had a reputation for being over-booked whenever a same-sex couple needed a cake (nothing that could be proven, mind you) so it was either a supermarket sheet cake, or this.

Though given the wail of frustration that bansheed out from the back...that supermarket cake was looking better and better. Even if we had to scrape "Congratulations, Graduate!" off the top.

Jacob picked up a filigreed metal hand-bell off the counter and gave it a shake. We both cringed at the ridiculousness of the tiny little tinkle it made. I called out, "Hello—Candy? We're here."

She poked her head around the corner and nearly deflated with relief.

While I try not to judge people on their looks, let's face it, we all do. Candy Myer annoyed me. Primarily her glasses. They were big and round and frumpy beyond belief, the type of frames that were the height of fashion...in third grade. They say all things old are new again, and while I could see the whole retro aesthetic working for her cafe tables, those glasses didn't do her any favors.

Since she was a high-maintenance vendor who'd insisted on multiple video chats before she even took our deposit, I'd been prepared for the glasses. What I hadn't banked on was the mom-jeans.

I truly don't get millennials.

"What a relief—you have no idea—I. Can't. Even!" Candy closed her eyes, took a deep breath, and said, "All right. I'll just come right out and say it. The strawberry coulis is not happening."

She needed a meeting for *that*?

Apparently, she took our stunned silence as some kind of recrimination. "There's normally another week left in the season, but with the heavy rain we saw a few weeks ago and an early warm-snap, all my local vendors are tapped out. And now I have *nothing* to put between your layers."

No doubt we could hit the grocery store and grab her a few perfectly serviceable cartons of strawberries. But sourcing local had been the subject of one of our numerous video chats, so I knew better than to offer. Those berries might have come from somewhere outlandish, like Michigan.

"What about raspberries?" I suggested.

As if I'd proposed filling the cakes with pterodactyl meat and dodo eggs, Candy said, "Raspberries aren't in season! They won't be for weeks."

"Vanilla frosting is fine," Jacob said—and he used his no-nonsense, authoritative voice, too.

Which didn't work on Candy....at all. "No it isn't. It's too sweet. Far too sweet. You've got to balance the sweetness. You need acid."

At this point, I definitely did—or at least a Valium. But I hadn't taken anything stronger than an aspirin since my encounter with the habit demon, and I wasn't about to start using again over something as trivial as a cake.

"Mascarpone?" Jacob suggested.

"With a Genoise sponge? My reputation will never recover."

"What about that?" I gestured to the nearest display cake—but not the kind with "naked" frosting, which to my mind looks like I attempted to frost a cake myself...with a hockey stick. "Can't we just use that one and call it good?"

Mom-jeans looked at me like I was soft in the head. "That's a facsimile cake. It's not real."

"I know what facsimile means." Back in my day, after I walked to the precinct—barefoot in the snow, uphill both ways—my desk would be covered in them. But before I got too snippy about it, an incoming text bleeped in my pocket.

It was our florist. And unlike Candy, he was the epitome of stoicism. The text read: *Call ASAP. Flowers DOA.*

Even with the complete lack of drama, it wasn't a message you'd want to receive two days before your wedding. I tilted the screen so Jacob could see, and he said, "They're just down the block. Divide and conquer? I'll sort out the cake filling—and don't worry. I'll make sure there aren't any raisins in it."

"I only use sultanas," Candy interjected, followed by some ramble about a vineyard in the Driftless Region. I wasn't really listening, though. Mostly, I was harkening back to the couples meeting we'd just come from, and the fact that not only did Jacob's personality complement mine, but he also knew me pretty darn well.

"Thank you," I told him—with no snarkiness whatsoever. Because to say Candy got on my nerves was putting it mildly.

Normally, I would have left it at that. But then Pastor Jill's comments about physical touch came to mind. And when could I show affection to my future husband, if not during the process of dickering about a wedding cake?

I caught his hand and went in for a kiss. He stiffened. This was not something we did outside our own home, in broad daylight—or maybe the car...which probably needed detailing now we'd gotten frisky in it. But we couldn't claim we needed to act professional for work. Not here, not now.

Jacob stiffened. We bumped noses, and my lips glanced off his.

I found myself weirdly disappointed. Yeah, it was just a kiss. But it seemed to me Jacob's big, gay hometown wedding was a statement—a triumphant affirmation of who he was. And at a time when he was questioning everything, he really needed to plant a flag in the ground and say, "This is who I am." Especially at a time when he was questioning that very thing.

I turned to go, but before I got away, he grabbed me by the shoulder and gave the whole kissing thing another shot. This one landed squarely where he'd been aiming, and lingered there, warm and just a little wet, while his strong, warm hand cupped my jaw and our bodies angled to fit our peaks and valleys together.

Turned out Jacob hadn't been apprehensive about the PDA—just startled. And once he got with the program, he was all in. And then some.

I pulled from his embrace reluctantly and left him to Candy's tender (and neurotic) mercies.

I could get used to this public kissing thing, I decided. I was still warm and fuzzy from our lip-lock by the time I strode up to the florist two minutes later.

Clauson's Flowers, the shop handling our wedding, was in a humid storefront close to the edge of the little downtown. It was nowhere near as artsy-fartsy as the cake shop, but the riot of color in the window made up for the lack of a fancy paint job on the building.

As I made my way through the forest of greenery inside, I remembered I like flowers even less than I like raisins. Luckily, when we placed our initial order, Jacob didn't have any strong preference either. I think, in theory, he *wanted* to have an opinion. The words *we should get something masculine* did leave his mouth. But when I challenged him to name a masculine flower and he came up blank, we picked out something inoffensive and called it good.

I guess we should've come up with a plan B.

At the sound of the door, Jim Clauson came from the back room with pair of pruning shears in his hand. The way the tool sat in his meaty paw, he looked more likely to gut a fish with it than trim flowers.

I waited for him to say something.

He stared at me and blinked.

"I'm Victor Bayne."

"Uh-huh."

"And you just texted me?"

"Uh-huh." That was it? *Uh-huh?* We stared at each other—but I'm great at staring contests, and after an overlong pause, he said, "The refrigeration on the truck went out. Your clematis didn't make it."

"Yeah. I gathered." More staring. It was tempting to see exactly how far the standoff would go, but I didn't have all day. "Now what?"

"Wanna see 'em?"

"Why?"

"Maybe you could use 'em somehow. Scatter the petals on the floor."

The mere thought was enough to make me break out in hives. "No. I don't want a bunch of dead flower petals."

"Okay." Clauson looked around. "Did you want a substitute?"

"Yes. I want a substitute. Because I'm having a wedding. And there should be flowers."

"Uh-huh. How about roses?"

My first impulse was to say, *Fine—just make sure they're alive.* But then Jacob's initial flower suggestion came to mind. "Do you have something more, uh, *masculine* than roses?"

"I've never had anyone ask for a masculine flower before." When I was just about ready to turn on my heel and grab a couple of random bouquets from the supermarket—along with a backup vanilla sheet cake—Clauson cracked a grin that transformed his whole face. And he struck me as a guy who didn't smile unless he really meant it. "It's a good challenge. Same color scheme as before?"

I'm sure the silvery muted lavender color we'd picked out in the first place was the reason our flowers needed to be shipped in special, and we couldn't afford another bad batch. "White is fine," I said. "Just white."

CHAPTER TWENTY-SEVEN

If Jacob and I had complementary skills, I'm not sure why, exactly, his sister needed to be so involved in our wedding prep. But Barbara insisted on "helping," so once the cake and the flowers were under control, we headed over to her place.

The plan was to go over her reading and our vows, since we were in such a time-crunch, we'd foregone the formal rehearsal. Pastor Jill said that with our simple, small ceremony, it would be no problem. Barbara, however, was absolutely convinced the church would fall in.

Weeks ago, Jacob and I had found our vows online and agreed they were exactly what we wanted. Maybe that wasn't as personal as composing your own, but since neither of us had the faintest clue where to begin, we both agreed that sounding normal was more important than being original.

Reading aloud in public was not my favorite thing, but at least the sentiment had been vetted by both of us, so I expected to be subjected to nothing worse than an awkward bout of public speaking. What we found at his sister's house was awkward, all right. But not because I'd stumbled on a word.

As soon as we got out of the car, we could tell we'd blundered right into the middle of an argument between Barbara and Clayton. Not because we were psychically sensitive to that sort of thing, but because we could hear them screaming at each other from all the way out in the driveway.

"I hate you!" Clayton hollered. It might've even qualified as a bellow, if his voice hadn't broken. "You *never* let me do *anything*!"

"And I don't intend to start, either—so long as you insist on lying to me about who you're with and where you're going!"

"It wasn't a lie! Some other guys showed up and we changed our minds and left—"

"For all I knew, you were dead in a ditch—"

Jacob cut his eyes to me and winced. "Maybe we should just move on to the next thing on the calendar."

The curtains rustled. "Too late. She's already seen us." I steeled myself, and we walked up to the house and rapped on the door.

Barbara yanked it open and said, "Well, at least *someone* made an effort to be where they said they would be."

Across the room, Clayton stood sulkily with his arms crossed and twin points of color blazing from his flushed cheeks. "Uncle Jacob, tell her to chill out. I was just across the street."

Barbara snapped, "Which you could have let me know with a simple text."

Clayton said to Jacob. "She gets all weird in front of my friends. It's embarrassing. I'm not a little kid."

At his age, I'd been left to my own devices—which involved playing kick-the-can with tetanus-riddled garbage and traipsing around on active railroad tracks. Jacob's parents were just as laissez faire. In fact, before he was even in high school, they'd given him a BB gun and a utility knife for Christmas.

But thinking back to those shots of Jacob and his sister at the Sacred Heart carnival—wondering what the hell had been going on behind the scenes of his seemingly idyllic childhood—made me suspect that Barbara was right to be concerned.

Jacob sat on the couch, tugged Clayton down beside him, and slung an arm around the kid. "Look, I know you think your mother is overreacting, but I'm with her on this one. If you weren't where you said you'd be when she came to pick you up, what's she supposed to think?"

"I was just across the street!"

"And how was she supposed to know that?"

"I don't know—whatever—she didn't have to have a total freakout—"

"You're right, Clayton, you're not a little kid anymore, you're a teenager—so I'll level with you. Maybe you weren't doing anything wrong, but it's not just your behavior that your mom has to worry about. Human trafficking is a real issue. And don't think that just because you live in a small town that it can't happen here. A place that's safe enough to make everyone feel complacent is the perfect place for a predator to look."

That spiel might've sounded canned from anyone else—but during Jacob's tenure working sex crimes...he'd seen some stuff. He hardly ever talked about it. And when he did, no one would dare contradict him. Even an argumentative thirteen-year-old, one who'd clearly inherited the family stubborn-gene.

"I'm sorry," he told his mother, only somewhat sullenly.

Barbara wasn't exactly prepared to be mollified. "Set an alarm on your phone next time and text me where you are—if I ever let you out of the house again. If I have time to go to work, and clean up after you, and plan a wedding on top of it, then you have time to set an alarm."

Jacob stood and dusted off his black jeans. "Barb, we've all had our plates full these past few weeks. Thank you for all your help—I really don't know what we would've done without it, handling this all from a distance."

Barbara blinked as if she'd never heard the words *thank you* before. Given the thankless task of parenting a thirteen-year-old, maybe she hadn't. "Of course. You're my brother."

"Look, we've all had a long day—and I'm confident we all know how to read. We're gonna head out and call it a night."

I was almost to the car when I realized Jacob had used the appreciation-speak we'd learned in Pastor Jill's office to throw his sister off balance and extricate us from the situation.

Talk about a quick study.

While it seemed awfully early to throw in the towel, I figured he was just angling for a quiet dinner. Evidently, I'd subscribed to my own suggestion to throw myself into the wedding and pretend it was our only pressing concern, because it hadn't even occurred to me that Jacob was just looking for an excuse to go back to Sacred Heart. It took a two-wheel maneuver on a hairpin turn of death for me to even realize that was where he was headed.

Well, we had maybe three hours of daylight left, though calling that last hour "daylight" would be generous. By the time we got there, fireflies had started to twinkle and the sky was already looking pink. The stretch of woods was actually kind of pretty... if you didn't know what lurked behind the trees.

Jacob pulled onto the gravel shoulder across from the old access road and said, "Pull up the map we found at the library yesterday and compare it to the satellite photo."

The image on the burner phone was small, but actually, that turned out to be pretty helpful in helping us spot the most obvious landmarks. The old roads from the plat map were gone now, but there was a creek running through the edge of the land that appeared in both images.

Jacob pointed to the satellite photo. "The hospital should be right about here. That farmer said they never tore it down, but there's nothing in that spot but tree canopy."

"You know as well as I do that when some old psychic testing ground disappears, there's a whole team of people behind the cover-up. I'm sure at least one of them is familiar with Photoshop."

We found a pen in the glovebox and started marking up the printout based on the library map, since neither of us was keen on getting lost in the dark. We were so focused on our task that a rap on the window nearly made me jump out of my skin.

Was it our friend, the helpful farmer?

Not at all   .

Not unless he was disguised as Barbara.

CHAPTER TWENTY-EIGHT

"You *followed* us?"

Jacob faced off with his sister on the side of the road, hands on hips and nostrils flaring.

And Barbara? Not intimidated in the least. "Can you blame me? Since when do you make a big deal out of thanking me for doing what anybody's sister would do? Obviously you were just trying to get rid of me!" She gesticulated at the trees. "But to drive way out here in the middle of nowhere—why?"

"You followed us. For an hour. Just to make a point."

It might've been a decent deflection, but Barbara wasn't taking the bait. Because the way she was now scanning the tree line, it was obvious she'd pieced together where we were. "Sacred Heart is closed, Jacob. It's been closed for years."

"Turn around—right this minute—and go back home."

Barbara ignored him. "The pelican." She squinted into the trees for a moment, then turned to me. "There *was* something weird about it. Wasn't there?"

I said, "All kinds of things seem weird until you find the explanation." Jacob shot me a warning glare. "Or not. Usually it turns out to be perfectly random."

She didn't buy it. "Like taking our picture in front of that stupid pelican year after year. Just random."

"Or maybe it was more like a tradition. Who's to say how *those* things get started. Anyway—"

"Barbara," Jacob snapped. "I don't have time to argue with you. We're losing daylight."

"What is so important about that hospital you need to go look at it right this...second...?" Barbara's eyes went round. *She knows something*, I thought. And Jacob must've thought so too, judging by the way we went all still and wary. Barb looked from her brother to the woods and back again—and then her hands flew up to cover her mouth as she sucked in a horrified gasp.

Well, shit.

You'll only have so much success sweeping something under the carpet if the other person knows damn well it's there. All I could do now was see where Jacob was leading with his damage-control and do my best to play along.

Shakily, she said, "Those things you told Clayton before—about predators. I figured you got that from your job. Not because it had happened to you."

"No one was molested," Jacob said firmly. "I just wanted to get some pictures of the old facade. I thought it might jog Grandma's memories."

Plausible. I could tell Barbara didn't quite buy it, though, so I added, "It would be a real shame if Jacob didn't get a chance to connect with her before we went back to Chicago." Or before she kicked the bucket—which even I was tactful enough to leave unsaid.

Barbara squinted off into the trees again. "Couldn't you just find a picture online?"

Jacob said, "We looked, but pre-digital events are tricky. It's old news—old *rural* news—and there just isn't anything out there."

There were so many holes in our argument you could play it like a flute, but the best way to distract Jacob's sister was to put a problem in front of her that needed solving. She glared at the trees across the way. "Look at that old road. It's disintegrated. You can see from here—completely overgrown. How're you gonna find the hospital in that jungle?"

"Don't worry," Jacob assured her. "We have a satellite map."

"Let me see."

Had we drawn anything incriminating on it? Not really—just a few squiggly lines and a circle where we expected the old building to be. Jacob gave me a subtle nod, so I pulled the folded paper from my pocket and passed it over.

Barbara scowled at the map. "This is terrible. How can you make heads or tails of anything?"

Jacob took it back before she could absorb the full extent of its vagueness. "Now you know why it's so important we get moving. We've only got an hour of light. Maybe less."

"Hold on. I have bug spray."

Barbara turned and jogged off toward her car.

In a low voice, he said, "We're not getting rid of her. She's too damn stubborn."

Pot, kettle. "Why didn't we see her tailing us?"

"She must've kept another car in between."

That, and she drove the same silver sedan everyone else drove. "Well, the hospital's not going anywhere. We can always come back."

"Agreed. We cut our losses for today—fumble around a little bit, let the light run out, and head back home."

Barbara came trotting back with a sizable Amazon box in her hands. I said, "That's a lot of bug spray."

She set the box on the car hood triumphantly and peeled open the flap. "Good thing Clayton picked today to get himself punished. Otherwise I wouldn't have his drone."

Well.

Talk about a game-changer.

Jacob edged toward the box as if he might grab it and sprint away. Clearly the wheels were turning, and he made a last ditch effort at scaring off his sister. "You took away his toy, and then you left him home alone?"

"Of course not. He's at Mom and Dad's."

Damn. There'd be no getting rid of her now. But on the bright side, at least the drone would let us take a better look at those woods.

"Do you know how to fly that thing?" I asked Barbara.

"Given that my son has been talking about it nonstop for the past week? I may have picked up a thing or two." People talk to me about all kinds of things—yoga, for instance—but that doesn't mean I'm capable of doing them. "Plus, he insisted on giving me a few lessons. Mainly to show off...but looks like it'll come in handy."

Apparently, Barbara was a quick study. She had the drone up in the air in two minutes flat. "Okay, we're good to go." The drone touched down on the gravel. "We should get closer before we send it up for real. There's only so much battery life."

Once she engulfed us all in a pungent cloud of bug spray, we were off.

The woods were no less imposing than last time, but Barbara was just as sturdy as her brother, and having her with us didn't slow us down. We did find occasional stretches of asphalt that corresponded with the squiggle that used to be a road, so it seemed we were on the right track. Until we came across a downed tree, anyhow.

It was huge.

Maybe the organization responsible for the cover-up had driven in with a tractor and pulled the thing down, or maybe Mother Nature had just been having a bad day. Either way, there was no climbing over, not unless we wanted an assful of pine needles. And taking the wrong way around could easily send us veering off in the wrong direction.

It was as good a time as any to launch the drone.

We all held our breath as it floated up into the air with a sound like a bunch of fans trying to blow away the smoke after a monthly sage smudge. The controllers looked like something from an old-school gaming system, with a bunch of buttons, a joystick for each thumb, and a pop-up viewscreen that showed a dizzying blur of vegetation.

Motion sickness doesn't generally affect me, but my throat fluttered at the sight of the topsy-turvy treescape. "It's real windy up there," Barbara said. "That's bad for the battery. I'll need to fly lower. We won't cover as much ground that way, but—"

A rooftop—a big one. We all saw it, just a flash, and then everything went wonky as Barbara struggled to stabilize the drone.

"Ope—jeez—" Images flashed by. Sky. Trees. A blinding flash from lowering sun. And then? Gravel.

"What happened?" Jacob asked.

"I must've crashed it." Barb jiggled the controllers. "On the roof."

Holy crap.

I couldn't say if that was good or bad. On one hand, our chances of getting rid of Barbara had just dropped exponentially. But on the other...at least Sacred Heart was still standing.

CHAPTER TWENTY-NINE

Losing a drone is not an uncommon occurrence, and Clayton's new toy was a high-end model with a GPS tracker. On one hand, it was completely reckless to let a civilian like Barbara go anywhere near the hidden hospital. But at the same time... neither Jacob nor I knew how to use the tracking app. Guided by her phone, we tromped around some more downed trees— and while I'm no expert, it seemed to me there were too many of them to be a coincidence. After a good fifteen minutes, we found traces of a road again. And five minutes after that? We pushed aside some undergrowth and found ourselves face to face with Sacred Heart.

Maybe, by Chicago standards, the hospital would be considered small. But out here in the middle of nowhere, with nothing around it but trees, it felt dauntingly big. No chance of searching the place in half an hour. In fact, it could easily take us at least a week.

It was a square brick building. Utilitarian—three stories and a flat roof, and the only ornamentation was a stylized heart and cross on the pediment. The ground-level windows were boarded up tight, No-Trespassing signs plastered the doors, and the whole thing was strangled in ivy.

Barbara shielded her eyes, squinted up at the roof, and powered up the drone. Or, at least, she tried to. "The connection's all screwy."

Like its battery was low...or like a signal-scrambling device had been planted by the cover-up crew?

While his sister struggled with the controls, Jacob appraised the situation. "We'll buy Clayton a new one."

Barbara snapped him a look. "Without so much as *trying* to get it down? This isn't just any old toy. His *father* gave it to him. And if I lose the darn thing, I'm the bad guy."

"Barb—it's all boarded up."

As if something as pedestrian as a plank of wood should matter. "You know how these buildings are, Jacob. I'm sure there's a stairwell inside that'll take you right up to the top. And it's built like a tank, all concrete and metal. It's not like you'd fall through the floor."

Jacob's jaw worked. "There's no way in."

"You haven't even looked!" As if to prove her point, Barbara stomped purposefully toward the old hospital, crunching through leaves and twigs.

The noise might've been intended to convey her annoyance, but it also let us hash out a quick plan.

"The burner phone," Jacob whispered. "Pull us up on the map and take a screenshot so we can figure out exactly where we are right now and come back later. I'll go distract my sister."

Compared to my super slick FPMP phone, the burner was cheap, unintuitive and laggy—but eventually I managed to pull up a map with a blue pin on it that represented my current location. And the clearing I was currently standing in—the one

I could see with my own two eyes? According to the satellite...it didn't exist. I fumbled around until I grabbed a shot of the map, then zoomed out until I could see the creek and took another one for good measure. I might've shot a few pictures of my feet in the process, but between the plat map and the screen grab, I was confident we could find Sacred Heart again when we had more time (and privacy) to really take a good look around.

Around the far side of the derelict hospital, voices were raised. (*Since when are you such a quitter?*) Barbara wasn't wrong about these square, institutional structures, and there would likely be a direct shot to the roof nearby—but everything in between would be locked up tight, and without a locksmith or a jackhammer, they'd be shit outta luck.

I double-checked the screenshots just to make sure I hadn't screwed anything up, then decided to grab another shot, just to be safe—a little triangulation since it was so easy to get turned around. To make sure Barbara didn't see me playing Spy vs. Spy, I went the opposite way around so the hospital building stayed between us.

The emergency bay protruded from that side of the building. The drive-up had been protected by a carport, once, but vines had crept through some delicate part of the structure. Bit by relentless bit, they'd pulled the roof down.

With that roof had come a good hunk of the door frame. The heavy plywood blocking the old emergency doors hung at a funny angle. And when I wiggled the board to see if it was still firmly attached, I found myself backpedaling to avoid getting flattened.

The doors behind the plywood had fared no better. The panels were safety glass, so they hadn't shattered, but they'd fallen out in big, crackled sheets.

It was dark inside, cold too, and my footsteps sounded crunchy. But one thing Barbara had been right about: it didn't feel like I was in danger of falling through the floor. Back in my patrol days, I'd picked my way through plenty of crackhead flophouses on the verge of falling in, and the floors here didn't have that same spongy give. Other than the messed-up door, everything felt solid.

I didn't think I'd find any crackheads here—too far off the beaten path—but wild animals were a distinct possibility. I bounced my pocket flashlight beam around the room, but nothing skittered away. The beam landed on a sign with arrows pointing to check-in, bathrooms...and stairs.

Since they were right there, I figured it couldn't hurt to take a look.

I tried the door. It opened. Some waning daylight filtered in through an upper-level window, so my flashlight didn't need to work quite so hard to get me my bearings. The stairwell was plain and industrial, and in surprisingly good shape. Other than the rodent turds caught in the textured grating of the steps, it probably didn't look much different than it had back when the building was still in use.

Just a quick look. Two minutes, tops. I jogged up the three flights of stairs to prove to myself they didn't lead to the roof... but ended up proving myself wrong. On the top floor, beside the door that led into the hospital, was another one marked *Staff Only*.

And that door opened, too. Without juice powering the electronic lock, the only thing standing between the hospital and trespassers was that old plywood. To its credit, the wood was awfully thick.

Well, I figured, I'd come this far. Might as well grab the drone before any covert government agencies spotted it with a drone of their own.

The final stairwell opened out onto an unremarkable flat gravel roof. I spotted Clayton's drone just a few yards away, next to a Frisbee that was sun-faded to an indeterminate shade of off-white. Jacob and Barbara's raised voices were audible. Still squabbling. I crunched over to the far side of the roof and called over, "I've got the drone."

Their heads snapped up. "You went in?" Jacob asked. Obviously the answer was yes, since I was currently chatting with him over the side of the roof. But what he couldn't say in mixed company was, *You went in without backup?* To which I answered, "Everything's fine, I'll be down in a sec."

I might've come off pretty blasé about my decision, but hearing the anxiety in Jacob's voice now had me reconsidering my bravado. The hospital administrator had offed himself...and suicides have got a habit of sticking around.

A shiver of dread crept down my spine and I opened my crown chakra wide, pulling down white light. It wasn't the quick flood of mojo I'd get when a ghost popped up in the vicinity and flooded me with adrenaline, but a slow and steady top-off, just in case. With the drone tucked under my arm, I headed for the stairwell. Going down is a lot easier than going up, I assured myself, and I'd be safely back outside in no time.

Maybe that would've been the case, if I hadn't paused at the second floor...and caught a glimpse of someone moving around in the shadows.

Adrenaline spiked after all, and the edges of my vision went bright and hazy as I formed a protective skin of white light and huddled inside it.

Finding a ghost in a hospital was like finding a needle in a sewing factory. Not only had this Director Mann checked out early, but plenty of other folks had died within those walls. And now the sun was setting. Spirit activity prime time.

Normally, I'd call Jacob and tell him to get his butt inside so he could do his bit as a human shield—but I had a white balloon around me, and his sister didn't. In fact, it might be a good idea to warn him away. But between the drone, my flashlight and my baggie of salt, I didn't have a free hand to send a text. And chances were, even if I did get him a message, he'd do the opposite of what I said and come charging on in.

The stairwell door was set with a tall, narrow pane of safety glass. I edged up to it and scoped out what lay beyond. Across the way, glass double-doors. When I angled myself for a better look, something moved again.

Something that looked suspiciously like my own reflection.

My head throbbed vaguely and I let my grip on the white light loosen, though I didn't drop my guard entirely. While the gawky mirror image in the glass might not pose much of a threat, the old director could still be lurking around. And thanks to whoever erased Sacred Heart, I had no idea what to look for. Young or old? Tall or short? Fat or thin? I didn't even know for sure he was Caucasian, though given the time and locale, it was likely. The only thing I was certain of was the gender.

I decided it didn't much matter. It wasn't as if I had time to confront the guy tonight. Not with Jacob busy diverting Barbara's attention.

I paused with the drone in one hand, salt baggie and flashlight in the other. I used to hide from the living folks around me when I talked to ghosts. Too much professional backlash when the other cops saw me doing my thing. But over the years, Jacob had managed to sneak in enough tendrils to pry off the heavy plywood of my distrust. Although I might need to constantly remind Jacob not to grab my white light, I'd still rather have him at my side to face off against the unknown.

Sacred Heart wasn't going anywhere. We'd have more time to poke around after the wedding. I turned to go, and when I moved, so did my reflection in the glass.

In the opposite direction.

A shock of pain lanced through my head as my adrenal glands opened up and white light thundered down. I needed more hands. I tried to shuffle the flashlight to my newly mended hand—the one holding the drone—but my muscles cramped, and the drone hit the floor with a plasticky clatter. No time to see if I'd broken the damn thing. I stuck the pocket flashlight in my mouth instead, freeing both hands, and tore open the baggie.

A spray of salt erupted and the stairwell lit up white to my inner eye, even with daylight rapidly fading. And in that flash-bulb moment, I locked eyes with the guy behind the glass.

CHAPTER THIRTY

Holy cripes, no wonder I thought I was seeing my own reflection. Our facial features were different enough, but his height, his frame, the way he stood? Just like me. Tall and awkward, ineffectively slouching like he was desperately hoping to be overlooked.

"You're the priest," I blurted out around the flashlight. No wonder Jacob's grandmother thought she knew me. This guy could pass for me in a lineup. He was so solid I read him as a living person and had a moment of disorientation—did he live here, or had he just come to catch us snooping around? But then, in the full light of my flashlight beam, he moved. And the jerky, stilted scramble of him backing away, scuttling like a startled six-and-a-half-foot cockroach, nearly made me inhale the damn flashlight.

It says something about how far I'd go for Jacob that my drive to find out what was behind his creepy carnival overrode my impulse to turn tail and get the hell away from that ghost. Like a cockroach, he might very well slip into a crack and evade me for good if I didn't act now. I switched the flashlight to my hand, then elbowed through the stairwell door and into the hall, where now I could see the glass double-doors were marked *Chapel*.

A chill tingled down my spine.

I nudged the chapel door with my foot and it grudgingly opened. I slipped through, focused on the spot I'd last seen the skittery priest...and nearly jumped out of my skin when I caught a figure looming beside me.

Bloody. Agonized. And entirely harmless, since that particular figure—Christ on the cross—was nothing more than plaster and paint. Dregs of fading daylight eked in through the stained glass windows, and the dim half-light played tricks with my eyes. I swept the chapel with my flashlight beam. Pews, kneelers, the whole nine yards. A pair of alcoves surrounded the seating, and in each one was a figure. The Virgin Mary, and Jesus again—but he looked a lot less tortured now than he did on the cross...except for the gory, anatomically correct heart hovering at chest level, painted blood red, swathed in flames and wound around with thorns.

I was so focused on the damn heart, I didn't see the priest until he was practically on top of me. He raised a skeletal hand. I flailed, scattering salt, while white light thundered down. Dealing with both the salt and the light was like walking and chewing gum—while being pounced on by a dead priest. I let the salt fall where it wanted and focused on wrapping the light around me. His hand swooped. I flinched...then realized he hadn't been grabbing for me at all. He was making the sign of the cross.

"...and forgive us our trespasses, as we forgive those who trespass against us..."

Not only that—he was *praying* for me.

I've got a lot better chance at connecting with a sentient ghost when I know their name.

"Father Paul," I said.

He faltered, then added, "And deliver us from evil. Amen."

"Father—do you know what's going on?"

He jittered like someone had jostled whatever was projecting him into my plane of being, but his eyes stayed fixed on mine. "That's usually my line."

"How so?"

"Ever since my heart attack, I've been helping lost souls find their way. You'd be surprised how many people don't realize they're dead."

"Unfortunately not."

"What's going on?" He jittered again, this time like he'd taken a step backward and then snapped into place again, as if his hold on three dimensions was no better than my hold on the salt. "Have you come to take my place?"

Only in my worst nightmares. "I'm here to get some answers."

He solidified a few inches to the right of where I expected. "I knew it was too good to be true. I haven't helped anyone find their way to the Lord in ages—but maybe that's just how it feels. Purgatory is so cold and dark and confusing, I've lost track of time."

"That's what this is to you? Purgatory?"

Another jump—several inches closer, with a wry twist to his mouth. "At least Purgatory is temporary. I'd rather not consider the alternative."

Ghosts who stick around to help others find the veil aren't as common as your typical intersection repeaters, but every once in a while, they do turn up. Not only are they lucid—they're strong. Even topped off with white light, I was no match for crossover ghost...though this one didn't seem nearly as stable as the others I'd encountered.

Maybe that was worse. Throwing him out of whack could easily lead to a possession. And if this ghost decided to take my body for a spin, he'd find it a disturbingly good fit.

The salt—or what was left of it, maybe a handful—was the only weapon I had that could even touch it. I backed up a few steps and dumped white light into the crystals.

Cautiously, I said, "I might not be your replacement, but maybe you can earn a few brownie points with the man upstairs by setting the record straight. The malpractice scandal—the one that shut down the hospital. Did it have anything to do with...psychics?"

The ghost blinked out of existence so fast I swore I felt my eardrums flex.

So much for the direct approach.

On the off-chance the priest wasn't really gone, just hiding, I called out, "A lot has changed these last couple of decades. Science figured out that not everyone hearing voices is actually crazy. Good to know. But the way they got their information, at least back in the early days, left a lot to be desired." Footfalls on metal stair treads sounded, growing closer. Jacob. Barbara, too. But it was okay. The priest had bailed, and I was only talking to myself at this point. Even so, I indulged myself by adding, "A hell of a lot. I should know."

"Vic?" Jacob called out.

"In here."

The stairwell door opened. Jacob's flashlight beam danced across the wall as he swept the hallway, never mind that he wouldn't see anything. Police training didn't just evaporate when the potential threat was dead.

"Well, thank gosh you found Clayton's drone," Barbara exclaimed. Why the hell had Jacob let her tag along? I shook my head at Jacob urgently as she bent to pick it up. Jacob wasn't looking at my face, though. He was staring at the baggie in my hand and putting together the reason for my delay. His eyes went wide.

As realization dawned on him, the dead priest flashed into view again—right between us. I lobbed the salt. But with him skittering around a couple inches to one side or the other like he'd lost hold of his ability to fix himself in place, I missed him entirely.

The baggie smacked Jacob in the chest, dousing him with salt.

Another flashbulb moment—this one emanating from Jacob. Just a glimpse, but a glimpse was enough. The priest, staggering back like he'd taken a sucker-punch to the gut. But he wasn't the only one. A few noncorporeal entities had been hanging in the air like a cloud of stink. Not the jellyfish-type habit demons that hooked into people with their invisible tethers, but vaguer things. Random splots. Some wavy tendrils. A few hazy, insubstantial blurs.

It was like looking at pond scum through a microscope—and only for half a second. But that glimpse was enough for me to see that we had company...and whatever Jacob *did* when the salt hit him? It blew that etheric flotsam out of the water.

True Stiffs were most definitely underrated.

"Would you two quit horsing around?" Barbara said. "By the time we get to the road it'll be pitch black out."

She didn't need to tell me twice. As she headed back down the stairs, I pulled in enough white light to leave me woozy and got as close to Jacob as I could manage without accidentally stumbling into him. We weren't wasting any time, and I figured we were home free.

Until the priest appeared in the doorway in front of Jacob.

I grabbed the back of Jacob's jacket and white light jumped between us.

The priest flashed utterly solid and lifelike, but only for a moment. When I found my equilibrium, he was insubstantial and jittery. "I know what I did was unconscionable!" he said.

Jacob, however, felt like he was cracking with power. "Don't blast him," I snapped. "He's talking."

Jacob cocked his head as if he might hear. Unfortunately, he'd need to listen through me.

The priest was distraught. "I had no good choices. We study those problems in seminary, but the real world is exponentially more complicated."

"You were in cahoots with Kamal?"

"He was very convincing! His father was on a team that dismantled landmines in the second World War—and Dr. Kamal carried on his late father's work. There was nothing wrong with his methods...not at first. But we were still at war."

"With who?"

"Take your pick! Russia, China, North Korea. They're all a massive threat to our very way of life—and they're all training psychics of their own. It was a question of the greatest good for the greatest number. Just a few families were involved—and no real harm came to any of them."

"No *real* harm," I repeated.

"They intermarried voluntarily. Look, we all need to make sacrifices. And sometimes that means getting off your theological high horse and making the best of a bad situation."

Bad enough to kill yourself over? "This Director Mann—suicide or murder?"

"He took his own life. God rest his soul."

"You crossed him over, didn't you?" Damn it. That meant the only answers I could hope to get were from this half-degraded holy roller. "What did he do?"

"One of the original group passed away—cancer took her— and Dr. Kamal wanted to study her body. She was a devout woman who would never have consented to such a thing. Dr. Mann falsified her records. The family challenged them—and he got caught."

"So Mann forged some signatures," I said. "What did *you* do?"

"I did nothing."

"Sure. And that's why you're in purgatory."

That got his attention.

The ghost flickered jaggedly, then solidified for just a moment and with great sorrow, said, "Dr. Kamal violated the sanctity of life...and I did nothing while he played God."

"What violation? Surgeries? Drugs?"

"No, nothing like that!"

"Then what?"

"Eugenics. And I did nothing to stop him."

They say confession is good for the soul. The problem with Catholics is that they think they can do whatever they want, and the minute they fess up to it, all is forgiven. For someone who believed condoms were a sin, eugenics had to be a major offense. And yet, once his big confession was off his chest, the priestly ghost made himself scarce. Whether for now or for good, I couldn't say. But it was pretty clear we'd get no more answers tonight.

"The priest is gone," I told Jacob, but I suspected he already knew. He'd been uncharacteristically quiet. Instead of his usual armchair quarterbacking, he'd been listening. Or focusing. Or whatever sense it was that connected him to his elusive talent.

"What did he have to say for himself?"

"Pretty much what you'd expect. Not my fault. Just going along with the program."

Not a particularly satisfying answer. Especially after the amount of effort we put into getting it.

We took the stairs down two by two and found Barbara scrutinizing the drone by the light of her cell phone. "The plastic is a little scuffed. I'll never hear the end of it."

We all turned and headed toward the cars. As we picked our way through the nearly-dark woods by our flashlight beams, Jacob let Barbara pull ahead, then leaned in and whispered, "I'm so sorry—I didn't mean to grab the light—"

"Never mind, it wasn't your fault. I'm the one who grabbed *you*. It was the priest. He popped up right in your path...and for the record, we don't look *that* much alike."

"Right when your light hit me—for that initial burst of energy—I got gooseflesh all over. I swear, I could feel him." Him, and a bunch of etheric dust bunnies. "What did he say?"

"Some rationalization about choosing the lesser of two evils...." The word *eugenics* felt too big for this conversation. "And not a whole hell of a lot else."

Up ahead, Barbara called, "Would you guys put a move on?"

Urgently, Jacob said, "Listen—I want you to drive back with my sister."

An hour alone in the car with Barbara? My stomach sank. "Why?"

"To make sure Father Paul hasn't followed us home. Barbara wasn't on Kamal's list. She'd be easier to stick to than I would."

Since Father Paul was a crossover ghost, it was unlikely he'd stray from the hospital. But if riding with his sister made Jacob feel better, fine. It took a few minutes for me to catch up with Barbara, and all the while, I did my best to refill my tank with white light. I'm not sure if etheric fatigue is an actual thing, or if it's my physical and emotional resources that dwindle. Either way, I had to buck up and hold the light as best I could. I'd hate to learn the hard way that the priest decided to leave his post after all.

Barbara was surprised I wanted to drive back together, but when I fed her a line about wanting to double-check our to-do list with her, she seemed to buy it.

Once I actually looked at our docket, I could see why. Between our final meeting with Pastor Jill, our rescheduled manicure and our bachelor party, we'd need to stick to our timetable.

Still, there was only so much to discuss. We fell into an easy enough silence with nearly forty-five minutes to go, with me focused on my white light levels and Barbara watching the road. The moon was out, the deer were scarce, and the radio was playing innocuous pop songs.

I'd relaxed, figuring I was home free, when Barbara turned down the radio and said, "It was funny seeing Sacred Heart all boarded up like that."

Also funny how I'd forgotten that Barbara had Sacred Heart memories too. "I'll bet."

"Mostly, I only went inside to use the restrooms—except the one year I tore my arm open on a chain link fence and needed stitches. The walls were such a funny shade of green and the whole place smelled medicinal. But compared to the carnival outside where it was hot and humid and full of these annoying little gnats, it felt so cool and quiet in there." She shivered. "I guess it still is."

I didn't know what to say, but it didn't seem like she was

expecting much of a response. We drove on, with the trees on either side of the road so high they nearly formed a tunnel, and road curving out in front of us in the headlights.

"I met Derrick just inside those front doors."

"Your ex?" I'm not sure why that would surprise me—obviously, she had to have met the guy somewhere. But that somewhere being a location where the chaplain was complicit in some sort of psychic scandal didn't bode well.

I said, "You don't need to talk about him if you don't want to." It was a cheap ploy I'd learned for my undercover work—but it worked especially well with contrary subjects.

Contrary...and stubborn.

"I was barely twelve, and Derrick was starting high school, so it was hardly love at first sight—not on his part, at least. I thought he was so mature and self-assured—and he wasn't much older than Clayton is now. I couldn't wait to see him the next year—but then that was the year the whole thing shut down."

"So how did you end up reconnecting?"

"At the Catholic church. I used to go whenever I stayed over at Grandma Marks's house. I can't imagine why everyone thought I was so pious! I just wanted to see Derrick."

Maybe Barbara's parents had been fooled...but I somehow doubted her grandmother was in the dark.

"Once we got married, the first few months were like a dream come true. We bought a four-bedroom house, honeymooned in Hawaii, and even got a rescue dog. Scooter. He was such a great dog." She trailed off as she lapsed into memory.

It was tempting to prompt her—forget about the dog, what's the deal with Derrick? But that same undercover work that had showed me how to steer a conversation also taught me that sometimes the best response is none at all.

A few miles up the road, Barb picked up her story again. "You know how some new mothers have postpartum depression? Sometimes I swear that was Derrick. We had this wonderful life—a storybook life—and one day he up and says, 'I can't do this anymore.' And by the end of the week, he was gone."

"Men are...strange."

"Tell me about it. I figured he was seeing someone on the side—I was still carrying a lot of baby weight, not that that's any kind of excuse, but it would've at least been a reason. But he's never remarried. I would never ask him, myself, but he's been chatting with Clayton once a month ever since the kid could talk, so I get the inside scoop on my ex whether I want it or not. It wasn't money problems. It wasn't an affair. 'I can't do this anymore.' That's the only reason I ever got."

"That sucks."

Barbara sighed. "Yeah. It really does."

CHAPTER THIRTY-ONE

The thing about hanging all your hopes on a ghostly confession is that dead people have an unfortunate knack of talking about everything except the facts you need to know. Father Paul thought he was sacrificing a few kids to save the rest of the country from the Red Menace. But that still didn't help us figure out how Jacob's talent was actually supposed to work.

I'd filled Jacob in on the conversation as best I could remember. And we were both more than a little surprised to have the eugenics allegations that landed Andy Parsons in the woodchipper corroborated by someone else. Partly because we'd presumed Andy was a screwup, partly because Jacob was the one on the roster, and not me.

The next day, as we sipped our early-morning coffee at his parents' kitchen table, I hazarded my best guess as to what it all meant. "Plenty of covert psychic research was going on even before the Ganzfeld Report blew the field wide open. Mostly an attempt to train our guys as remote viewers and use them for espionage."

Jacob frowned. "But remote viewing is basically some sort

of long-distance clairvoyance, right? We both know full well how they test for that sort of thing. Matching cards. Naming colors. Drawing pictures. If anything like that happened to me, I would remember."

As someone who'd had big hunks of his adolescence erased, I wasn't so sure. But Jacob was upset enough as it was without me giving him something more to doubt. And anyway, if Dr. Kamal had been hoping to breed himself a human shield, I shuddered to think what that testing process might involve.

Jacob fiddled with his coffee mug. "Every time I feel like we're closing in on an answer, we get nothing but more runaround. Why wouldn't Father Paul give you any details about what they were testing for?"

"Too busy trying to exonerate himself?"

"Or maybe he didn't know. Back then, the six-talent, seven-level system didn't exist, and everything fell under the blanket term of 'psychic.' Think about it, though. If everyone else was training up remote viewers, it would make sense to try and counter their telepathy with a True Stiff."

Made sense...on paper. But the way the etheric pond scum reacted to Jacob when he was full of mojo—hell, the way the dead priest reacted, too—it seemed shielding wasn't the only tool in my future husband's toolbox.

Bad enough Jacob was secretly bred by Kamal to be a psychic.

What if the aim wasn't to create a psychic shield...but a psychic *weapon*?

If I went particularly quiet trying to un-think that thought, Jacob didn't notice.

It was one thing to learn to handle a weapon. Most cops I know hope they'll never need to pull that trigger. But being the weapon? I couldn't even imagine a scenario where Jacob's self-image survived intact. The fact that he had the healthiest ego of anyone I knew only made it that much worse.

I did my best to put it from my mind. There'd be no time to delve into it now anyway. We had a full docket, starting with our final premarital counseling session.

At the church, Pastor Jill greeted us with a warm smile. "All ready for your big day tomorrow?"

"Here's hoping," I said.

"It wouldn't be a wedding if everything went to plan. Some people find weddings to be as stressful as funerals." Probably not psychic mediums, but I took her point. "For our last session, I thought we'd work on communication skills—because it's a lot easier to handle a stressful situation with clear and honest communication."

Jacob and I sank down next to one another on the love seat. "Let's talk about assertiveness," Pastor Jill said.

My face must've telegraphed exactly how I felt about that, because she turned all her attention on me. "No two people express themselves in exactly the same way, Vic, and it's pretty safe to say you're more of an introvert than Jacob."

"Wow. You're quick."

"Opposites really can make great partners, since they've got a broader range of emotional tools to draw on. Being quiet and thoughtful and having a big internal life are likely the very things that attracted Jacob to you to begin with."

Sure, and the fact that I saw ghosts had nothing to do with it. I didn't bother contradicting the pastor.

She said, "Not everyone does all their processing internally, though. And when conflict arises, it's important to let your partner know what's going on inside. It might not feel comfortable, but in the long run, that moment of discomfort while you're speaking your truth is well worth it."

I may have been grimacing.

"Now, given the little deflection you did when I pointed out you're an introvert, I'm thinking that expressing your preferences verbally might be a growth area for you." Pastor Jill turned to Jacob. "Think back to the last disagreement you had regarding the wedding."

"It's been going pretty smoothly."

"Really? So many moving parts—and you were in a real time crunch. There's bound to be a confrontation that cropped up."

Jacob shook his head. "No—my sister's been on edge about getting everything done. But Vic seems fine." He turned to me. "Are you?"

"About the wedding?" Weird response. Jacob's eyes widened as if he thought I'd blurt out just how stressful it is to be ghost hunting in the woods. "It's fine. Uh...really fine, not just let's-drop-the-subject fine."

Pastor Jill wasn't satisfied. "Think back on some typical stressors. Guest list? Menu?"

I shifted uneasily. "The baker was a little...out there. But Jacob handled her."

"So you let Jacob handle your confrontation?"

"I was dealing with a flower emergency. Divide and conquer. In terms of the cake, so long as no one sneaks in any raisins, I don't really care—"

"Hold on," Jacob said, "My mother's bran muffin—the one you spat out—was a potential confrontation. You told her it was good."

"I don't remember saying that."

"You made a noise that sounded...good-ish."

"That's debatable. And what difference does it make? It's a muffin."

Pastor Jill folded her hands sagely. "In the book of John, Christ said, *The truth will set you free*. But truth can also be used as a weapon. You don't need to go out of your way tell your friend her haircut is unflattering...or your mother-in-law that her muffin is less than stellar. But what about the next time a muffin you don't like comes your way?"

"I'll say I'm not hungry."

"You certainly could, and if your main motivation is to be gracious, that might be the best response. But what if the muffins then become a regular thing? Every time you visit, she bakes another batch. What if she's made them just for you—and she's gonna stare at you until you eat one? Truth has a way of coming out. The longer you keep up the lie, the more awkward it will be when the *prevarication* runs its course." She wagged her eyebrows at me.

"Yeah, I was in law enforcement. I'm familiar with the word."

The pastor narrowed her eyes in assessment. "Oh, the stories the two of you could tell. If you ever need to talk to someone, keep in mind that I'm bound by confidentiality as clergy."

I liked Pastor Jill...so I wasn't about to suck her into the psychic vortex. But I did appreciate the offer.

She said, "Trust is important in my relationship with you both—but it's even more crucial between the two of you. Any job that requires such a water-tight NDA must be stressful. Not only are you working together, but living together. Loving together. And the bedrock of all these relationships is trust." She pulled a bandanna out of her desk drawer. "Let's try a little trust exercise. Who wants to wear the blindfold?"

A Camp Hell flashback flexed against the surface tension of

my memory. I massaged the back of my neck. "I don't really go for that sort of thing."

"Oh?"

"It's complicated."

"I'll do it," Jacob said quickly.

Pastor Jill must have thought he was fighting my battles for me again, but she handed him the bandanna anyway. She led us across the hall to a sort of church rumpus room, with a coffee station, tables, and shelves full of board games and books. "Normally, I have the participants switch places halfway through. Even without the role reversal, though, you'll still get something out of the exercise. Go ahead, Jacob, put it on."

He did as he was told, and she spun him around a few times like she was prepping him to take a swing at a piñata. Then she looped her arm through mine and let me across the room. "Okay, Vic, I'd like you to guide him through the tables with nothing but your words."

That seemed too easy. Probably the blindfold game was a distraction and the real exercise was something else entirely, but it seemed harmless enough. "Two o'clock," I called out. "Three paces. Eleven o'clock. Ten feet—okay, stop. One o'clock." Within a few seconds, Jacob was at my side, and I turned to Pastor Jill, fully expecting another shoe to drop.

She looked at me strangely and said, "How funny. I've never seen anyone navigate the room so fast—and he didn't even touch a single piece of furniture." She should try it with a roomful of ghosts. That was a real barrel of laughs. "Whatever it is you guys do for a living...I'll bet it's never dull."

I shrugged. "You could say that. So, what's the next part?"

"There is no next part. Usually at this point, someone's still wrapped around a folding chair. The good news is that Vic can be assertive when the situation calls for it."

Well, sure, crackheads and vengeful spirits don't take you seriously unless you channel your inner badass. The pastor must've seen whatever it was she wanted to see, since she let us out ten minutes early for good behavior.

We climbed into the car and Jacob paused with his key just resting against the ignition and a faraway look in his eyes. I waited. Eventually, he said, "The thing that's bothering me most about Kamal's notebook isn't that I don't know what it is I'm supposed to be. It's that I'm worried I've been living a lie, and my parents aren't together because they want to be, but because someone forced them together, or paid them off."

I jostled his knee. "Come on, we know your dad and Uncle Leon are inseparable. Jerry would've married Shirley just to keep him in the family."

Jacob smiled sadly. "My grandmother knows something."

"Yeah. She does. But she can't tell us."

"Even if she could, I doubt she'd be willing to." He caught my hand and ran his thumb over my pale knuckles. "Vic, when I was blindfolded and you guided me through the chairs, I felt just as confident as I would've felt looking through my own two eyes. The sound of your voice was the only thing that mattered. And I'm worried that in all this useless digging around, I've lost sight of what's important: me and you. Us."

"Jacob...." *It's fine.* The words were on the tip of my tongue. But I forced myself to bite them back, to stop trying to deflect the feelings Jacob was struggling to express. "I'm here for you. Whatever you need. I'm here."

CHAPTER THIRTY-TWO

Pastor Jill might have intended that trust exercise to teach me something about assertiveness, but it ended up convincing Jacob that he needed to clear the air with his parents. Despite the fact that we'd been staying under their roof these past few days—and in a none too comfortable fold-out bed—we'd avoided them pretty well.

When we got back to their place, both cars were in the driveway. We sat out front, peering through the windshield at the front door. "You don't actually have to confront anyone," I told Jacob. "Take it from a long-time avoider. Sometimes the best course of action is to simply drop it."

Sometimes...but not this time. Jacob took a fortifying breath and we headed into the house.

We found his parents in the living room watching the news, each in their respective recliner flanked by a pair of TV trays bearing the remains of an early lunch. Shirley snapped down her footrest and said, "Are you hungry? I can make you a sandwich. We didn't realize you'd be back—we would have waited."

Shirley did make a mean sandwich—in addition to the mayo,

she buttered the bread—and I realized that yeah, I could eat. "That sounds great." I slid a glance to Jacob, who looked to be second-guessing himself, and decided that divide-and-conquer would give him the best opportunity to make his move. "I'll help."

I followed Jacob's mom into the kitchen while he and his dad headed downstairs. God knows what Jacob claimed he needed in the basement, but it gave the two of them some privacy to really talk.

Sandwich-making didn't require any actual assistance, but Shirley let me join in anyhow, even if it did take longer to hand things to me and explain how to do it instead of just doing it herself.

"Make sure the butter goes all the way to the edge," she instructed, and I gave the slice of bread I was holding a more thorough spreading.

I then blurted out, "I'm not a big fan of bran muffins."

I hadn't realized just how much my relationship with Shirley meant to me until I threatened it by practicing confrontation. There was half a heartbeat in which I expected her to whack me with a slice of ham and call me an ingrate, and a poor excuse for a son-in-law to boot.

Thankfully, my panic was short-lived. "Oh, Jerry too—he says they taste like sawdust. Dry the lettuce leaf with a paper towel, otherwise when you bite into it, all the insides will slide out."

Well...since we were talking.... I blotted the lettuce, steeled myself, and said, "How did you and Jerry meet?"

If Shirley thought the question was a non-sequitur, she didn't remark on it. "We went to high school together."

What about the author of the love letters? The bran muffin confrontation was bad enough. I wasn't sure how I'd handle it if Shirley lied to me...if the trust I thought we'd built up was worthless. "High school sweethearts?"

"Oh, no—back then, each of us was going steady with someone else. We ran into each other a few years later."

"Where?"

"At the bowling alley. It really wasn't any big deal—like I said, we already knew each other."

"But there must've been a moment when you realized you thought of Jacob's dad as more than just a friend."

Shirley smiled softly to herself. "His brother, Fred, had a buddy—this was before the big to-do happened where Fred got a free ride to college and Jerry got nothing—this funny kid, Norm."

Norman...Krimski. I went very still and did my best to not hyperventilate.

"Norm was a real cut-up. He just blurted out whatever was on his mind. He saw Jerry helping me get a knot out of my bowling shoes, with Jerry down on one knee in front of me, and out of the blue, he says, *You'll kick yourself if you don't propose to that girl.* We all laughed it off. But then Jerry got our number from Leon and called the very next day to ask me out."

I'd always figured Camp Hell's Director Krimski sprang into the world as a fully-formed middle aged man—and the only time someone would refer to him as a "cut-up" was if they were on the receiving end of a fatal stab wound.

I said, "How much time did you actually spend with this Norm guy?"

"Not much. He ended up moving away. Chicago, actually." Shirley gave the sandwich its finishing touch: a diagonal cut. "Wonder what he's doing nowadays?"

Yeah. Me too.

She handed me the knife, then paused and tugged up the sleeve of my sweatshirt. "How's your hand?"

"Fine." I flexed it a few times. "Uh...mostly. I'll need some physical therapy to recover my grip. But after all that time under plaster, it's weirdly...pale."

If I'd been fishing for reassurance that I was just being self-conscious, I'd cast my line in the wrong spot. Shirley gave my hand a thorough scrutiny, then brightened and said, "I have just the thing!"

By the time I wolfed down half a sandwich, she'd bustled upstairs to the bathroom and come back with a tube of self-tanning lotion.

"First thing in the summer, my legs always look like fish bellies, so I need a little help. It'll be our secret."

I probably should've hung my left arm out the car window and let nature take its course, but that would've been some trick from the passenger seat—and besides, it hadn't occurred to me.

"Give me your hand."

I wasn't entirely sold on the idea, but I obeyed. Shirley slathered the offending limb with lotion, then washed her hands. "It doesn't look any different," I said.

"Because it takes a few hours for the tan to develop. Just make sure you wash it off at bedtime, otherwise it'll stain the sheets."

I flexed my hand a few times, then said, "So Grandma Marks didn't have anything to do with you and Jerry getting together?"

Shirley nearly choked on her sandwich. "Just the opposite." She lowered her voice, and in confidence, told me, "That woman did everything in her power to keep us apart. But I think that only made Jerry more determined to marry me."

So, other than a good sandwich in my belly and a hand that smelled like self-tanner, what did that leave me with?

More questions.

Why had Jerry's mother discouraged him from getting together with Shirley? Was Shirley meant for some other set of initials on Kamal's roster—or did the old woman's reasons have nothing to do with Kamal's experiments? Hard to say. The machinations ran so deep it was hard to imagine anything else might be the cause.

Once Jacob ate—he denies that he loves butter as much as the next guy, but I know better—we headed out to check and double-check that our wedding would go off without a hitch. But our suits had been pressed, our flowers were on track, our decorations had been delivered, and our annoying millennial baker was only having a minor meltdown.

The prep work was done. Out of our hands. All that was left to do was show up for our bachelor party...if Jacob ever managed to pull away from the curb. He'd frozen with his hand on the ignition, lost in thought. And I was pretty sure it had nothing to do with the bakery.

Eventually, he said, "I asked my dad about those love letters."

I wondered when we'd come around to that. As much as Jacob might have been chagrined about letting our wedding take back seat to his investigation, he wouldn't be Jacob if he just let the matter drop. "What did he say?"

"That Leah was just a high school sweetheart—a friend of the family his mother was gung-ho about him seeing."

"I have a hard time picturing your grandmother being particularly fond of anybody."

"Which means that Leah could have been part of Kamal's experiments too—someone my grandmother was encouraging him to...*breed* with. If we track her down, maybe we can get some answers."

"Hold on." I pulled Kamal's notebook out of the glovebox and refreshed myself on the strings of initials. "Even if Leah's return address had her married name, there's nobody with a first name that starts with L."

"Which means my Uncle Leon wasn't on the list."

I thought back to the last conversation I'd had with Grandma Marks. "*Only one child.* That's what Father Paul promised your grandmother."

"What's that supposed to mean—something genetic, a trait that only shows up half the time?"

I shook my head. "That wasn't the impression I got. It sounded more like some kind of sick bargain."

A text from Crash pinged my phone. *Just about ready for the big shebang—what's your ETA?*

As much as Jacob might want to put this Kamal business behind him and just focus on the damn wedding, I could tell his compartmentalization skills were failing him miserably. I said to my phone, "Tell Crash we're running half an hour behind." And once I was positive the phone was done listening to me, I told Jacob, "You won't get any peace until you've exhausted every possible avenue. So let's go talk to your grandmother one more time."

When we got to the nursing home, a group of old ladies was just finishing up their dinner.

Jacob's grandmother was not among them.

The nurse at the desk in Grandma's ward headed us off on the way to her room. "Just so you fellas know, Mrs. Marks has been sedated."

"Why?" Jacob demanded.

"For her own protection. A few hours ago she fell again, and she keeps trying to get up and wander around even though her balance is out of whack. There's no reasoning with her, poor thing, so we had to restrain her—and the doctor thought it was cruel to just let her struggle."

Maybe so, but at least we could have still taken a stab at making her talk.

The nurse said, "You can still visit her, though. I know it's real tough to see your loved ones when their minds start to go."

Since the nurse had more experience with the elderly than either of us had, I figured it couldn't hurt to pick her brain instead of continually running around on a wild goose chase. "What are the chances we'll get to have a lucid conversation with her?"

"There's no way of knowing. Sometimes you'll get a little glimpse. Sometimes it seems like they're not even themselves anymore. But I like to think the person you love is still there, somewhere inside. That's the part of them you talk to, even when it seems like nobody's home. I've been in hospice over twenty years now, and one thing I can say for sure is that no one regrets getting to say their goodbyes."

Hospice? Beside me, Jacob tensed.

No one said anything to us about hospice.

We made our way to the room. Asleep, Grandma Marks was a heck of a lot less intimidating than she was with her eyes open and glaring. The sight of a wrist restraint cinching her to the bed made my spine prickle.

Jacob clung to the bed rail, fuming. "What do you wanna bet she dies just to keep from telling us anything we can use?"

I dunno. If she died, maybe she'd feel the urge to come clean.

Or at least feed me her justifications. But the way our luck had been going, she'd cross over and leave me hanging. "If you need to be pissed at anyone, be pissed at Kamal. He got what was coming to him." I shuddered at the memory of his corrupted spirit fused with an outbreak of habit demons. "And then some."

"The more time I spend with my dad these days, the angrier I am that she just threw him to the wolves like some sacrificial lamb for Uncle Fred's benefit."

"Look, Jacob." I pried his hand from the rail. "Kamal is gone—you shoved him through the veil yourself—and your parents are okay. Your *dad* is okay."

He grunted a half-hearted agreement.

I said, "You may not get any answers here—or at least none that you like. I'm sorry your origin story is as screwed up as mine. But that doesn't change how I feel about you—not for one single moment."

CHAPTER THIRTY-THREE

On our way out the nursing home door, another text came in from Crash: this one containing the address of our bachelor party.

As if we weren't under enough stress.

Back when Jacob and I decided to tie the knot in an official church ceremony instead of just sneaking off to City Hall for a private elopement, I knew I'd be called upon to do plenty of things that were way outside my comfort zone. What I hadn't fully appreciated was how high on that list a stag party would be.

And that was before I knew the party planning duty had fallen to Crash.

Bad enough he was flirty and opinionated and unabashedly gay. He reveled in making me squirm. Maybe that's what friends are for...but I'd rather not have to endure the agony in front of what few other friends I had.

Visions of muscular, oiled strippers waving their junk at me while people I knew looked on nearly had me begging Jacob to pull over so I could flee into the woods, never to be seen again.

But when Jacob mapped the location, I could practically feel the tension drain out of him. "We're meeting at the park."

That seemed awfully...tame.

I wasn't entirely convinced that there'd be no strippers involved, but if we were in a public park, at least they wouldn't be completely naked.

The road to the park was as treacherous and winding as they come, but the closer we got to our destination, the more Jacob relaxed. "I haven't been here in years. Camping with the Scouts... fishing with Uncle Leon. Sunset over the bluffs...and after, when the stars come out...I can't wait to show you."

A park shelter had been reserved, and most of the cars in the adjacent lot had Illinois plates. My friends were mainly work friends...which made me doubly apprehensive about any indignities I might suffer in front of them. At least until I noticed a skinny girl of maybe ten or eleven lobbing pine cones at Clayton.

Jacob's breath caught. "That's one of Carolyn's daughters."

What a relief, and not just because it was a family-friendly event. Carolyn hadn't RSVP'd before we headed up to Wisconsin. Having her here would mean the world to Jacob.

Funny. I'd always figured that between the two of us, I was the one who had the most trouble making friends. And yet, scanning the small crowd, I saw that I had just as many as Jacob. My old partner Maurice hovered by a smoking charcoal grill while his wife Nichelle was laughing over something with Jacob's mom. Agent Peter Garcia, who was convinced I'd saved him from sure death at the hands of The Assassin, was slicing a watermelon. Hopefully he would put my mind at ease by checking it for surveillance devices while he was at it. My fake husband, Bly, was chatting with Jacob's gym rat buddies...and he had a tall, thin woman with ramrod posture on his arm. Apparently he'd paid attention to my tip-off about Bethany.

Hopefully he could learn to enjoy yoga. And hopefully Jacob's sister didn't give him too much hell for bringing along a last minute plus-one.

I didn't make friends easily. But maybe I held onto them better because I didn't alienate them by always having to be right.

Crash, with his spiked peroxide blonde hair, stood out among the crowd. He perked up when he saw us and slow-jogged over in his combat boots, metal bracelets jangling. "Greetings to the guests of honor. As you can see, your emphatic plea to *keep it simple* was received and heard. Hamburgers and hot dogs to the right. Taco bar with vegan options to the left. And all the fizzy-water you care to drink. The strippers canceled, but we did manage to arrange for a scandalous event called *cornhole.*"

"It's a game," Jacob supplied, for my benefit. "A G-rated game."

Would I ever get a handle on whether Crash was just teasing or not? Unlikely. But I could live with that.

Red looked up from the taco bar he was arranging and came over to greet us. If you ever need evidence that Pastor Jill's "opposites attract" theory plays out all the time, look no farther than the guy Crash settled down with. Red Turner is the most gracious person I know.

So when he gave my left hand a long-suffering look and said, "Oh, Vic..." I realized I'd really screwed up. "What did you do?"

I glanced down at the hand in question...and immediately regretted the self-tanner.

Crash, of course, felt compelled to weigh in. "Fuckin-A, his knuckles are even darker than yours. Is that sunless tanner or a skin disease?" Due to my arm marinating in a plaster cast all those weeks...a little bit of both. "Did neither of you notice your hand was turning fifty shades of brown?"

To be fair, we were both phenomenally distracted. "Now what am I supposed to do? Everyone will be looking at it tomorrow."

Crash shook his head. "Get a load of those blotches—it's like a Rorschach test. Did you exfoliate before you put it on?"

I'd never exfoliated in my life. "Can you help me or not?"

Red said, "Don't worry, Vic. We got you."

Crash scrutinized my sorry hand. "A tanning remover would be your best bet—but I can't even recall the last big drugstore I saw." He cast a critical eye over the barbecue. "But maybe your dead skin cells can work to your advantage. We just so happen to have something in our bag of tricks that combines citric acid with a sugar scrub."

Realization dawned on Red. "The lemonade mix. There should be plenty left."

"Come on, goofus," Crash said to me. "Let's go fix your hand."

Crash snagged a plastic tub of drink mix from the picnic table and herded me off toward the toilets. It was the perfect setup for a lewd comment. Glory holes, wide stance—the possibilities were endless. But as he hauled me over to the sink and shoved my hand under the tap, he was uncharacteristically non-antagonistic....

Until he met my eyes in the mirror, cracked a naughty grin, and said, "This is gonna sting."

He dumped the lemonade crystals on my hand and the powder immediately brought to attention my every last ragged cuticle. I steeled myself and said, "It's fine." Though my eyes might've been watering.

Crash pulled a travel toothbrush from his pocket, angled my hand toward the light, and began to scrub. I winced, but only on the inside. He said, "Let's face it. The greatest rewards in life always involve a little pain."

His tone implied he was referring to the bedroom, but that was just a defense mechanism. Crash and I didn't do mushy. "You probably think this whole church wedding is ridiculous."

He scoffed and scrubbed even harder. "I swear, sometimes it's like you don't even know me at all. Of course I don't think it's ridiculous—I think it's brave."

"Really? In what way?"

"Well, let's face it. The second you and Jacob bought a place together—especially one as pricy and unsaleable as the cannery—it was obvious the two of you were in it for the long haul. The deal was sealed. And yet, you're voluntarily taking another oath. Not only in front of your whole social circle, but church and state. I wouldn't do it—but that's just my inner anarchist."

Time was, I would've also figured myself for an anarchist. But that was at least a lifetime ago. "Last February, during my big undercover gig...wearing a wedding band for a month without being able to come home to Jacob? It really did a number on my head."

"Yeah, I figured there was some sort of catalyst. Makes sense. I wouldn't have necessarily pegged you for the marrying type—but Jacob? You'd think he'd be in his glory. Not stressed out and fuming."

I cringed as the lemonade lit up a tiny scrape on my knuckle. "Maybe he is in his so-called glory and you just can't feel it. And that's not some nasty dig about your abilities either, since we both know he's a True Stiff."

"Even so—I'm well-versed in his facial expressions and body language. And I can tell when his emotions are locked up tighter than a folder of porn on the family computer."

Knowing full well he could read my emotions like a big, anxious billboard, I simply said, "Things have been a lot more stressful than we'd bargained for."

"Other than saving you from the world's most ridiculous tanning fail...anything I can do to help?"

I trusted Crash one hundred percent—but we were swimming in the deep end of the psychic pool now, and as valuable as his feedback might be, it was just too dangerous to keep pulling him in. "You've already done plenty."

I wouldn't go so far as to say my hand looked good when Crash was done with it, though it did look about ninety percent better. He assured me a once-over with a concealer stick would get the rest of the job done, though I'd need to refrain from buffing my knuckles on my wedding suit or I'd have more problems than a self-tan gone wrong.

We emerged from the toilets to a party in full swing. The first hot dogs were coming off the grill—they smelled incredible—and a cluster had formed around the taco bar. The evening was blessedly stripper-free...though the "cornhole" beanbag toss went cutthroat, fast. It was clear that practice made perfect, as all three generations of the Marks family blew everyone else out of the water. As for me, I was content to stuff myself with watermelon, catch up with Maurice, and watch the fireflies come out.

We were among the last to leave. Although we had a big day lined up tomorrow, I would have happily stayed up well past my bedtime. Even Jacob was more content than I'd seen him since that damn notebook came into our lives. Probably endorphins. I think he may have even allowed himself a brownie.

I drifted off on the way home, and snuffled awake in his parents' driveway when Jacob gave my lemonade-scented hand a gentle squeeze. "It was a good night," he said simply.

And I had to agree.

It didn't really register that it was way too late for all the downstairs lights to be on until we walked through the front door.

Jerry was on the land line looking grim while Shirley hovered at his side. When we came in, they both looked up as Jerry finished up the conversation with a vague, "Okay. Uh-huh. Thank you." He hung up the phone and stood there with his hand on the receiver, gathering his thoughts. A moment later, he took a deep breath, then turned to us and said, "That was the nursing home, Jacob. Your grandmother just passed away."

CHAPTER THIRTY-FOUR

Everyone processes grief in their own way. Granted, not everyone would announce, "I'm going for a drive," at midnight like Jacob did...but since his folks were grappling with their own feelings, they didn't seem too surprised.

"Are you okay?" Shirley asked. "Do you want me to come with you?"

"Stay here with dad," Jacob said, and swept out the door before she could suggest they both come along.

In the car, he said, "Where would her spirit be? The nursing home?"

"Maybe," I said, but the part I didn't say was, *if it's still in this plane at all.* Etheric bodies are the stuff of ghosts, and everyone's got one. But while it might seem like everywhere I go I'm tripping over a wayward etheric form, the vast majority of folks find the veil within moments of their passing.

Hopefully, the notorious Marks family stubbornness would work to our advantage.

The streets were empty, and Jacob blew through all the stop signs and both traffic lights. We squealed up to the nursing home in ten minutes flat, and I power-loaded white light all the way there. But my salt was gone, scattered in a doorway back at Sacred Heart, and I wasn't eager to find out that Jacob's grandmother wanted to get under my skin.

There were automatic glass double-doors at the front of the building that normally whisked open at our approach, but tonight they didn't budge. Jacob pounded with the flat of his palm until a rumpled security guard came out to see what all the fuss was about.

"Can I help you?" he called through the glass.

"I need to see my grandmother."

"Visiting hours start at eight—come back in the morning."

"I need to see her *now.*"

A night nurse in cheerful flowered scrubs came and peeked around the corner, then hurried over to join the guard. "Are you here about Mrs. Marks?"

"I'm her grandson. Has the funeral director come yet?"

"He'll be here in the morning." The nurse made a sympathetic face. "I'm real sorry for your loss."

"I've got to see her one last time. I live out of town and I won't make it to the funeral. Please. I...just need to say goodbye."

In Chicago, this little ploy would never work. Night watch-men are too hardened by their exposure to the type of dirtbag who'd weasel his way in with a sob story, whip out a knife, and make off with all the narcotics. But here, in this little hamlet of small-town decency?

The employees exchanged a look. The guard clicked open the lock, and the nurse told Jacob, "I'm not supposed to...but we can give you a few minutes."

The nursing home felt different at midnight—just as deserted as the streets. Maybe that was a good thing. The fact that it had the potential to be swarming with non-physical entities hadn't really registered until I was halfway to the body.

People don't die neatly. The fact that Jacob's grandmother was lying on her back with her hands folded atop the blanket attested to the fact that someone had already done a cleanup job—that, and the fact that the room smelled of antiseptic air freshener and not bodily fluids.

"Is she here?" Jacob whispered.

I doubled down on my white light and triple-checked all the shadows. "I don't think so."

Jacob shook his head in disgust. "I didn't think I felt the pull of the veil, but I was hoping my perceptions were skewed by my own emotions. They literally just called my parents—"

"Maybe so. But judging by the level of housekeeping that took place here, it looks like they weren't in a big rush to deliver the news."

"Do you think they were covering something up?"

His grandmother's eyeglasses were neatly folded on the pillow beside her so the funeral director didn't forget them. That didn't smack of a cover-up. Just a bunch of hospice workers who saw so much death, they no longer shared the level of dread and anxiety harbored by the rest of the population. "Looks to me like they were just doing their job."

"So she's gone. And that's that."

"I...don't see her."

Desperately, he grit out, "Try harder."

It's one thing to fail at something you don't know how to do—no one expects you to play the piano by sheer force of will if you've never once touched a keyboard. But I'd had years of practice with this particular instrument, so it galled me that the second we needed it most, all my efforts were met with a resounding silence. With his grandmother crossed over, I was as powerless to talk to her as everybody else.

But was that really true? I'd bet Darla would be able to make contact. So why couldn't I?

Maybe, in the end, Darla was just the higher-level medium. On paper, she was officially considered a strong level four, almost as high as me. This was a major upgrade for her too, since she'd struggled her whole life to be taken seriously, while I'd come by my five seriously downplaying my ability.

But maybe her level was as underestimated as mine, given how useless my talent currently felt. Not only were we in the location of his grandmother's death, but we were in proximity of the body. I pulled down white light until my head hurt...fat lot of good it did me. "Jacob, if there were anything to pick up on here—I would. But there's nothing. She's gone."

"Why am I not surprised she'd take her secrets to the grave?"

"Don't...bury...me...."

A chill danced over the back of my neck as the words registered, faint and far away, and suddenly all the white light I'd been pounding had a bead on where to focus. I swung around to face the room's entrance, and spotted motion down toward the floor. With focus came recognition, and a jumble of abstract flickers resolved themselves into the semblance of Jacob's grandmother, bisected by the bathroom door.

"Vic?" Jacob asked cautiously.

"She's still here."

The ghost on the floor crawled forward, maybe an inch, struggling in death as much as it might in life. Half pathetic old woman, half Japanese horror flick...as if she wasn't scary enough before she died. And then we locked eyes.

I'd been full of white light to start with, but now another

volley poured in. A spike of pain lanced through my head and I swayed on my feet. It wasn't an entirely rational fear—obviously, she was in no state to possess me. But unlike the hospice workers, I'd never developed a comfortable relationship with death.

Probably because I could see what happened when the exit strategy got botched.

"Please," Jacob's grandmother forced out as she struggled on the floor. "I'm begging you. I need to be cremated."

"You're white as a sheet," Jacob said.

I opened my mouth...closed it again.

"She's talking to you, isn't she?" Jacob scanned the room, searching as if he was listening with his whole body. He could see where I was looking, which guided his awareness just as surely as my directions in the blindfolded obstacle course. "Is she lucid?

"Promise me," she begged. "They'll desecrate my body."

"Who will?"

"The doctors. The government. They can't be trusted—none of them can!" How bad is it when something that should sound like a paranoid delusion rings absolutely true? "When my husband died, the vultures came for his body—tried to talk me into donating it to *science*. I had him cremated after the viewing so they'd never get their hands on him. And now they'll come for me."

"Ask her why she chose Uncle Fred over my father," Jacob demanded.

"I didn't! God forgive me, I loved Jerry best."

"Hold your horses," I told Jacob, then asked his grandmother, "Didn't you send Fred off to college to put distance between him and Kamal?"

"Where do you think we got the money for his tuition? My

husband was a good man. A hard worker. But he was gullible, and he bought into all of Dr. Kamal's promises."

"Like what?"

"That he was doing the patriotic thing."

"In what way?"

"To help the war effort. A bunch of us tested—why not, they paid us each five dollars, too—but not everyone got in. My brother joined. I joined. My steady boyfriend joined. We thought we were doing what was right. It was nothing but a bunch of silly tests...until they started dictating how we should marry off our children. Do you know who else did that? The Nazis, that's who." She clawed her way forward another few inches. "I wanted to be done with it, but my husband insisted one of the boys stay. I gave them Fred so I could save Jerry... who went and married that Shirley Larson anyway! After all I did to keep him out of the experiments, he sealed his own fate by marrying her!"

"If you wanted out so bad, why the carnival? Why Sacred Heart?"

"All I could do was stick to my grandchildren and protect them as best I could. There was no way those people would let the third generation alone, not with *both* parents in the program."

"What is she saying?" Jacob snapped.

"Hold on," I insisted, then asked his grandmother, "Third generation what?"

"Psychics!"

Jacob's patience was wearing thin. "Vic—*what is she saying?*"

Damn it. "Psychic *what?*"

"Please," she begged, "don't let them take my body."

Half a conversation was so much worse than none at all.

Jacob stopped just short of grabbing me—but he was so worked up, I wouldn't have put it past him. I huffed out a frustrated sigh and waved him off. "I don't think she knows. And...she's really suffering."

Jacob flinched. "Can she hear me?" he asked. I nodded. His focus went wide, like he was seeing something off in the distance—and his voice was soft when he said, "Grandma? You didn't make it easy for any of us to love you...but I do anyway."

Something inside me unclenched. Not the part holding the white light, but the part that wasn't a hundred percent certain Jacob was above torturing his own grandmother to get what he wanted.

His grandmother's anguished face relaxed into a smile, albeit one that was mostly regret. And as it did, a faint shimmer appeared on the opposite wall just a few feet from where she lay.

"The veil," I murmured...but Jacob already had eyes on it. Whether it was his love—his forgiveness—that gave his grandmother the strength to rally, or whether he was actually doing something non-physical with that elusive talent of his, I couldn't say. But one moment the veil was just a vague disturbance bending the light, and the next it was a blinding glow that flared white hot, and was gone...along with the ghost of his grandmother.

CHAPTER THIRTY-FIVE

If I had any ideas of how my wedding day might go, they all flew out the window when Jacob's grandmother died. The family was subdued, Barbara's eyes were red from crying, and Jerry had a really hard time wrapping his head around the whole cremation thing. We'd decided to fudge the truth and say Grandma had confided in us while she was alive. The family might be keen on my abilities, but even the most ardent psychic groupie cools their jets when my talent hits too close to home. Psychic groupies or not, Jacob's folks would be unsettled by any post-mortem announcements. I'd worked hard to be comfortable among them. I didn't want to screw it all up by being honest.

We were due at the Lutheran church for our wedding before the funeral arrangements were finalized. And while part of me thought that if the old woman was so afraid of landing on the dissection table, she should have made the proper arrangements herself, I had nothing in place either...and maybe I should. So who was I to cast stones?

The church had a couple of separate rooms set aside for the bride and groom to ready themselves for their big walk down the aisle. Judging by the pint-sized seating, mine doubled as a cry room for kids too rambunctious for service, but it gave Crash somewhere to make up for the manicure reschedule that I missed and mash my hair into place. I always suspect he pulls it harder than he technically needs to...but I can't argue with the results.

He was shoving goop through my hair when Jerry opened the door and Leon stepped through, bearing a small box with great reverence—two-handed, though of course no one saw the ghost arm but me. I hadn't had occasion to wear a boutonniere since a junior high dance. Mama Brill had jabbed me but good when she pinned the crushed carnation to my lapel. Hopefully Leon wasn't planning on giving it a stab. Etheric limbs can only do so much.

Of course, no one was as aware of that limitation as Leon. He handed things off to Jerry, who fiddled nervously with the box, cleared his throat three or four times, then said, "Anyways. I always wanted another son—so I suppose you'll do."

We all pretended we didn't notice he was choking back tears as he pinned on the boutonniere...without stabbing me even once. Leon gave me a mostly one-armed hug, and the two of them went off to shed their manly tears in private.

Crash gave the flowers a critical look—if you could even call them flowers. Mostly it was a bunch of green stuff with a few white fronds tucked in. Clearly, I should've been more specific with the florist, but there was nothing to do for it now. At least in the overall scheme of things, the boutonniere would be too far away for people to notice it looked like something I pulled out of my lawn clippings.

"Eucalyptus," Crash announced. "Interesting choice."

"Yeah, I get it, I screwed up. You don't need to rub it in."

"I'm serious. Not only is the plant associated with all sorts of good esoteric vibes, from protection to healing to dispelling negativity—but these herbal arrangements are remarkably on-trend."

I wasn't entirely convinced he was being serious, but before I could challenge him, Pastor Jill poked her head in and said, "How's everything going in here?"

"Fine," I said, then thought better of it and added, "if nothing else, my hair will look good."

"Charmer," Crash said.

Pastor Jill grinned. "Chin up, Vic. It's a felicitous day to constellate!"

"Uh...turn into stars?"

"To gather together...though I don't mind your definition. How great it would be to let go of the need to achieve and do, and simply shine our light on God's creation."

Crash said, "I'm not one for organized religion, but if I lived up here, I'd definitely check out your sermons."

"You're welcome anytime."

As the pastor made to leave, I said, "Before you go, I was wondering, what are your church's views on cremation?"

"Well, it's up to the individual. We believe in the Resurrection— but also that God is perfectly capable of resurrecting your body whether or not you've had it cremated."

"So the same would hold true with donating your body to science."

"Exactly. We consider organ donation an act of sacrifice and love."

There's organ donation...and there's dissection. But I wasn't about to split brains. "And what about Catholics—aren't they pretty particular about being buried intact?"

"Traditionally, yes. But times are changing. The Vatican says cremation is fine, so long as you don't do anything crazy with the ashes. It's all about respect. It's one thing to reduce the body to ash...another to scatter those ashes to the wind from a jet ski in Aruba."

"Would you mind mentioning that to Jerry? He's having a hard time with his mother's final wishes."

Pastor Jill gave me a soft smile. "It's kind of you to be thinking of him when you've got so much else to worry about. I'll bet he's real pleased to be gaining a son-in-law like you."

When she was gone, I told Crash, "Thanks for not rolling your eyes."

"What? I'm not a total heathen, y'know—and I have a softer side, too." That said as he tugged hard enough to make my eyes water. "Okay, I suppose that's as presentable as your hair's gonna get. Now, be honest. Did you soak and moisturize your hand like I said?"

I sighed heavily and presented the offending limb. The skin was blotchy and the knuckles were creased with brown.

"Yeah, I figured as much. Lucky for you, I found a decent cosmetics counter at the mall." He pulled out an array of concealers. "And, by the way, these cost easily as much as a professional spray tan, so consider it your wedding present."

Nothing to gather dust and take up space? I couldn't ask for a better gift.

Barbara bustled in as Crash was trying to achieve just the right blend of Fresh Beige and Golden Sand. "Hand makeup? Is that a thing?"

"Don't worry about it," I said. "What's up?"

"I was just at the supper club to set up your decorations...guess what I found?"

"No idea."

"A bunch of random weeds and the most boring decorations I've ever seen in my life. You said you took care of it!"

"I did." At least I thought I had. Though I could see now I probably should have picked actual flowers, and maybe a real color.

Crash said, "If you guys get everyone to loiter around the church after the vows, Red and I can go on ahead and try to zhuzh it up."

"Fine," I said, then turned to Barbara. "Is that it?"

Slightly mollified, she pulled out her phone and called up her to-dos. "Last-minute checklist. You have Jacob's ring?"

"Of course." Though obviously she wasn't going anywhere until I proved it.

"I'll grab it." Crash dug in my pocket and flashed the ring at Barbara, then said to me, "Don't be touching yourself with your makeup hand, not until you wash off the concealer. I got you the most smudge-proof, bulletproof stuff I could find—but it'll still leave a skidmark on your black suit." He must have felt my rising anxiety, because he added, "Keep everything within reach with your right hand and you'll do fine."

"Check for the pastor?" Barbara prompted.

"Already delivered."

"And your vows?"

Jacob and I were in agreement that we didn't have the mental bandwidth to memorize our vows, and had printed them out a while ago. I peered into my right pocket and double-checked the paper was right where I'd left it. "Here."

"Okay. And try not to mumble." Barbara gave me a meaningful scowl. "Good luck."

We locked eyes. I could've told her how much I appreciated all her help—bossy or not, she got the job done, while dealing with everything that was going on with her grandmother. And I could've said how much it meant to me that she was treating me as part of the family nowadays. Hell, I realized I could have told her I loved her—and meant it. But Barbara Marks didn't do mushy. So I had to settle for, "Yeah...thanks."

Even that earned me a tight smile that bordered on a wince.

Once she was gone, Crash gave my hair a final tug, then dusted his hands together and said, "Well, Psy-Pig, I suppose you're as ready as you'll ever be. Time to get the show on the road."

CHAPTER THIRTY-SIX

Jacob was already waiting in the vestibule, shifting foot to foot and tugging at his cuffs—and not because his cufflinks were sitting funny. He looked more nervous than I felt...but he also looked unbelievably hot. While Crash had been insulting me and pulling my hair, Red was working his magic on Jacob. A couple of weeks ago, when Crash announced, "The nineties called—they want their goatee back," Jacob had agreed to grow out his stubble. I wasn't necessarily convinced a full beard was the way to go, but Red assured me that facial hair was among his specialties. Apparently he hadn't been exaggerating. Seeing Jacob now, polished and pressed, everything groomed and styled, not a hair out of place? I felt stirrings that were most definitely not appropriate for church.

When Jacob spotted me, his eyes widened. His expression shifted from its intense hyperfocus to a broad, all-encompassing look that bordered on wonder. And when the doors to the sanctuary opened to reveal all our friends who turned to check us out expectantly, I experienced my own moment of wonder as, despite all that we'd gone through these past few days, weeks, months...my heart felt impossibly full.

The ceremony was about as simple as they get—we'd opted for no major fanfare, just some basic recorded music, with no wedding party and no elaborate choreography. We walked down the aisle side by side. Fewer than twenty people were in attendance—and most of them had spent the previous night with us playing cornhole, eating hot dogs and swatting at mosquitoes. The church was mostly empty, aside from two clusters up front on either side of the aisle, though the space seemed as full as my heart, because everyone there was someone I truly cared about. Neither side was exclusively Jacob's, or exclusively mine. Our lives were so intermingled, it was hard to say who belonged to whom...other than Jacob's biological family. Though soon they'd be stuck with me, too.

Pastor Jill awaited us at the altar, beaming at us as we approached, looking surprisingly official in a liturgical gown. And while I half-expected her to whip out some strange vocabulary word, she did the reading as planned without taking any creative liberties. It was your typical religious passage about love—and while the words washed over me as more of a gentle cadence than an actual string of sentences, it wasn't because I was zoned out, disconnected, or retreating inside my own protective shell.

Just the opposite. I felt like I'd been broken wide open for the world to see, in all my vulnerability. Because nothing's even half as vulnerable as happiness—and despite the weeks of frantic planning, this thing we were doing, Jacob and me, hardly felt real.

"Vic," Pastor Jill was saying, which brought me back down to earth. "The vows you prepared?"

There was brief moment of panic in which I thought I'd

end up covered in concealer, but a comforting papery crinkle assured me that I was practically in the clear....

Until I unfolded my vows and discovered they weren't vows at all, but instead the map to Sacred Heart covered in scribbles I'd stashed to keep it out of Barbara's hands. Seriously? How had I managed to grab *that*? "Uh...hold on a sec." That was the last thing Jacob needed to see. I folded it back up and tucked it away, then reached around to pat my left pocket with my right hand. But as I already suspected, it was empty.

"So...the thing is, I...uh, I'm finding myself more than a little bit out of my depth right now. The prewritten vows feel a little stilted...so I think I should just speak from the heart."

Jacob stared into my eyes, one dark eyebrow slightly quirked. Baffled. Yet intrigued.

"I, uh... I never saw myself getting married in church."

Jacob's eyes narrowed as he wondered where I was going with this.

Him and me both. "Frankly...I never saw myself getting married at all. And I especially never saw myself finding a man who loved me for exactly who I was, not in spite of it. I will always have your back, Jacob. And whatever life throws at us, it's my solemn promise I'll be right there by your side."

Pastor Jill looked at me expectantly, and I muttered, "Uh, that's it."

"And what about you, Jacob?" she prompted.

No doubt his pre-prepared vows were exactly where he expected them to be...but he could hardly follow my ad lib with a reading. He leaned in, and his short whiskers ruffled my cheek as he pressed his lips to my ear and playfully whispered, "You'll pay for this later, mister."

As if the illustrious Jacob Marks is ever at a loss for words.

He eased back to arms' length and cocked his head as if he was trying to figure out what to make of me, then gathered his thoughts, cleared his throat and said, "Vic...I set my sights on you without knowing if my overtures would be welcome, let alone reciprocated. You were so independent, it seemed like you didn't need anyone else—like you didn't even want the complications a relationship would bring. And then you let me into your life anyway. I thought I knew what to expect...but I was wrong. Being with you has been an adventure. Always. And even better, I feel as though our journey together has only just begun. I vow to be the partner you deserve, every step of the way."

Pastor Jill said, "Victor and Jacob have chosen rings to exchange with each other as a symbol of their unending love. Vic, if you would place the ring on Jacob's finger?"

Don't get makeup on your suit.

Wait, other hand.

A moment of panic, and then my fingers closed on a platinum band, plain and solid, warm from my pocket. Cameras flashed as I took Jacob's hand in mine, and our hands became the center of everyone's attention—but as far as I could tell, my left hand was passing for normal. And thankfully, with my nails neatly trimmed and buffed, it looked remarkably okay.

Jacob's ring caught on his knuckle, but I wasn't afraid to give it a good shove—and this part of the ceremony, we *had* memorized, since there'd be no easy way to consult our notes. Once I jammed the ring home, I took a deep breath, looked into his eyes, and said, "I give you this ring as a symbol of my love. Let it be a reminder that we have joined our lives together." And then I presented my left hand, whispering, "Watch the makeup."

It wasn't my first time in a wedding band—and not just the

fake one I nearly ditched on a dozen occasions. We'd modeled them for the dog photographer just a few days prior. And yet the sensation of the band sliding on felt momentous, as though from this day forward, everything was new. And while there was a slight hitch at the knuckle...between the sweaty palms and the makeup, it didn't put up much of a fight.

Jacob held my hand reverently in both of his and said, "Let this ring be a symbol of my promises to you and a reminder of my devotion. I am honored to call you my husband."

On paper, they'd seemed like just so many predictable words. But hearing Jacob say them with such emotion, such love, nearly made me tear up.

Okay, my eyelashes might've actually felt a little damp. But the only one who'd be able to tell was Jacob. And I trusted him with my life.

With our vows safely out of the way, the pastor smiled broadly and spread her hands in benediction. "Those whom God has joined together, let no one put asunder. Victor and Jacob, you have given and pledged your faith. I pronounce that you are now married, and may seal the promises you have made with a kiss."

We both leaned in for the requisite kiss, and as we did, it occurred to me that a discussion of exactly how much tongue was appropriate would have been useful—but I figured I'd just follow Jacob's lead. And for a guy who'd introduced himself to me tongue-first, here in front of everyone who mattered, even he felt uncharacteristically modest. His lips pressed against mine, soft, even reverent. And as our mouths relaxed into one another and Jacob allowed himself to breathe, the sweet spice of cinnamon gum, just a hint, flitted across my tongue.

Our first kiss had been bitter, tinged with the aftertaste of

Auracel. But now I couldn't even recall the last time I'd swallowed one of those noxious pills. I didn't need to drown out the ghosts anymore, and I didn't need to avoid being who I was.

Not with Jacob at my side.

CHAPTER THIRTY-SEVEN

I'd love to say that with the vows out of the way and the ring on my knuckly finger, I felt confident the rest of the wedding would be smooth sailing, and was currently awash with relief. But in my opinion, public speaking ranks up there with getting your balls waxed (which, for the record, I've never done—though I have seen videos). While everything had managed to work out, I was still tacky with flop-sweat and shaky around the knees. And I was hoping to air myself out before we headed over to the reception.

Unlike me, my new husband thrives as the center of attention. When I slipped out the side door and into the church's overflow parking lot, I was surprised to find Jacob had stepped outside, too. Until the door clicked shut behind me and he turned toward the sound—and I realized it wasn't Jacob at all I'd just blundered across, but a ghost from the family's past.

Though not the type who had me reaching for my baggie of salt.

"Uncle Fred." A statement, not a question...because he and Jacob really did look alike, plus or minus twenty years.

"You know who I am?" Fred gave me a self-deprecating grin, the likes of which you'd never see on his nephew. It made him look like less of a doppelgänger, which was a relief. "Well, how about that? I thought my name had been permanently struck from the family vocabulary."

"They say it, all right...but not in the most complimentary way. Is that why you're lurking around out here?"

"I didn't want my presence to overshadow my only nephew's big day."

"I'm sure everyone will get over it."

He smiled sadly. "Shirley called last night and told me everything that was going on—the wedding...the funeral. It's a lot. I'm not quite sure how to feel."

"I'm sorry about your mother."

"She had a long life. I'd love to say it was a happy one...but it sounds like you've met her, so why bother sugar-coating the truth?"

"Maybe she had good reason for being unhappy."

A silence hung between us, one that could go either way. I'm a lousy judge of character, but having Jacob as a point of comparison made me think I could get a read on Fred. Where Jacob was glib and calculated, Fred seemed open and honest. It could've meant he was just a better actor. But I didn't think so.

I gave them Fred so I could save Jerry. Fred didn't appear with the rest of the family in Kamal's journal, either—and not because he'd been excused from the experiment. What if the list we were looking at was more like a control group—the family members carrying a recessive gene, but not psychics themselves...at least as far as anyone knew.

Unless that was all a lie. And no one was ever really spared.

Confrontation was not my forte, but I wasn't about to give

up my chance at finding some answers. I said, "Were you aware that Jacob was a PsyCop?"

Fred smiled. "Sure—I saw him on the news."

"Well...I was a PsyCop too. Which means the stress of being in a psychic program? It's not lost on me."

A civilian would take that for a total non sequitur...and a Psych bound by umpteen confidentiality agreements would pretend to do the same. But Fred Marks gave me a shrewd look instead.

And then he looked even more like Jacob.

"What can you tell me about Dr. Kamal?" I asked.

"It's been a few years since I've heard that name." His tone was easy, but his wheels were clearly turning, wondering exactly how much he could say.

Maybe it was naive of me to trust him just because he was the spitting image of my husband. But he *was* family, after all. I said, "I had my own run-in with Kamal, but I'm guessing yours happened a few years earlier, so it might provide some much-needed perspective."

"That big project of his? There's not really much to tell—I was nothing more than a statistic. My psychic potential never amounted to anything."

I wrestled with the urge to let things drop—nothing to see here, folks—but whether or not Fred had talent, I suspected he at least knew what he was bred to be. Him...and, therefore, Jacob. Whether Jacob would be able to handle that knowledge, I didn't know. And me?

I'd have to be strong enough for both of us.

"The potential Kamal was looking for...what exactly was it?"

"Telekinesis." The look on my face must've been pretty priceless, because he added, "Moving things with your mind."

"I'm familiar with the term." I was also well aware that TKs were the unicorns of the psychic rainbow. My initial reaction was disbelief. Back at Camp Hell, Movie Mike got a killer headache from sliding a stupid penny across the table. And Mike was the only telekinetic I'd ever seen actually move something.

But I'd run across a few True Stiffs in my time...one of whom was Patrick Barley.

The Assassin.

What if Patrick not only trained to hold a weapon...but to *be* a weapon? Dread filled my belly as I wondered if good aim was the only reason the Marks family annihilated their competition at cornhole.

Cautiously, I said, "I'm guessing you've....*endured* your fair share of psychic tests."

"Actually, I'd say *failed* is the word you're looking for. Big waste of time. And about fifteen, twenty years ago, they stopped testing me altogether."

When Kamal landed himself at Camp Hell. I dry-swallowed. "Those tests of yours. What did they entail?"

"Nothing your typical ten-year-old couldn't handle."

"As in...carnival games?"

Fred seemed surprised. "Sometimes. Yes. Was that how you trained to be a PsyCop—with games?"

"Not exactly." Not unless being locked in a room with a dead body was your idea of fun. "So, those games of yours...what was the point?"

"The military wanted to develop an elite anti-landmine crew—psychics who could sense the mines, maybe even deactivate the charges remotely. I know, it sounds far-fetched nowadays, what with all the current research into the field of Psych—but during the Cold War, newer and deadlier mines were being created all the time, and Dr. Kamal was convinced he'd stumbled into some ingenious way to defuse them without any loss of life."

My relief at stammering out a passable ad lib marriage vow? That was nothing compared to the relief of hearing Fred's news. Whether Jacob was a dormant telekinetic or a True Stiff—I'd still need some time to piece together that particular puzzle—he hadn't been bred to take lives...but to save them.

And his Uncle Fred seemed like a genuinely nice guy.

"What about your kids?" I asked. "Do the men in black still run them through a gauntlet of tests every year?"

Fred's easy smile slipped. "I never had kids." Neither had Leon—possibly because of his arm—so if both Fred and Leon had been chosen for the experiment, the generation of TKs Kamal had been hoping to cultivate from either of them had never come to be. "Whenever I met someone who was gung-ho about having a family, I'd hear my mother's voice telling me, *You'd make a terrible father*...and I'd find a way to sabotage everything."

So, that remark about Jacob making a terrible husband hadn't been aimed at Jacob after all. "I suspect your mother said the things she did because she was dealing with some serious issues of her own. But Jerry and Shirley are two of the nicest people I know. And I think you should take advantage of the wedding to try and mend fences. Plus, I'm sure Jacob would love to properly meet you."

Fred might have been leery of wearing out his welcome, but if ever there was a time to bury the hatchet with the rest of the family, it was now. I added, "Shirley wouldn't have invited you if she didn't want you to come. And Jerry is beside himself with joy, so what better time to reconnect?"

Better now than at the funeral. At least at the reception they could avail themselves of the open bar.

CHAPTER THIRTY-EIGHT

There was only so long we could linger around the church to give Crash and Red time for their "zhuzhing", and eventually we had to head over to the supper club.

Unfortunately, when we walked through the door, it seemed like all the time in the world wouldn't have been nearly enough.

The banquet room that had seemed comfortingly simple upon my initial inspection now looked cold and stark. And everything on the tables, white on white, blended together—all but several towering weedy-looking bundles of greenery. It looked like a prison wedding, if such a thing existed, and even the most talented stylists we knew couldn't make it right.

And there was no one to blame but me.

Jacob is well accustomed to my inclination for austerity, but judging by the way he tensed at my side, even he was taken aback. But before he was forced to lie through his teeth and tell me everything looked great, Crash called over to Red, "They're here, hit the lights!"

And with the flip of a switch, the barren expanse of a banquet room transformed like magic.

Tiny white lights played across the tables and walls, some solid, some gently twinkling. They threaded through the greenery, which just moments ago looked like so much yard waste, but had morphed into something trendy and sleek. And while the overhead lights were off, it was only mid-afternoon, and ambient daylight from a few high windows lit the rest of the room well enough that it didn't provoke my typical panicky gut reaction to the dark.

By the time our guests filtered in behind us, my heart had stopped hammering enough for me to unclench. Kill enough lights and most anything can come across as romantic.

The reception turned out to be surprisingly normal. No one complained about the seating arrangement, our requisite slow-dance was excruciating, and the relish trays were truly a thing of beauty. Who knew pickled green beans could be so addictive? I was scoping the room to see if any of the other tables had failed to notice how good they were and see if I could insert myself when Jacob snagged my attention. He led me out onto the dance floor and eased a hand around my waist, and I fell into position reluctantly. "We had our big awkward dance already," I said, but without much steam behind the complaint. I'd never gone to a dance with a date, after all—certainly not with a guy—so I might as well try to enjoy the experience of sharing a voluntary dance with my husband, if only to say I'd done it. Not done it *well*, by any means. But people cut you a certain amount of slack on your wedding.

"I just wanted to make sure I actually got to see you at some point tonight," Jacob murmured in my ear. "How are you holding up?"

"Fueled by pickles and adrenaline. You?"

"Good." He leaned his temple into my cheek as we swayed

on our postage stamp of real estate. "More than good. I can't imagine anything more...perfect."

I turned to see where Jacob's attention had wandered and found Bill Kaiser trotting across the banquet room, heading right for us. "It's the owner," I told Jacob. "And he's awfully nervous."

Kaiser halted at the edge of the tiny dance floor like it was made of lava, and then proceeded to look profoundly awkward. Because he'd never seen two guys dance together? Or because he had some unwelcome news to deliver?

Possibly both.

I never thought I'd be loath to disengage from a public slow-dance, but I could hardly enjoy pressing up against Jacob while someone stood five feet away wringing their hands. I pulled away reluctantly and approached the hovering man with cop-like brusqueness. "Mr. Kaiser. Anything I can do for you?

Not gonna lie...I got a kick out of him thinking I was the boss.

He dithered for a moment, blanched, then said, "I think you and your *husband* will need to come see for yourselves."

Worst case scenario, the kitchen was on fire and we'd all be evacuated. But even if that happened, we could order a mess of pizzas and relocate the gathering to the Markses' backyard. But given the absence of smoke and alarms, it didn't look like the impromptu pizza party would be a go. Our check had cleared... so I couldn't imagine what it might be. "You didn't forget the vegan option, did you?"

"No, no, of course not. The artichoke linguini is all ready to go." He paused at a final doorway and gave a pained smile. "It wasn't our fault at all...though maybe we could have noticed the issue while there was still time to correct it."

"Correct what?"

With an apologetic wince, Kaiser whisked aside a curtain to reveal a godawful train wreck of a wedding cake.

I wasn't sure how it had anything to do with anything...until it registered that since ours was the only wedding reception at Kaiser's that night, the cake monstrosity was ours.

"I've called the baker about the mix-up—she's awful high-strung—but the other reception has already cut the cake. Your cake."

"So we're stuck with...this?"

"I'm real sorry."

The changeling cake was a triple-tiered beast, big and ungainly, with that ridiculous "naked" frosting that made it look like someone with a massive sweet tooth had absconded with all the icing. "Can't you just put some frosting on it?" I asked Kaiser.

"But...isn't it supposed to look that way?"

Jacob said, "If you knew that much, then how did you even notice it wasn't our cake?"

"Well obviously, it's the topper."

There hadn't been a cake topper in our original plan, just a simple mound of piped flowers. Straight couples had a gazillion hetero bride-and-groom toppers to choose from. We had four—three of which would need to be special ordered.

We leaned in for a closer look at the couple on our cake.

Two brides. Huh.

Jacob settled a hand on my shoulder. "I know, I know...you had one preference—normal buttercream—and everything else was negotiable. Well, aside from the raisins. But is it really so bad?"

I pried off the brides and a hunk of cake came with them...but frankly, unless you were really searching for a bald spot, you wouldn't know it.

Well...at least I wasn't the one who'd screwed up. I shot Crash a quick text, and moments later, he and Red joined us in the kitchen. Red gave a low whistle. "That is one sexy cake."

And given that he doesn't do sarcasm...he must've been sincere.

No doubt his boyfriend would soon set him straight. But instead of the scathing remark I expected, Crash patted his belly and said, "Since it's clearly bursting with eggs and butter, Red can only eat it with his eyes. I, however, will make sure his piece finds a good home."

Before I could pipe in with my low opinion of the frosting, Jacob said, "There was a mix-up with the cake topper. Can you work your magic?"

"No problem," Red said. "We'll add some botanicals and it will look perfect."

It seemed awfully early to start dinner, but either the guests had skipped lunch or they normally ate at six, because when servers rolled out the buffet trays, they lined up to wait eagerly with their plates. Even Jack Bly, who normally approaches mealtime with the same enthusiasm I feel about driving through repeaters. I peered over his shoulder and said, "Are you putting *pasta* on your plate?"

"Bethany's given me a new motto—everything in moderation." He and the yoga lady locked eyes, and I was practically scorched by the explosion of pheromones. I could only imagine how powerful it must feel to an empath. Whatever carbs he might consume, I had the feeling he'd enjoy working them off later.

The meal went off without a hitch. A true foodie might have pointed out that we could get a much fancier dinner in Chicago—but apparently Kaiser's chefs really knew their way around a big hunk of beef, and nobody was complaining. I must've been hungrier than I thought, or maybe those pickled green beans weren't really all that filling, because by the time the obligatory toasts came around, I was neck-deep in a food coma. Uncle Leon—with surprisingly good comedic timing—offered up a story about the time they nearly lost me at the farm implement store, and Maurice offered some heart-warming, if meandering, insights about following your dreams.

While he rambled on, the light through the windows began to fade, and the twinkle of the fairy lights intensified. I watched the nearest bulb wax and wane as within its tiny glass tube, the filament pulsed with light. Don't get me wrong, I was stupidly grateful for the kind words—especially coming from my stand-in father, though Maurice made for a much more relaxed parent than Harold ever was. But something about that tiny pulse of light was dragging my attention back to my conversation with Uncle Fred.

The one where he felt the urge to define the word *telekinetic*.

Back when Jacob and I forced Dr. Kamal's ghost through the veil, the lights in the pharmacy were blinking like a Christmas tree. I'd taken note of it at the time—but it hadn't occurred to me to wonder why. Maybe I figured it was some kind of fallout from the nonphysical entities. Or maybe a side-effect of the GhosTV.

What if it wasn't?

I shifted my gaze to the crowd. A disproportionate number of them were certified Psychs, which was part and parcel of our vocation. And a few of them were equally talented, but undocumented.

And then there was Jacob's family.

Back at PsyTrain, I'd scanned a roomful of Psychs under the range of a GhosTV, and they'd all lit up with talent. Jacob had been the only True Stiff, pumped up and coursing with red energy. But by its very nature, PsyTrain wouldn't have recruited any Stiffs, so no wonder he was the only one. If I could get a GhosTV-powered look into this room? Quite possibly he'd have some competition.

If only I could figure out how to unlock my mediumship. Not just for the sake of keeping out possessions—which would be a pretty big deal in itself—but the other oddball things I'd managed to do once or twice under duress...then never managed to accomplish again.

If only I could help my new husband.

If I weren't so limited, I could've spoken to his grandmother in the astral when she was too stubborn, or too confused, to give us a good answer. I could figure out if Uncle Fred had only failed his testing because Kamal was looking for the wrong thing. Hell, I could reach through the veil and get some answers from Kamal himself. But I'd spent so much of my life trying to dumb down my own talent, I couldn't figure out how. Without a psyactive drug or device, I was still a one-trick pony.

Jacob's hand fell across the back of my neck and he gave my shoulder a squeeze. He leaned in and whispered, "Time to cut the cake." What a relief to have something to focus on other than my own insecurities. "And keep in mind, people will be taking pictures."

"Are you saying I should save my eye-rolling for later?"

"Just giving you fair warning...though if you want something good to think about, feel free to imagine what I'd rather be doing when I'm feeding you the cake."

True to his word, Jacob gave me a look hot enough to set the decorative weeds ablaze as he tucked a morsel of cake into my mouth, though I had nowhere near enough confidence to lick it from his fingers with an equal amount of sex appeal.

Not in front of the parents.

I will say this for the mistaken cake—it tasted pretty darn good, though Crash had to explain persimmons to me several times...and I still wasn't quite sure I could picture them in the produce aisle. There was plenty of cake to go around, given the size of the thing, so we encouraged everyone to help themselves to seconds. Crash was actually on thirds—and I'd never known him to have much of a sweet tooth, but Red brought out the side of him that was willing to dial back the snark and eat lots of cake. Although he did sound plenty acerbic when he muttered, "I knew telling you to keep from pawing at yourself was too much to ask."

A flesh-covered handprint lay smack in the middle of my right sleeve—though how I'd managed to press the *back* of my left hand to it was is anyone's guess. But if there's a perk to my job as a federal agent, it's that I now own a multitude of decent black suits. Thankfully, I'd had the foresight to bring a couple of spares.

Since everyone now had a persimmon cake sugar-high or was tipsy on brandy old fashioneds, they were less likely to shoot an incriminating photo of my hand. I hit the can, scrubbed off the makeup as best I could, then headed out to the car to grab another jacket.

The fireflies were done sparking for the night, but the cicadas were in full chorus. Up here in the hinterlands, there's a vast solitude to nighttime that you don't get in Chicago. And while it was peaceful, I fortified myself with white light anyway. Just in case. Because nothing kills solitude like getting ambushed by a ghost.

I beeped open the Crown Vic and traded my foundation-christened jacket for a new one from a garment bag on the back seat. But as I was switching over the boutonniere, a phone rang...and not my phone, either.

It was coming from the glovebox...where we kept the burner phones.

CHAPTER THIRTY-NINE

Maybe it was the unaccustomed solitude, or maybe the fact that I was already hoarding white light. Or maybe I'd just seen too many slasher flicks where the call was coming from inside the house. Either way, at the sound of the ringer, my blood went cold.

It's probably nothing more than a dumb robo-call saying my car warranty has expired.

Probably.

And yet, I wouldn't rest easy until I knew for sure. But before I could get to the front seat, the ringing stopped. Since I hadn't set up voicemail on the burner phone, I supposed I'd never know exactly what flavor of telemarketing I'd almost been subjected to.

And then it started ringing again.

Which has never before happened to me with a robo-call.

I sucked down a fresh dose of white light—a reflex action, because obviously it wasn't as if a ghost was calling me. Then again, ghosts were always figuring out new and horrifying ways to be scary. I was just beating myself up for my lack of long-distance reception, but you know what they say: be careful what you wish for.

I grabbed the phone that was lit up and checked the readout to see if I recognized the caller. A random jumble of numbers showed that wasn't even the right amount for a phone number. Now I had to know. Heart hammering, I jabbed the talk-button and cautiously said, "Hello?"

"Vic—what a relief! The sí-no wasn't sure if you'd pick up or not."

Relief flooded me so fast it left me giddy. Relief, and surprise that she'd thought to sí-no the number to my burner phone. And longing. Because I really thought I'd get to see her. "Lisa. Damn. I miss you like crazy."

"I'm sorry. It wasn't safe for me to come." It wasn't worth asking why. If telekinetics were unicorns, Lisa was a flying unicorn on steroids. No doubt plenty of unsavory folks were eager to recruit her talent...or silence it. Or at least cut her open to see if they could figure out how she ticked. "I really wanted to be there."

"At least now I know Crash can relay my messages."

"No, he can't."

"Nice try—but you weren't just sitting around sí-no-ing when I'm about to get married. Uh...were you?"

"Of course not. And I would never put Crash in danger like that—especially not after Constantine went through so much effort to keep him undocumented."

"Well then how—?"

"Your *boss* told me."

Well, shit. "How is that safe? Don't the feds have Laura right in their crosshairs?"

"Only as a regional director they can bully. They don't know they're dealing with The Fixer. Laura is sharp and resourceful, and people underestimate that because she's a woman. Even her own people."

The appeal of flying under the radar was not lost on me. Given how FPMP National reacted to Con Dreyfuss's show of competence, it would be stupid to do otherwise. And Laura Kim was most definitely not stupid.

Nearby, another familiar voice joined Lisa's—one I would have been just as happy to never hear again. But given that Lisa married Dreyfuss with the blessing of the sí-no, I doubted they'd be in divorce court anytime soon. "Three minutes till the next satellite sweep."

"We don't have much time," Lisa told me. "So if you had anything to ask the sí-no, ask it now."

Was this a special dispensation for my wedding day, or was she giving out sí-nos again? I didn't bother asking. Lisa's existential struggles resulted in all kinds of mental gymnastics, and a sí today might very well be a *no* tomorrow. So instead I blurted out, "Is Jacob telekinetic?"

Silence.

"Lisa?"

"I'm here. I'm just confused."

"As to where I'd come up with such a crazy idea?"

"No...it's an interesting question, but it seems like I could answer either way."

"So he's *kind of* a TK."

"That's one way of putting it. Or maybe he's something more. Like Constantine. Con is clairvoyant, obviously. But his talent reaches a lot farther than it should. And it keys in on people he's never met."

And his eyeballs left tracers behind when I saw them near an active GhosTV, which made me think his subtle bodies might be as loosely connected as mine.

She said, "The six-talent, seven-level system works, more or less. Psychs tend to fall into certain categories, and some have more talent than others. But at the same time, it's really limiting. Like at PsyTrain, the Light Workers each seemed to have totally different abilities, you know? Like super-different, from spirit walking to lucid dreaming to astral projection. It would make sense that other talents might fall between the cracks."

"So that's what Jacob has ? A seventh talent?"

Lisa sighed. "No."

"Two minutes," Con piped in.

Lisa said, "Maybe it can't be a seventh talent if the six talents are basically bogus."

I knew someone who could probably spin out a pretty good theory as to what it all meant. But unfortunately, I doubted Dr. Kamal would be joining the call. "Listen, if we can't figure out what Jacob is, maybe we can make it so that I can do it myself."

"How?"

"I need to be able to talk to the dead."

"But you already can."

"Not like I do now, when a spirit is still hanging around. I need distance. Like Con. I need a line to the other side."

"No. This isn't something you could do."

"Not now, not at my current capacity. But if I could figure out how to tap into that superconscious state—if I had a decent psyactive, or a GhosTV, or—"

"Vic, no. It wouldn't matter."

"Are you sure? There's gotta be some way I can power up. What if I did *yoga*?"

"You're at the top of your game. I'm sorry."

I had to admit, the fatigue of being continually "on" was something I'd really been grappling with lately.

Ego is a funny thing, though. If you'd asked me two minutes ago, I would have said I didn't even possess an ego. But hearing Lisa tell me—definitively—that there was nowhere for me to go but down?

She must be mistaken.

"One more minute," Con informed us.

"I can't be maxed out, Lisa. You've seen me on psyactives—"

"I've seen you faint from chasing an astral body around a nursing home."

"I didn't *faint*." More like blacked out. Which is totally different...or at least less wussy.

In the background, Dreyfuss said, "Is he seriously using his last thirty seconds to argue with you?"

"Okay, okay. Lisa, can anyone among the living definitively tell me what Jacob is?"

"No."

"And does F-Pimp National have any idea what he can do?"

"Not really." She mumbled to herself in Spanish. "They just think he's a really good Stiff."

But how could that be, when Kamal was part of F-Pimp, at least for a while, and Jacob's initials were in Kamal's notebook? "The list Jacob is on—no time to explain—were those the subjects, or the control group?"

"They weren't the subjects."

Which meant that when his grandmother said Fred was the one she'd offered up to the study, she'd been telling the truth.

I was relieved for all of half a second, until I thought of Barbara being absent from that list. And the husband she'd met at Sacred Heart. And the way he kept up their sham of a marriage only long enough to procreate.

I was about to ask about Clayton's father when the sound of phone-fumbling filled my ear. Dreyfuss took the phone from Lisa and said, "And that brings today's visit to a close. Congratulations, mazel tov, and don't go swallowing any questionable pills. And one last thing—my very talented spouse and I trust Laura with our lives. Things might be easier for you and yours if you did the same."

CHAPTER FORTY

Was I disappointed that, according to Lisa, I'd maxed out my abilities? Somewhat. But was the sí-no *entirely* accurate? One hundred percent of the time? Or might I achieve the same goal by working more creatively with what I already had?

And I wasn't entirely convinced about the whole telekinetic thing either. Flickering lights, carnival games and cornhole. I was turning them all around in my mind when Shirley cornered me very purposefully over by the bar.

She put on her sternest face (which wasn't very stern at all) and said, "Now, I know this isn't the type of thing you'll want to discuss with your mother-in-law, but it needs to be said." Uh oh. "It's your wedding night. And Jerry and I wouldn't feel right if the two of you didn't get some time to yourselves."

To do the nasty. She was right—I was entirely mortified to think what she might be picturing.

"We've booked that bed and breakfast we told you about. Not for you, since you were so against the whole idea—but for us. You'll have the run of the house. And it's getting late...so no one would think twice about it if you wanted to get going."

"Please never advise me on my love life again. And...thanks."

"You betcha."

Jacob seemed keen enough to call it a night, so I was able to convince him to forego the pleasantries and slip away without any lengthy goodbyes. But as we headed out to the parking lot, we blundered into another guest who'd had the same idea.

Laura Kim. Who neither of us had said two words to all night.

"It's getting late," she said awkwardly, and Jacob, usually the smooth one, didn't seem to know how to answer that.

"Thanks for coming," I said. "Sorry we didn't get a chance to—"

"It's not as if we won't see each other at work."

"Yeah, but still. At work, we talk about work. You made the trip up here and all...so how about breakfast?"

Jacob tensed.

So did she. "I'm sure the two of you will be really busy."

"There's a local joint that does some really amazing hash browns," I insisted.

She knew something was up. But she also trusted me. "That sounds...great. Send me the time and place and I'll see you both there."

It occurred to me that when I had access to the sí-no, I should have asked if there were any surveillance devices in the car, but it was too late for that now. It had been a good day, a memorable day—but an incredibly long and stressful day, too. Jacob and I rode back to the house in silence that was more weary than companionable, but it was punctuated by the brush of our pinkies across the bench seat, and somehow even that tiny bit of contact was reassuring.

The night was cool, but we headed for the backyard anyhow. We dragged a couple of patio chairs well away from the house and planted ourselves at the far edge of the lawn. The obnoxiously bright motion sensor light by the garage kicked in, but by the time we were settled, it winked out and plunged us into darkness. And as my eyes adjusted, the night sky blossomed with stars.

I told Jacob everything. The conversation with his uncle. The phone call with Lisa—the parts related specifically to him, at least. And the fact that I didn't think we were going to get a better answer than the one we already had.

"Telekinetic?" he scoffed.

"*Sort of* telekinetic." I could see he wasn't buying it. Frankly, neither had I, but I thought we could at least give Lisa the benefit of the doubt. "Listen, we know you've got something way more than just a non-ability."

He made a grudging sound of agreement.

"Have you ever tried to move something with your mind?"

"I'm doing it right now." He gestured at a stray flower petal on the grass. "And nothing's happening."

"It'll probably take time and practice."

"Will it? Did you practice getting a visual on ghosts—or did you happen across the site of a car crash and see it plain as day?"

He did have me there. I said, "You're not starting from zero. You can sense the veil."

"Forgive me if I don't find that very exciting."

"It's not nothing. When you forced Kamal to the other side, it was a hell of a lot more." I thought back to our last encounter at The Clinic's pharmacy. The GhosTV was playing, and I had a front row seat of Jacob bursting with red energy. But the GhosTV didn't really do much for any other psychs, not unless it was tuned to the channel that sent everyone on an astral jaunt at bedtime. The technology had been designed to augment psychic mediums.

But it had a pretty big effect on Jacob, too.

Under the TV's lambent glow, not only had he blasted Kamal's ghost right through the veil, he'd pulled a habit demon off my neck and torn it in half. And all the while, the lights were flickering and the electronics were going berserk. He was on Kick at the time—so it could have been the drug.

And yet there'd been other times he'd really outdone himself with nothing more than the TV. Like when Richie was possessed and he'd stopped Jennifer Chance's ghost from sliding out from under Riche's skin...or in the FPMP morgue, when he held her ghost inside her semi-frozen cadaver. "Jacob...what if you never knew you were telekinetic because you couldn't see what you were moving?"

"I don't follow."

"We already know you're kinesthetic and not visual. But what if there's more? What if your talent isn't focused on the physical...but on the etheric?"

"What are you saying—I'm some type of medium? And that's how I ended up in Kamal's notebook with Sergeant Warwick's nephew?"

"That connection seems thin, at best. We know Kamal had his fingers in way too many psychic pies. So forget his damn notebook for a second and think about what we actually know first-hand. Think about *us*. Sometimes it seems like my subtle bodies are just rattling around inside, threatening to fall out. But yours are fused solid, locked in tight. Where I'm vulnerable, you're strong." I took his hand in mine and smoothed my thumb across his wedding band. "Cliché as it sounds, maybe opposites really do attract."

We sat with that idea for a while, until finally he said, "This is all incredibly theoretical."

It was. And if anyone knew how hard it was to test something non-physical, it was me. "Maybe theoretical is for the best. That way, the powers-that-be don't need to know about your talent until you're ready to tell them. If ever."

"If that's how you feel...then why did you invite Laura to breakfast?"

"Look, mister, you were the one who joined the FPMP, I just tagged along when I saw which way the wind was blowing. And as much as I balk at authority, I don't feel right sneaking around behind Laura's back. I like Laura—and I think she'd be more willing to help us if you'd stop being so weird around her."

"I'm not being weird—"

"You totally are. You can't keep blaming Laura for being possessed. She wasn't the only one Jennifer Chance used as a hand puppet. Richie and Darla, too—and those are just the ones we know of."

"I don't blame Laura. If anything, I feel sorry for her. I can't imagine how hard it must be, knowing that her finger pulled the trigger when Roger Burke was killed...that her body was nothing more than a weapon." Huh. Maybe he did get it after all. "I just feel bad for how hard I went at her. Even though I was right."

Jacob wouldn't be Jacob unless he pointed out that he was right. "I trust Laura," I told him, "and not just because Con and Lisa vouch for her, either. I think you'd feel a lot better if you started trusting her again, too."

"Are you saying you want me to hand over Kamal's notebook?"

"And endanger your whole family by putting them under the microscope? No. I do trust Laura. But once we open up that particular can of worms, there'll be no stuffing them back inside."

Would there be more to glean from the notebook? Maybe. Maybe not.

Under the peaceful chill of the starry night sky, we agonized over our next decision—and came to the conclusion that in the scope of what we'd figured out, any additional insight we might gain from the notebook was just too risky to justify holding onto it any longer.

Good thing Jacob's parents had decided to afford us some privacy, though we didn't end up using it in quite the way they might have imagined. Instead, we dragged our lawn chairs over to the brick fire pit in the center of the yard, and with a squirt of lighter fluid and a handful of kindling, made sure that Kamal's notebook would never fall into the wrong hands.

CHAPTER FORTY-ONE

Breakfast with Laura the next morning was only somewhat awkward. I managed to draw her out by prompting stories from her tenure as The Fixer. The hash browns were particularly crispy and good. And I believed her when she reassured us that F-Pimp hadn't planted any surveillance devices in our car.

Our stuff was packed and we'd already said our goodbyes to the family, and the only thing left to do was drive back to Chicago. Jacob double-checked a traffic app before we hit the road. I figured he was just mentally navigating around some construction, so I was surprised when he looked up from the map and said, "We could hit the library on our way home."

"Your stack of unread paperbacks is so tall it's threatening to bury you in your sleep," I said, though we both knew he wasn't hoping to discover his new favorite author.

He wanted to revisit that ghost.

Whatever etheric capabilities a True Stiff might have, they'd be just as hard to test and train for as mediumship talent. Precogs can predict the flip of a card, and telepaths can glean thoughts from helpful volunteers. But if there were any benign etheric entities floating around that we could safely practice on, I'd never encountered any.

Ghosts were as different from one another as the people they'd once been. Occasionally, I come across one who doesn't inspire me to start chugging white light—but those enlightened spirits are few and far between. The dead librarian wasn't in the same category as, say, Miss Mattie. But she *had* helped us locate the hospital, and she didn't feel aggressive. She'd be a good candidate for test-driving Jacob's talent.

And yet...the thought of doing that to Frieda just didn't sit right. "Jacob...I get that you want to open up your talent and see what you can do. Like you pointed out back at the library, she's sentient. Neither of us appreciated being used as a lab rat. Is it really fair to do the same thing to a ghost who's not an active threat?"

"What about Father Paul, then?"

"He's a crossover ghost. They only leave when they're good and ready."

"Then what? We look for repeaters?"

"We'd have a heck of a lot more guinea pigs to choose from, that's for sure. But repeaters aren't quite the same as ghosts. They're more like afterimages. If the sentient part of them is already crossed over, I think they'd be even harder for you to get a bead on than regular spirits." Heck, for all I knew, they weren't even etheric, but some other plane I was seeing with an entirely different subtle body.

Jacob stroked his short beard...which really did look even sexier than the goatee. "So if the ghost were an active threat... you'd have no qualms about me getting rid of it."

"You realize this is the equivalent of handing a gun to a baby, yelling, 'Good luck,' and throwing it in a pit of scorpions. You have no training whatsoever."

"That's not true—you've been training me."

"If that's what you call training—"

"You have," he insisted. "And I might not be able to see the etheric, but you can. You're my eyes."

"Jacob, this isn't some goofy trust exercise in a church basement. A pissed off spirit is a lot more dangerous than a folding chair to the groin."

But my overconfident husband was not to be dissuaded... which was why, later that night, we pulled up in front of our local ATM with a fresh bag of salt and a whole lot of trepidation. Last time, the ghost of the dead mugger took us by surprise, but we weren't about to make the same mistake twice. Not only had we gorged ourselves on mugwort tea—supposedly a natural psyactive—but I'd found a pump spray-bottle with really good range and filled it with Florida Water.

We'd even done a few yoga poses.

We'd done our research, too. The mugger had been haunting that particular stretch of concrete since my Police Academy days, and us none the wiser. He had no family to speak of, and the officer who'd gunned him down had succumbed to a coronary last year.

There was no reason not to show him the door.

We'd decided to don our black G-man suits. They might attract more attention than our street clothes, but if we needed to clear out any civilians in a hurry, they'd be more likely to take orders from us if we came across like authorities, and not just a couple of guys carting around some really weird props.

It was late and the hardware store was closed. Foot traffic was sparse. The few people who did stop for cash were dissuaded with a vague warning about official business. I'd pulled down so much white light I was feeling a little spinny. And yet all of our prep work was starting to feel like one big, disappointing exercise in futility.

I had my eye on the spot I'd seen our mugger before. Jacob was ranging up and down the sidewalk, feelers out, trying to get a signal. And both of us were picking up a whole lot of nothing.

"Maybe he's tied to a particular time," Jacob said.

I checked my watch. "If he is, that time has come and gone."

"Day of the week, then."

It didn't seem likely that a ghost would only appear on, say, a Wednesday. That simply wasn't how humans marked their big events. The anniversary of their death? Maybe. But I didn't particularly care to stand there for an entire year to find out.

Holding onto the white light, especially in the absence of panic, wears me down. Especially these days, now that I no longer take periodic breaks from my talent with Auracel and Seconal. By the time it was dark enough for the street lamps to power on, I had a dull throb pounding deep in my head. No matter how many times I reminded myself to top off, my light reserves felt slippery and low.

"Do you feel a chill?" Jacob asked.

"I do...but I think it's just a breeze off the lake."

"Maybe we can summon him."

I'd never been able to do anything like that before. And given the sí-no's assertion that I was already at the top of my game, I wasn't too confident I could suddenly learn. "Look, it's possible that when we tangled with this guy before, we got rid of him for good."

"You didn't seem too sure of that at the time."

"Maybe not. But if he made it across the veil, he's gone."

"If," Jacob repeated. He didn't want to throw in the towel—he was pulling the stubborn-face I knew so well—but he was also smart enough to realize that standing out there all night wouldn't prove a damn thing if there was no ghost to prove it on. He mulled it over for a moment, then gave in with a sigh of disappointment. "We'll come back tomorrow. In the meantime—I'm starving, and I've got a serious craving for Thai."

Now that he mentioned it, after a week in small-town Wisconsin, I was pretty steak-and-potatoed out. Our favorite Thai joint was just a few blocks away, and their green curry chicken was so good I could shovel it down until it hurt—but the cashier gave you the stink-eye when you tried paying with plastic. "Do you have any cash on you?" I asked.

"Not much."

"I blew all of mine on tips when I was feeling especially magnanimous."

"Pastor Jill would be proud."

Of my vocabulary choice? Or the fact that I'd bestowed a windfall on so many local busboys? I swiped my card through the reader and turned toward Jacob to ask—only to realize it wasn't Jacob standing right over my shoulder...but shadowy guy in a hoodie.

The temperature plummeted, and I sucked down white light for all I was worth. But my reservoir felt shaky and unstable, worn thin from hoarding white light for hours with nowhere to turn it loose. Mojo oozed from the seams like green curry through a soggy takeout container. And even the adrenaline of panic wasn't enough to fill my energy quicker than it leaked out.

"The mugger," I gasped. The words left my mouth in a cloud of frost, and suddenly I didn't have nearly enough hands. I dropped my cash card and dug for the salt, spritzing Florida Water left-handed for all I was worth. So naturally, the trigger-squeeze was one of the particularly atrophied gestures I should have been working on with a physical therapist, and the spritz fell woefully short.

"Gimme the money, asshole! Gimme the fuckin' money!"

I dropped the Florida Water and went for the salt, but I'd put it in a heavy freezer bag, and the plastic didn't tear. I fumbled with the zip-lock while my vision narrowed stupidly to the bloody, blown-out eye socket. I pawed at the plastic, slippery with sweat, and strained for more light—but it was no good.

I'd hit the upper limit of my ability. And that level was nowhere near enough.

"I'm here," Jacob barked, stern and commanding and way too full of himself for his own good. "Be my eyes."

My biggest enemy isn't ghosts—it's despair. And Jacob's show of confidence distracted me from it enough to let him try and help me.

"Don't grab my light," I reminded him, "pull in your own." Jacob's gasoline is a different octane from mine, or maybe an entirely different fuel, this crackling red energy he draws up from the earth. I might not be able to see the energy now, but I could picture how he looked with it coursing through his bulging veins.

"Where's the veil?" he asked.

"I don't know—damn it—"

I backpedaled, nearly dropping the bag, and the ghost was matching me step for step.

"You think I'm playing? I will blow you away right here. How fancy is that suit gonna be when I put a bullet hole through it?"

"He's lucid, and pissed off, and—eleven o'clock—"

In a move better choreographed than anything we might have managed on the dance floor, my True Stiff stepped in, as close as he could possibly come without his shoulder blades brushing up against me. The eye-shot mugger was crowding me so bad, Jacob didn't quite slide between us, but rather, *into* the ghost. With a crackle of energy, it jolted back a couple of paces.

And now it was livid.

"What the fuck was that? You think you're some kinda tough guy? Huh?"

More testily now, Jacob repeated, "Where is the veil?"

"I don't *know.*" And I couldn't wait any longer for him to find it. I freed the salt—finally—and grabbed a good handful. Filled it with light. Pushed with all my will to disrupt the angry spirit and flung it over his shoulder.

If this were a carnival game, my toss would've bounced harmlessly off the rail.

But where I was running on fumes, Jacob had just now powered up. And when the street distorted behind the mugger with a subtle bending of light, I didn't know if we'd found the veil, or if Jacob had somehow forced it to appear.

"Dead ahead," I told him.

It might be harder for him to spot the veil, but with me pointing him in the right direction, he could lock onto it with his other senses. As Jacob focused, it became more solid to me. I wasn't just guiding him...we were guiding each other.

"You got it," I said. "Push him through!"

Without a psyactive or a GhosTV, I couldn't quite see Jacob's energy—but I could feel it. Just barely. Not because it was subtle, but because it was operating on a level that was a real stretch for me to perceive, like the long, low rumble of thunder in the far distance.

Jacob gathered himself—and he shoved.

Bullseye.

The streetlight beside us flickered. The atmosphere flexed. And the ghost reeled backward, flailing, his one remaining eye wide with shock as he was pulled, inexorably, through the veil.

I backed up a few feet and caught my breath, and considered telling Jacob he'd done it—but I sensed he already knew. Traffic had slowed to watch a couple of guys in black suits gesticulating and yelling, and Jacob did his best to look casual as I pocketed my salt, retrieved my ATM card, and withdrew a wad of cash. It seemed weird to be doing it right where the mugger met his demise—but, hey, it was no longer haunted, so why waste time tracking down a different machine?

We climbed into the car and sat there for a moment, absorbing what we'd just accomplished. All those sessions with Pastor Jill had seemed like so much red tape, something to plod through for the sake of getting to the altar. But looking back on the experience, I now suspected that Jacob and I got a lot more out of it than we'd bargained for. And while Lisa might've been technically right about my psychic talent being maxed out, she hadn't accounted for how much I could do with it if Jacob was helping me.

If we were helping each other.

Jacob had just smashed a hostile ghost through the veil, so he had every reason to be smug. Yet he actually came across as diffident, even humble, when he asked, "Is it okay to touch you now?"

"Yeah. More than okay."

We both leaned in for the kiss and met in the middle—and as our mouths found each other, a tingle of energy passed between us that might have been etheric…or maybe it was purely physical. I was lucky beyond belief to end up with a guy who was so much like me in certain ways, and so completely different in others.

Someone I trusted with my life…and loved with all my heart.

ABOUT THE AUTHOR

Jordan Castillo Price prefers the pace of Wisconsin living to the hustle and bustle of Chicago...though she does miss the Thai restaurant by her last Chicago apartment.

She has never had occasion to use a self-tanner.

http://jordancastilloprice.com

ABOUT THIS STORY

I've lived in Wisconsin for twenty years now, and it's always fun when Vic and Jacob visit, because I get the opportunity to have them interact with a setting that's very different from the big city. I experienced quite the culture shock moving to Wisconsin from Chicago. The sense of urgency here is greatly diminished. I still remember being disgruntled about the way people would chat with a cashier while I was waiting in line behind them, or the fact that I couldn't get my Sunday newspaper on Saturday night. Thankfully, I've since relaxed.

Jacob's hometown is a fictionalized (and unnamed) city somewhere in southwest Wisconsin. I picture many of its specifics as the small city of Mount Horeb, though without its close proximity to Madison. Mount Horeb is also full of big wooden trolls, which don't exist in Jacob's hometown, and would make the city seem more quirky than I need it to be. The bachelor party took place in Wyalusing State Park, which is gorgeous—definitely visit if you're in the area. And Historical Marker 21 is not specifically about walleye, but the Wisconsin River Headwaters.

Driving down the two-lane, I often find myself intrigued by abandoned structures. Unused barns and silos start leaning and crumbling, and derelict houses slowly fall in. I'm usually surprised there aren't homeless people squatting in these places—at least they seem totally abandoned as far as I can tell—I suspect because they're just too far off the beaten path.

Though Jacob grew up in small-town Wisconsin, I think he's more of a Chicago guy now. Will being married to Vic change him at all? Since Jacob is a serial monogamist, he probably had his mind made up by the third date and the wedding just made things official. Still, maybe he'll have less to prove now. And although Vic never saw himself as the marrying kind, I think he'll make a fine husband.

More ghostly PsyCop adventures are planned for the happy couple. I've always thought Vic and Jacob were a formidable team, and I'm pleased that both of them are beginning to realize it, too.